BARBARY

Allan

SILVER MOON BOOKS LIMITED
PO Box CR25, Leeds LS7 3TN

SILVER MOON BOOKS INCORPORATED
PO Box 1614 New York NY 100156

New authors welcome

Silver Moon Books of Leeds and Silver Moon Books of London are in no way connected.

ALSO BY ALLAN ALDISS
from Silver Moon
(These novels may be read in any order)

ISBN 1-897809-01-8 BARBARY SLAVEMASTER
ISBN 1-897809-03-4 BARBARY SLAVEGIRL
ISBN 1-897809-08-5 BARBARY PASHA
ISBN 1-897809-14-X BARBARY ENSLAVEMENT

If you like one of our books you will probably like them all!

For free 20 page booklet of extracts from our first 16 books (and, if you wish to be on our confidential mailing list, from new monthly titles as they are published) please write to:-

**Silver Moon Reader Services, PO Box CR 25
Leeds LS7 3TN**
or
**Silver Moon Books Incorporated
PO Box 1614 New York NY 100156**

Surely the most erotic freebie ever!!

Barbary Revenge copyright Allan Aldiss
First published 1995

CONTENTS

PART I: MERCHANDISE

- 5 1-Enter Prince Rashid
- 9 2-A Long Line of Slave Dealers
- 15 3-Hassan Atala Makes Plans
- 19 4-A Secret Slave Establishment
- 26 5-Sheik Turki
- 29 6-The Bitter Truth
- 32 7-Inspected
- 34 8-Sold!

PART II: CONCUBINE

- 38 9-The Golden Cage
- 46 10-Concubines & Odalisques
- 51 11-The Prince's First Wife
- 57 12-The Master
- 66 13-Sky Blue Gets A Trainer
- 70 14-In Her Master's Bed

PART III: MAID SERVANT

- 75 15-Princess Leisha
- 80 16-The Prince Gives A Party
- 86 17-A Night Of Love
- 90 18-New Orders
- 93 19-The Prince's Majlis
- 98 20-Judged To Be Ready
- 101 21-The Teaser
- 106 22-A Shock For Amanda
- 108 23-Escape?

PART IV: THE ISLAND

- 110 24-Arrival
- 113 25-In The Pens
- 118 26-Sold Again!

PART V: BROKEN IN

- 121 27-Discipline
- 126 28-Drilled
- 131 29-More Humiliation
- 135 30-Put To Work
- 142 31-A New Trick

PART VI: GALLEY SLAVE

- 146 32-Amananda Learns The Truth
- 154 33-The Sporting Club
- 159 34-Row, Girl, Row!
- 164 35-A Little Psychology
- 165 36-Tour Of Inspection
- 168 37-Taken By Her Master
- 177 38-Final Training
- 182 39-Amanda's First Race

PART VII: SPECIAL CONDITION

- 188 40-New Rules
- 193 41-Amanda Is Prepared
- 200 42-Mated
- 204 43-Sheik Turki Entertains
- 210 44-A Little Light Distraction
- 215 45-Escape!

PART VIII - ENVOI

- 219 46-A Chance Meeting?

PART 1: MERCHANDISE

1 - ENTER PRINCE RASHID

The nubile young woman awoke naked and terrified, gagged and blindfolded.

All around her a ship creaked and groaned and the engines vibrated beneath her.

She quickly discovered that her hands were tied together and confined in thick mittens which denied her the use of her fingers.

There was dread in her heart as she lay trembling there and wondered what had happened to her and where she was being taken.

She had no way of knowing that they were steaming into a modern version of the days when the Barbary corsairs carried so many women away to slavery in Arabia -

His Excellency Prince Rashid bin Murad al Salia sat back on a long sofa in the private office of his large palace, sipping his sherbet, triumph lighting his thoughts. Outside, in the grounds of his palace, the sun shone down upon fountains and date palms and beyond that heat shimmered on the endless sand dunes.

He smiled as he studied the photographs of Amanda Aston, together with her passport which had been furnished as proof of identity, and contemplated Hassan Atala, the dealer, who stood diffidently before him on the priceless rugs.

"Yes! That is the one that brought shame upon me! You have done well!"

Hassan bowed respectfully, rubbing his hands in anticipation of profitable business.

He coughed, a wary eye on the Prince. "Your Highness will, I trust, bear in mind that the abduction of this particular woman was extremely difficult and expensive. I had to wait until she was on holiday in the Mediterranean by herself - and then move fast and bribe many people to turn a blind eye, so that she just disappeared and cannot be traced."

He paused and coughed again, even more significantly.

"Your Highness will be aware that several other leading Arab personalities have also been insulted on her television show and have expressed a desire to get their hands on her."

"Very well, Hassan," the Prince replied at last. "You are a trader and your price will be high. Name it!"

"But Your Highness!" protested Hassan. "It is a little early yet for that! I just thought that Your Highness would be interested to know that she will shortly be on the market - but not yet! Indeed, she is still on her way. Then I shall make a video -"

"We need not wait for that. I wish to buy her now."

"Oh, Your Highness!" exclaimed Hassan with a gesture of despair. "There is nothing I would like to do more than to oblige you, but that would cause grave offence to some of my oldest and most influential clients. I have had to promise them that she will be sold by auction to the highest bidder."

Prince Rashid's lips tightened and he frowned ominously and Hassan rushed into nervous speech.

"Sheik Turki, for example, has expressed interest -"

"That - that upstart!"

The Prince jumped to his feet and strode up and down, mastering the inner rage which it would be demeaning to show before this mercenary rogue who dared argue with him.

"I am sorry, Your Highness. Truly, I had no choice."

"Very well, Hassan. I am not pleased, but I shall be there. What do you think she will fetch?"

"Your Highness, I will do all that I can to help you acquire her, but I must warn you that bidding is likely to start perhaps as high as a quarter of a million dollars."

Prince Rashid nodded nonchalantly. "I shall be there, Hassan. The higher the price the sweeter the revenge!"

Hassan bowed deeply, hiding his inner delight.

"There will be several other white women, Highness, including a most attractive and unusual couple - an aristocratic English mother and daughter, and couple of beautiful blonde Norwegian nurses."

There was no reply. The Prince was no longer interested. He had turned away. The interview was over.

At the door Hassan salaamed again.

The matter was going well, but there remained much to see to.

Prince Rashid was very rich and very influential. He was a leading member, some people said the leading member, of the ruling family of Shamur, a geographically small but very rich sheikdom that had in recent years become one of the largest oil producers in the world.

He was a tall, well built and very good looking man in his early forties. His face was long and thin, with a small black beard, pointed and carefully trimmed. His dark eyes were alert and kindly, intelligent and observant, but they also portrayed the natural dominant and commanding aspect of his character. His voice was pleasant but nevertheless firm, typical of a man who was very sure of his position and his views. His charming manners and courtly smile, combined with his striking appearance, made him a popular and attractive figure - not least in the eyes of the women he met on his frequent visits to Europe.

He had been partly educated in Europe, and had travelled widely in the West as a trusted Minister of the Government of Shamur and had had several discreet affairs with European and American women.

Back in Shamur, his large and luxurious palace near the capital contained a spacious harem wing, which housed his three wives, half a dozen odalisques or senior concubines, and thirty junior concubines. His wives were all Princesses from the ruling families of Shamur or of the neighbouring states, though he usually kept the position of fourth wife vacant in order to encourage his concubines into greater efforts in pleasing him.

The concubines were all beautiful young women from Egypt, the Lebanon, Turkey, Morocco, Iran or Pakistan. To be considered for promotion to the much sought after position of odalisque, a concubine must first have borne the Prince a son, for, despite his Western veneer, he still had the the traditional urge of the desert leader to father many sons from carefully chosen women.

Some of the concubines had been bought from dealers. Some had been given to him as presents by other visiting Arab leaders or business associates. Some were women who had caught his eye on his travels and who had willingly entered his harem to enjoy the life of ease that it promised.

Although he was a well travelled, cultured and sophisticated man of the world, the Prince's attitude to women was basically the traditional Arab one of regarding them with compassion as inferior creatures who must be protected from their own passionate natures, and whose purpose in life is simply to give pleasure to men and be the mothers of their sons.

Until now, the Prince had not seriously considered permanently acquiring a European concubine, despite the many attractive offers that Hassan had made in recent years.

Amanda Aston, however, was a quite different matter.

She had called him a ruthless despot. A despot he was, but a benign one who saw to the welfare of his people, poured money into schools and hospitals and roads.

She had called him a despicable womaniser and an abuser of women, which in his eyes he was not. He saw nothing strange in denying his women the right to leave the harem, or to write or talk to other men or even see another man at close quarters. He considered it quite normal for the women immured in a rich man's harem to adore and worship their Master and love only one man, whilst a man could be interested in, and even love, quite a large number of women at the same time.

She had said other scornful things also, she had used her television program to humiliate him - unfairly and in public.

She deserved to be punished. She also needed to be silenced, for her words were poison.

Oh yes, it was unquestionably his duty to acquire, humiliate and punish this young woman for what she had said about him and, worse, about Islam: he would acquire much merit.

The fact that she was very beautiful would, admittedly, add to the pleasure!

2 - A LONG LINE OF SLAVE DEALERS!

Hassan Atala was pleased. His forbears would have approved of the way he had handled the Prince.

The fortunes of the House of Atala had started during the revival of the white slave trade by the Barbary pirates of North Africa during the long French Revolutionary and Napoleonic Wars. Suddenly large quantities of Christian women had flooded onto the slave markets of the Middle East. Many were simple peasant girls, snatched from their homes and coastal villages by the raiding Barbary corsairs. But amongst them were some well educated, and even aristocratic, Italian and Spanish women captured whilst they were summering in their family villas by the sea; or blond Northern women, the wives of German and Scandinavian sea captains, captured when their husband's ships were boarded by the Barbary pirates.

It was by handling these desirable and highly valuable women that the House of Atala had originally made its name - both with the buyers, chief black eunuchs who knew that they could return a woman whom their Masters spurned, and with the Reis, or Captains, of the corsair ships who knew that they would get an extra good price from the agents of the House of Atala for a special woman.

Then in the nineteenth century, when the Barbary corsairs had been suppressed and the Khedives, Beys and Pashas of Egyptian became yet more wealthy, the attention of the Atala's had switched to Constantinople, the capital of the cruel Ottoman Empire. Here the slave markets were often well stocked with women from the Balkans - the wives and daughters of unsuccessful Christian rebels. Once again, some were well educated women, condemned to slavery as part of the punishment of their menfolk and to set a terrifying example.

Like the old Barbary Corsairs, the dealers who followed the rapacious Turkish Army knew that they could sell such women on at a handsome profit to the Constantinople agents of the House of Atala.

So it was that after yet another revolt, a steady stream of good-looking young European women would be driven up onto the sales block in Cairo: beautiful Hungarian countesses who had married angry young Macedonian chieftains; tall blond women educated in the best schools in Vienna who had been caught up in the confusion of a Balkan war; or striking-looking upper class Greek and Romanian girls whose menfolk had been caught out plotting against the Ottoman rule.

Most of the women had become the pampered concubines, or even wives, of the wealthy Egyptian Beys and Pashas and had enjoyed a life of ease and luxury. But there had always been some wealthy Levantine gentlemen who really enjoyed having a recalcitrant white woman forced to labour on his estate under the whip of a black overseer as part of a chain gang of otherwise dusky skinned maidens - as an enjoyable and erotic alternative to forcing her to share his bed.

The fall of the Ottoman Empire at the end of the First World War made little difference, for now large numbers of beautiful but destitute White Russian refugees, often well educated and aristocratic, were flooding into Istanbul, as it was now called.

Sometimes by trickery, and sometimes out of sheer despair, some of the more attractive of these women came into the discreet hands of the House of Atala. This had been a very profitable business whilst supplies lasted, for the demand from the Egyptian Beys and Pashas for these outstandingly beautiful women, with their pure white skins, their passionate natures and hot tempers, seemed unlimited - as did the the enjoyment of their black eunuchs in disciplining them.

The second World War had seen Cairo and Alexandria full of attractive young refugees from many countries. Penniless and without protection, some were an easy prey for the well organised House of Atala.

The war had also seen the introduction of a growing number of British service women in Egypt. Hassan's father had specialised in a more limited, but lucrative market: pretty young British naval Wrens, often from good English families. In the chaotic circumstances of the war the occasional disappearance of a pretty young nubile Wren could be staged as a swimming or car accident.

It was all highly profitable for the British were little liked by the Egyptians and the idea of actually owning a pretty woman member of the hated occupying forces was particularly piquant for a wealthy but somewhat jaded Pasha - especially if the young woman was actually an officer.

Indeed Hassan's father had found that his wealthier clients were particularly ready to part with their money if a furious but frightened Wren officer was paraded for their inspection, naked except for her well pressed uniform jacket, embroidered with the correct number of blue stripes for her rank, and wearing her distinctive tricorn hat.

It had even been rumoured in certain circles that a member of the royal family kept a royal barge on his estates, bordering on the Nile, that was manned exclusively by young adducted British Wrens, supplied by Hassan's father and kept, wearing only their naval caps, chained to their oars. It was said that it was the sight of these naked English girls, sweating at their oars under the whip of a black overseer, that would compensate him for the many humiliations that he suffered from the British as a member of what they regarded as a mere puppet ruling family.

When, after the war, Nasser had overthrown the King and the old ruling class, Hassan had to seek further afield for his clientele. Fortunately for him, it was just at this time that the huge oil revenues had started to pour into the pockets of the ruling families.

As this vast wealth spread among a growing number of Arab Princes and Sheiks, so too did a new demand for many things Western: cars, yachts, modern palaces, racing cars, private jets and white women - especially white women.

These newly rich Princelings, however, soon tired of semi-professional European courtesans, dancers and call-girls. What they wanted, and what they were willing and able to pay high prices for, were beautiful but respectable white women, even if they were unwilling. This was the demand that Hassan was now specialised in meeting.

From his new headquarters in the Red Sea, an establishment discreetly disguised as a private nursing home for women, Hassan supplied a small but steady stream of reluctant and horrified white women to the harems of many of the wealthiest men in the Arab world.

It was, of course, a business that had to be carried on with great circumspection and discretion for Arab men never discuss their women or their harems, nor do they wish to become involved in some scandal regarding the disappearance of a white woman. But once such a woman was locked up in their harems, they would make sure she never escaped to tell her story.

It was a business that earned Hassan very considerable profits, for most of the women fetched high prices, being strikingly beautiful, well educated and of good families - even if they were appalled at the life that lay ahead of them. Often indeed it was their very unwillingness that made them worth so much more in the eyes of their cruel Masters.

Part of this new business was to arrange, for a considerable fee, for the disappearance and abduction of a particular European woman who had caught the eye, or, in the case of Amanda, the wrath of several wealthy Arabs.

Much of his success depended on effective agents in Europe, able to advise him on the potential availability of suitable women. Equally important was the discreet liaison he maintained with his clients, or potential clients, in the Middle East, or more usually with the black eunuchs in charge of their harems - sending them detailed information and, if possible, videos, of women coming onto the market.

Hassan, had no qualms of conscience about his trade. On the contrary, he felt, like his forebears before him, that he was providing an essential service. In the Moslem world, middle-aged rich men had been buying young women for their pleasure, and keeping them locked up in their harems, for centuries. Moreover it was a tradition that was being given a new boost by the fundamentalist drive sweeping the Arab world, one of whose tenants was to put women back into the veil, the chador - and the harem.

Hassan liked to regard himself as the Sotheby's of the white slave trade, selling a relatively small number of really top quality goods to a limited clientele.

3 - HASSAN ATALA MAKES HIS PLANS

Hassan inserted the video cassette that had been made for his approval and switched on the player.

The screen showed two very pretty tall young women on a little stage. There was a background of Arab music. The women were dressed in long nurse's uniforms that buttoned down the front. Their hair was hidden by their nurses' caps.

Hassan smiled approvingly. He liked his clients to be first shown white women as if being auctioned but dressed as they would normally have been if they had still been free. Not only did this serve to show the client the background of the woman being displayed, but also accentuated the fact that a once free Western woman could now be bought as a mere concubine.

The women were smiling nervously at the video camera.

"My name is Ingrid," said one of the young women in a charming Scandinavian accent.

"And my name is Brigit," said the other in a similar accent.

Their lips had been painted scarlet, and their eyes had been carefully made-up and outlined with kohl in the Eastern fashion. Their eyes seemed unnaturally large - thanks to drops of belladonna.

Again Hassan smiled approvingly. The sight of respectable European women erotically made up like Arab dancing girls never failed to arouse interest.

But even more erotic was the sight of each tall woman now being led round the stage by a small black boy holding a dog lead fastened to a collar round her neck. The black boys were dressed in red baggy trousers, embroidered waistcoats and big silken turbans. The Eastern opulence of their dress acted as a further erotic contrast to the simple Western uniforms of the women - and so did their small size and the little dog whips with which they were tapping the buttocks of their tall charges.

The women were in fact a couple of Norwegian nurses who had been working for an aid organisation in Eritrea. They had been captured by guerillas when the isolated village in which they had been working was overrun. The guerillas very short of money had sold them to Hassan's local agents.

Now being sold as a matched pair, Hassan was confident that they would reach a good price at his next auction - provided the video showed them off well. Copies of the video would be discreetly sent to the chief black eunuchs in charge of the harems of certain wealthy Arab clients whom Hassan thought might well be interested in this pair. At the auction telephone bids would be taken as well as bids from those present in the auction room.

The video continued to show the two young women being walked up and down by their small black keepers, their high heel shoes showing off their carriage. The video now zoomed in to show each of the young women's breasts wobbling entrancingly under the thin nurse's uniforms and on their excitingly swaying buttocks.

Then a larger and stronger-looking black boy entered. He was carrying a pair of shiny metal handcuffs. He gripped the wrists of one of the young women and pulled them behind her back, making her grimace.

"No! No!" she shouted. She started to struggle but there was a clicking noise and her hands were now helplessly fastened behind her.

Hassan nodded approvingly. It was important that the video showed the woman off as if she was being auctioned.

The larger boy, still standing behind her, now gently removed her nurse's cap, letting her long blonde hair tumble down. Then he expertly arranged it so that it hung entrancingly over one shoulder.

The sight of this silken cascade of honey coloured hair made even the jaded Hassan catch his breath. Blonde hair always had an electrifying effect in the Arab world and this would really make the rich viewers sit up!

Then her small black keeper, still holding her lead in one hand, slowly began to unbutton the front of her uniform. The larger boy, still standing behind her, suddenly jerked the top of the uniform down over her shoulders, baring her breasts. The young woman wriggled with delightful embarrassment as she vainly tried to cover them with her hands.

"Be still!" the boy shouted giving her a hard tap across her buttocks with his dog whip. "Head up! Shoulders back!"

The terrified woman's firm breasts were now thrust forward. They were surprisingly large. Her nipples were also surprisingly prominent - and painted the same shade of scarlet as her lips.

Again Hassan smiled. Arab men liked large breasts and nipples. Clearly, the breast enlargement and nipple stretching treatment that he had ordered for these women had been a great success. The latest laser American equipment had been expensive, and so he had been sending one his black assistants to learn how to use it. But it had been well worthwhile, and a little breast enlargement and forming was now standard for most of the white women who passed through his hands.

It was a more difficult decision to decide whether or not a particular woman should have another certain little operation - one that greatly increased the value of a woman in the eyes of some men. It would much reduce the pleasure felt by a woman, but without reducing her ability to give pleasure. Indeed it made the girl concentrate more on the pleasure she was giving to her Master. It also largely removed the temptation to deceive her Master with another woman, or even with another a man or by herself. Above all, it greatly increased the feeling of power felt by the Master, and although it was cruel and sadistic, it had been considered perfectly normal in much of Africa and Arabia for centuries - and still was.

In its simplest form, it was such a simple operation - just a little snip and a woman's main source of pleasure was removed. Many African women had the operation done when they were children, but the idea of it being done to a grown white woman was one that greatly appealed to some of Hassan's clients - but not to all. Many men preferred the feeling of making his woman respond, even against her wishes.

Hassan often liked to offer in each sale at least one white woman who had been cut and to offer to cut another free of charge if bought by the same customer, either before delivery or if she was subsequently brought back for it to be done.

Hassan rubbed his nose. Should he have had these Norwegian girls cut? Probably not. He turned back to the screen.

The small black boy was continuing to undo the buttons. Soon a narrow waist and flat belly were displayed. Hassan had ordered both of the young women to be put on a strict diet and kept well exercised. He was delighted with the result, for the contrast between the prominent but firm breasts, the slender waist, and the hint of the swelling but still hidden hips was very arousing.

The larger boy now went over to the other young woman.

Despite her protests, she too was handcuffed, and her equally lovely blonde hair carefully arranged. Then the top of her uniform was undone and jerked back over her shoulders to display her big firm breasts, stretched nipples and slender waist.

They really were a matched pair, thought Hassan, and as such would sell very well indeed.

The two black boys delicately finished unbuttoning the uniforms and then dramatically pulled them back to disclose long white legs and hairless mounds, under which their equally hairless but scarlet painted beauty glistened provocatively.

Then, not giving the viewers more than a glimpse of these delights, the camera came behind the two young women, displaying their long backs, slender waists and voluptuous buttocks.

Hassan lent forward and switched off the video. It would do very nicely and copies should be sent out immediately to the black eunuchs in charge of the harems of a dozen or more potential buyers. By working through these influential personages he was able to ensure a steady flow of continuing business with his clients, since the eunuch was able to take the credit for finding these new acquisitions for his Master and would be keen to arrange for a repeat order!

By keeping in touch with these black eunuchs he was also able to keep himself better informed of the individual desires, disappointments, and new requirements of his clients. Arab gentlemen do not discuss their harems with other men, but their black eunuchs do!

Hassan mentally patted himself on the back for having acquired this delightful matched pair here in Africa. It was a trend that was increasing. On the one hand, the increasing famine in the black African states meant that more young white women were going there under the auspices of various small aid organisations. And, on the other hand, the increasing chaos and fighting was throwing up more opportunities for these women to disappear and end up in the hands of an agent of a white slave dealer.

It was really a continuation of the centuries-old slave trade that had brought women from all parts of black Africa to the Red Sea and on to Arabia - a trade with which he maintained close links despite his family tradition of dealing only in top grade white women. He was able to offer its dealers a ready market for the more exotic of the women they had captured. He had, for instance, recently handled an educated black English Princess from Uganda, a pretty young university graduate from Sierra Leone, and even a younger member of the Ethiopian royal family who had escaped from the prison in which her family were incarcerated, only to find herself imprisoned in a harem.

He also maintained a useful link with a certain terrorist organisation which periodically raided the outlying settlements of Israel. They often had nubile young Israeli women on their hands, whom they were anxious to dispose of for a good price, or pretty girls from many countries who had strayed one evening a little too far from the carefully guarded walls of the kibbutz.

Hassan chuckled to himself as he remembered how after one Arab-Israeli war he had even been able to sell to a certain black potentate a complete captured platoon of young Israeli girl soldiers, together with their young woman officer. The potentate had enjoyed putting the entire platoon into a chain gang to work half naked under the whip of a black overseer on his private estate. It had been spectacle that was also much enjoyed by visiting Arab dignitaries, smarting from the humiliation of Arab defeats.

All this would so impress the influential Arab visitors from rich oil states that they would recommend, on their return, that further funds be sent to the African potentate for the further development of a country whose anti-Israeli sentiments were so strikingly displayed.

But, of course, the mainstay of his business remained his chain of agents in Europe.

These were expert in spotting, abducting, holding and dispatching suitable women. His previous sale had included a young French model, the brilliant but errant daughter of a penniless Irish peer, and a promising young ballet dancer from Denmark. It was their background, as well as their beauty, that had attracted the attention of his clients and had resulted in all of them reaching a high price in his auction ring.

He chuckled again at the thought that his next sale would include not only the controversial young journalist Amanda Aston, but also, as a special pair, the niece of an English peer and her pretty teenage daughter.

Partly by judicious bribery, he had been able to keep his operations highly secret and out of the public eye. They were based on a remote island in the Red Sea. A simple code enabled details of what was required in the female line, and what was available, to be passed by telephone in an apparently innocuous conversation regarding equestrian matters. Virgins, for instance, were referred to as unbroken fillies, young married women were mares, women who had already had a child were brood mares, pregnant women were mares in-foal, harems were stables and chief black eunuchs were trainers, and so on. Hassan himself was a bloodstock dealer.

As a separate sideline Hassan would occasionally take advantage of the efficiency of his network of agents to accept a private and confidential commission to arrange for the abduction of a particular woman who had caught the eye, or perhaps the wrath, of a wealthy Arab sheik or prince. He chuckled at the thought of the well known young French show jumper whose pretty thighs had recently caught the eye of a visiting Arab ruler. Arranging for her secret disappearance had been a complex matter, but now she was devoting her talents to satisfying a cruel master in the strict seclusion of his stables.

Gerda von Brahm, a young girl who had been aboard the coaster that had recently delivered the infamous Amanda Aston and the mother and daughter, was another such case. At a gymnastic competition at Munich she had caught the eye of an elderly but wealthy sheik. Fascinated by the young girl's extraordinarily agile body, he had commissioned Hassan to acquire her for his harem, for a very large fee, in order to enliven his old age - a choice young fruit for an elderly degenerate.

Such commissions were not necessarily confined to the fair sex. He had been asked to deliver, neatly emasculated, a very good looking young ballet dancer a rich Sheik had admired at a gala performance. He had joined the Sheik's male harem of similarly castrated young men and youths - colts who had been gelded, as Hassan euphemistically described them.

Hassan was a great believer in the efficacy of cattle goads as a way of controlling white women. Once they were in the harem of their future Masters, then they would have to face the cane, the whip and even the bastinado. But meanwhile he preferred to keep them unmarked and for this the goad was ideal.

His thoughts were interrupted by a black servant boy announcing that the coaster was in sight.

Hassan strode onto a balcony. Yes, there she was. She would be anchoring soon and her secret cargo transferred to his 'nursing home'.

This was potentially a tricky operation, for he did not want a valuable young woman throwing herself into the shark infested Red Sea. Nor did he want any women being seen by prying eyes.

More importantly, he did not want any of the women to see where they were, or even what the coaster looked like. It was essential that even if a woman later escaped to freedom she could not tell a tale that might incriminate Hassan and his organisation.

The crew would have drugged the women, and put them into small innocuous wooden crates which the ships's cranes would lower into his launch, apparently as stores for his Nursing Home.

But half an hour later all four women would be safely locked up, and recovering from their drugs - having no idea where they were or how they got there.

4 - HASSAN'S SECRET WHITE SLAVE ESTABLISHMENT

Amanda lay on the bed of her locked room. She was naked, except for her gloved hands and the leather collar round her neck by which she was chained to a ring at the head of the bed, terrified, helpless and totally bewildered.

The gloves were really mittens, thick and fingerless, and made it impossible for her to grip anything. Indeed everything, even her most intimate toilet, was being done for her by two little black boys who spoke no English.

The room was attractively furnished and air conditioned - all part of Hassan's policy of allaying the natural fears and anxieties of the mainly white women he handled. There was a chintz on the comfortable armchair and an attractive silk cover on the bed. The dressing table and curtains made a pretty sight. In an annex off the bedroom was a modern bathroom.

It might have been the guest room of a country house bedroom were it not for the carefully locked door, the bars across the window, and the high wall that completely shut off the view. There was also the noticeable absence of anything made of glass, of anything sharp, of picture cord, or indeed of anything which a person under stress might use to harm themselves.

It was now two days after she had been taken off the Arab registered coaster from Sicily which had crossed the Mediterranean, and made a rendezvous off Crete with the caique bringing the unfortunate young Gerda von Brahm. Nor had she realised that they had traversed the Suez Canal, for all the time they had been kept gagged and confined to a secret compartment. Then the ship had gone down to the Red Sea to Hassan's private island.

Drugged, Amanda and her companions had not felt the ship slowing down, nor the shaking as the anchor cable ran out, nor the sudden vibration as the engines were put astern. Shortly afterwards they were put into little wooden crates that were nailed down before being lowered into Hassan's boat. None of them would ever be able to pinpoint the location of this strange Nursing Home.

It had therefore been an astonished Amanda who, naked and with her hands still encased in the thick gloves, had slowly regained consciousness in the room in which she was now chained. She had no idea where she was, nor why, and only a vague idea about what had happened to her companions. She was also mystified by the presence of two grinning young black boys with electric cattle goads.

Hassan's so-called nursing home was situated in a discreet and half hidden position between two hills in a little island some miles off a small port on the mainland. The port gave the coaster an excellent excuse to call in periodically to unload its genuine cargo of European goods: refrigerators, clothes, electric light bulbs and so forth.

A helicopter landing pad had been built on the island near the nursing home, and near the port was a convenient landing strip. Not only did Hassan sometimes receive his merchandise by air, but also his clients, or their black eunuchs, often came by private aircraft or helicopter to view the merchandise for themselves or to attend an auction.

No questions were ever asked about the silent and heavily veiled figures who sometimes embarked in, or disembarked from, the helicopters or aircraft, nor about the coffin-shaped trunks that often formed part of the luggage of departing Arab dignitaries.

For the first day Amanda had been left lying chained to the bed with her hands still helpless in the gloves. The black boys had fed and potted her like a baby. It had only needed one of them to raise his goad menacingly, whilst simultaneously putting his finger to his lips, to make her stop protesting and asking questions. But she could not help noticing how they had grinned at each other as they constantly felt her relatively small breasts.

But on the second morning after they had washed and bathed her, they dressed her in a pretty negligee that made her feel more like a pampered woman, and a lead was fastened to her collar.

They unlocked the door and the first boy led her down the corridor. The second boy followed close behind her, his goad raised. Nervously she followed close behind the first boy.

She saw to her consternation that the thick glass windows looking into her room bedroom and bathroom were one way ones. She must have been under constant but unseen observation!

At last they came to a door. One of the boys opened it and led her inside. It was a modern beauty parlour!

A pretty young black girl dressed in a white house coat walked across and took Amanda's arm reassuringly. She led her towards a hairdresser's chair.

"Now we make you beautiful!" she said in broken English.

"You speak English!" cried Amanda. "At last! What is happening?"

"No questions!" the young black girl said. "I am not allowed to answer questions. You will learn all in time." She pointed to the goad held by one of the black boys. "No more questions!"

At the sight of the goad, Amanda instantly became silent. One of the black boys went out, leaving his companion standing by the door, his arms crossed on his chest, his goad at the ready.

The young negress started to wash Amanda's hair.

Half an hour later, as she sat under the drier, the black girl took off one of Amanda's gloves and started to give her a manicure. Amanda was thrilled to feel her hand free again. But instantly the black boy came up and stood by her, waving his goad, as if warning her not to try and take advantage of her hand being released. Minutes later the black girl, strapped the glove back onto Amanda's right hand and took off her left one.

Amanda was now made to stand up and the black girl, helped by the boy, took off her negligee, making her feel very naked and ashamed. She was told to lie down on a couch. Her legs were waxed. Her toe nails were painted. Then the black girl, bending over her, started to work on her face, using a variety of creams, of foundations, of rouge, of eye-brow pencils and eye shadows, of mascara and kohl, and of lipsticks.

She caught a brief glimpse of herself in a mirror. She certainly looked superb in a heavily made-up Eastern way, her long blonde hair glistening like spun gold, her eyes huge and sparkling, outlined in black, her high cheekbones set off by clever shadowing, her lips painted scarlet.

Then suddenly the second black boy came back. Before Amanda realised what had happened her wrists had been strapped to the side of the couch, and a strap fastened across her naked belly and another across her throat. She was now held down helpless on the couch. She could not even raise her head to see what they were doing to her.

The black girl pulled down a strap from a metal arm that hung over the couch. One the black boys raised Amanda's ankle and the other boy fastened the strap round it. Then they repeated the process with her other ankle.

Her knees were now held raised, and wide apart. She saw the young black beautician coming towards her with something in her hand. She heard a humming noise. An electric razor!

"No! No! Please not there!" Amanda shouted as she suddenly realised what was going to be done to her.

"Oh yes! We make you smooth like little girl! Arab man like that!" The black girl bent over Amanda's body and carefully began her task, first with the electric razor and then with special burning creams.

Just as she was finishing, a black man dressed like a surgeon came into the room. To Amanda's horror, she saw that he was holding a syringe in his hand, and was followed by two white robed Arabs wheeling a trolley.

The man exchanged words with the black girl, nodded and then came towards the couch, his epidermic syringe raised. Amanda started to scream as she felt a little prick in her arm, but her scream died on her lips as she collapsed into unconsciousness.

Once again Amanda had slowly regained consciousness lying naked on the bed in her room. Once again she was chained by the neck to the head of the bed, and those awful gloves were still on her hands. Once again the two black boys stood grinning by her bedside.

As her head cleared, she felt a slight pain in her breasts. They felt somehow heavier, somehow larger. She glanced down. Her normally small nipples seemed huge!

She felt strange between the legs and raised her head to look down properly. She was as smooth as a baby girl! Horrified she remembered what the black girl was doing to her when the black surgeon had come in. She remembered the girl's strange remark about Arab men. But what had Arab men go to do with her?

To her embarrassment one of the boys started to stroke her now smooth beauty lips whilst the other, equally admiringly, felt her apparently heavier breasts and stretched nipples. They were talking excitedly to each other.

She longed to question the black boys. But she knew that it was a waste of time. There was no one she could speak to.

For two whole days the black boys kept her lying on her back silent and helpless, periodically feeding her with fruits and milk.

Then, without a word of explanation, she was taken out of her room again and taken on a lead back along the passage, and once again she was led on into the beauty parlour where the black girl was waiting to do her hair. Once again she was strapped down on the couch and any little hairs that might have re-grown were carefully removed.

Then the two black boys came over to her as she lay with her legs raised. Chattering to each other in some strange language, and one of them carrying a little notebook, they started to examine her intimately.

Her head held back by the strap across her throat, she felt the cold of a probing instrument being inserted. She felt herself being stretched and she felt hands and fingers.

It was too awful being treated in this way by mere boys, even if they did seem to know what they were doing. They were conferring and writing notes - notes about her, about her body!

It was as if someone wanted a full and intimate report on her. And this indeed was the case, for Hassan never sent a video of a woman to a rich client's chief black eunuch without also supplying her full details - the sort of intimate details that an efficient black eunuch would want to have before recommending the purchase of a white woman to his Master.

Then once again the terrifying surgeon-like figure came in and once again she passed out as she felt a little prick in her arm. Once again she regained consciousness in her room and once again there was a dull pain in her breasts which once again seemed even heavier, and her nipples even longer.

Once again she was kept resting on her bed silent and helpless for a couple of days.

Then the whole process had been repeated again. But this time she was only left to recover for a couple of hours and then the black boys unchained her neck and gestured to her to get up.

Immediately she felt the strange extra weight of her breasts. She put her hands to them, but her gloves prevented her from feeling them properly. The black boys gestured to her to look at herself in the full length mirror. Her face and hair were beautiful and her now longer nipples had been painted to match her lips.

But she was even more embarrassed when she looked down at her shorn mound. It was quite hairless and bald, and had been rouged to match her cheeks, whilst her beauty lips had been painted to match her nipples and lips.

Suddenly she blushed prettily. Her body now looked strange, new, fuller, powdered, polished and painted. It was exciting but shaming! It was shocking. It was embarrassing. But she began to feel a curious pride in her new erotic look.

She would been less proud and even more embarrassed, had she known that the large fleshy figure of Hassan Atala the slave dealer stood looking through the one way mirror from the corridor side.

He was rubbing his hands with delight as he admired his latest acquisition, his latest investment. Bearing in mind that originally he had simply acquired Amanda, without thinking of her potential beauty, simply to satisfy the need for revenge of certain leading Arab dignitaries, he had wondered whether to bother to have her breasts enlarged.

Seeing the effect, however, he was glad that he had done so.

It was the next day that the little black boys showed her the row of beautiful dresses hanging in a cupboard in her room, together with stockings and shoes and hats.

They dressed her first in one dress and then in another, chattering excitedly like children playing with a doll.

Despite her anxiety, Amanda felt herself being drawn to these immaculately cut and very feminine dresses. It was all part of the routine that Hassan had used for years with many white women. He knew only too well that after nearly two weeks of being kept cooped up in the ship and in her room, wearing only a nightdress, many white women would find the sight of these beautiful but suggestive dresses irresistibly appealing, and somehow reassuring.

She would feel a woman again, and an attractive and well dressed one at that.

So it was that the next day found Amanda walking up and down her locked room, not so much like a caged and bewildered animal as like a proud and self confident woman.

She was wearing a simple well cut black cocktail dress with a swirling skirt split up one side that disclosed to perfection her long shapely legs, her slim figure, her large and firm breasts, and her now very white and very soft skin.

Amanda looked into the mirror. She saw a very beautiful and desirable woman. Certainly the dress made her feel very feminine. It was also one that had been chosen for her to wear when later that day the video tape was to be made. Under it the dress was allowed only an expensive looking satin slip that had been specially chosen for the erotic effective it would have when the dress was removed.

Under the slip she was quite naked, except for the her black stockings and black suspender belt, both which matched her big black hat and long black gloves - for once quite normal gloves.

Only the leather collar fastened round her neck showed that anything untoward was planned.

The door opened and in came the two black boys. With them was an older black boy she had not seen before. Snapping a lead onto her collar, they led down the corridor, but this time on past the beauty parlour. A door was opened. Amanda found herself standing on a little floodlit stage around which she was invited to parade.

At this stage Hassan wanted to catch the attention of certain clients by showing them a video of Amanda, a beautiful and intelligent young woman, unaware of her fate, unaware of just what had been done to her breasts, unaware that she was in the hands of a white slave dealer, and unaware of the retribution that was about to fall on her.

At an actual auction, or at private presentations, he liked the women to be paraded under the duress of the whip, to be paraded in a highly embarrassed and terrified state, a state which he knew of old was guaranteed to arouse potential buyers and persuade them to bid far more highly than they had intended.

For the English mother and daughter, who were to be offered at the same time, he decided that a similar scene should be shown. It would be aimed at making a rich client determined to own this attractive upper class English women and to have them broken in for his personal use. They would be shown being forcibly stripped, just as had the video of the two Norwegian nurses.

But in Amanda's case the video was to be different. It would show the woman who had so insulted Arab manhood in a more subtle and relaxed way. He felt his clients would respond best if she were shown as an apparently free woman, wearing pretty if suggestive European clothes, and undressing in apparent privacy - for, of course, it would still be important to show her naked.

Hassan felt that Amanda and her two companions, for unknown to them their other companion Gerda had already been despatched to the elderly sheik who had commissioned her abduction, were now ready to be filmed. Enhanced by powder and lack of direct sun, their bodies were now dead white and their muscles soft. They had all put on a few pounds as a result of their mainly milk diet, and whilst in no way fat or plump, their bodies had a slightly more rounded look - just the soft and sensuous effect that a Middle Eastern gentleman usually likes to see in a woman destined for his harem.

So it was that, confused as to why the black boys wanted her to do it but scared stiff of their goads, Amanda played along with them, walking up and down in front of the hidden cameras, smiling when they laughed, and letting herself be undressed, first down to her satin slip and then down to her stockings and suspender belt, gloves and hat.

Encouraged by the basic English of the black beautician, Amanda made a little speech giving her name. Then she almost wept when she said how she missed her friends and her boy friend - something which brought a smile of contentment to the watching Hassan, for he knew that this would greatly increase her attractions in the eyes of the cruel men who might buy her. For them the idea of using in their harem the woman of another man was deeply satisfying. This was something that went back to days of bedouin tribes raiding each other for their women.

The final edited video recording of Amanda was highly successful. Hassan arranged for copies to be taken to certain clients he did not need to speak to personally.

5 - SHEIK TURKI MAKES HIS PLANS

Sheik Turki was the opposite of Prince Rashid in almost every way: in appearance, in manners, and in his attitude to European women.

Sheik Turki was short and fat - a repulsive-looking man, with a hook nose and a full beard. Behind the dark glasses which he invariably wore, his eyes were cold and expressionless. His voice was soft and somehow chilling.

Sheik Turki had deliberately stocked his harem with reluctant white women. And whereas for the busy Prince Rashid his harem was an amusing little sideline, for the under-employed Sheik Turki it was the centre of his life.

He too was a member of a ruling family - of the nearby state of Sadek, which was almost as rich in oil revenues as Shamur. Ever since he was a young man he had been a frivolous playboy, interested only in his own pleasure.

He had schemed and plotted to become the Crown Prince and eventually the Ruler of Sadek but, after numerous unsavoury scandals involving white women, his reputation, both at home and abroad, had alarmed both his own family and other ruling families as well.

Prince Rashid in Shamur had been largely responsible for organising a counter coup to oust Turki from the succession. To keep him quiet, Turki had been granted a very large pension. He now lived in a neighbouring sheikdom where he had bought himself a large estate in the interior centred on a fertile oasis in the desert. Here he had built himself a well guarded, luxurious and spacious palace, which he liked to think surpassed in splendour even that of his arch enemy and rival Prince Rashid.

The harem of Sheik Turki was ruled over by his cunning and repulsive chief black eunuch, Mansour, a huge negro, six foot six inches tall. Mansour was a man of great physical strength, capable of picking up a recalcitrant woman and carrying her off under his arm for punishment.

Mansour spoke in the high pitched falsetto voice of a eunuch. It sometimes made a newly arrived white woman regard him as a pathetic figure of fun. But she soon learnt that there was nothing pathetic about his huge frame, nor about his brutal-looking face disfigured with tribal scars, nor about the cruel way he dealt with the women in his care, terrorising them into cringe fawning over Sheik Turki in their eagerness to provide him with pleasure and so earn Mansour a steady stream of bonus payments.

Beautiful bodies had no physical attraction for Mansour, but he had great pleasure in controlling a woman's every thought, word and deed, as well as from punishing them if they were impertinent or lazy, and training them to be his Master's most obsequious possessions.

Mansour shielded Sheik Turki from his women's tantrums, emotions, jealousies, female ailments and occasional rebelliousness - problems which largely stemmed from being kept cooped up, under constant supervision, in the sensual atmosphere of a harem, and from being forced to look to their repulsive and hated Master, Sheik Turki, for any hope of sexual relief.

Mansour bowed to his Master and handed him a video tape that Hassan had given him that morning.

"This is Amanda Aston?" Turki enquired eagerly.

"Yes indeed, Your Highness!"

Mansour disconnected the large television screen from the internal television cameras in the harem to which it was normally connected. The video tape started to play.

Sheik Turki lay back on the comfortable chair in his study, gloating. Mansour stood behind him. At the Sheik's feet, the naked back of a young white woman served as his footstool. The Sheik's eyes glistened wildly as he watched entranced. The young woman did not dare to move or make a sound as she knelt on all fours, her back beautifully straight, her palms flat on the floor, whilst hatred of her Master dominated her thoughts.

The video ended.

"I want her! I want her here. That little bitch! I'll teach her a lesson alright! She'll soon rue the day she ever tried to make a fool of me on her damn television show!"

Mansour coughed discreetly.

"I understand that Prince Rashid is also interested in acquiring her, Highness."

"Rashid?"

"Indeed Your Highness. She criticised him also. I understand that he is willing to pay a very large sum to acquire her."

There was a long silence. Mansour knew that his Master longed to revenge himself on Prince Rashid. Nevertheless he was getting a little overspent on his pension, having just bought a couple of lovely young French girls from Hassan.

"Perhaps, Your Highness, it might be possible to extract this young lady from the palace of Prince Rashid at a later date - and at little cost!"

"Kidnap her?"

Mansour spread his hands and smiled.

"Yes, indeed, Mansour! Kidnap her from Rashid! Just what I was thinking! We already have spies in Prince Rashid's palace. Let's give them something to do!. And it will humiliate him greatly to be deprived of his enjoyment of this bitch! Ah yes!"

In his excitement, Sheik Turki kicked down at the naked woman kneeling at his feet. But she was too well trained, and too frightened of Mansour's cane to do more than gasp and straighten her back.

"And if Your Highness were to allow Prince Rashid to outbid you for this particular young lady," said Mansour, "then, pending the completion of your other arrangements, I think Hassan would be able to offer you something else that might amuse you meanwhile."

Mansour replaced the video tape of Amanda with another. He knew his Master well.

"A pretty aristocratic English lady and her teenage daughter," he explained suavely. "Both being sold together as one lot in the same auction as the other English woman. They will go for a high price, of course, a white mother and daughter is a rare event indeed, and these are aristocrats! But think what you will be saving on the Amanda Aston bitch!"

He switched on the new tape. Sheik Turki watched in silence as the two women were paraded and then stripped. His eyes gleamed at the size of the mother's breasts - just as they had earlier at the sight of Amanda's. They gleamed again when Mansour whispered that the daughter was still a virgin.

The tape ended. There was another long pause.

"Mansour, I want you to go to the sale. Have a good look at the famous Amanda Aston, so that you can give me full report on her physical attributes. I want you to bid for her, until there is only you and Prince Rashid bidding. Then I want you to drop out, as if you had reached your limit, and let Prince Rashid buy her. In this way, when she disappears, he will go through the torment of suspecting that I am enjoying her, but will not be able to prove anything! And be sure you come back with the mother and daughter."

He rubbed his hands with delight.

"Yes, it will be a double revenge! Revenge on Prince Rashid and revenge on that bitch! I've got some special plans for her! Very special! The high and mighty Amanda Aston! She's really going to suffer for her insults!"

The Sheik leaned forward and started to whisper into the eunuch's ear. Mansour's eyes became larger and larger.

"Excellent, Your Highness, excellent!" he laughed. "Life in the Prince's harem would be child's play by comparison!"

6 - AMANDA LEARNS THE BITTER TRUTH

It was time to start rehearsals for the auction, time to confront the women with the truth about what was going to happen to them. In that way they would be suitable shamed and horrified by the auction - something that would make it all the more the more exciting for the buyers, and so push up their bids.

Hassan lifted his house phone. A few minutes later Amanda, wearing only her negligee and the mitten gloves, was led in by her two young black keepers. They led her up to a large desk and then unfastened her lead and stood back.

Amanda started when she saw the large flabby figure of Hassan sitting smiling behind his desk like a successful businessman - which of course he was.

"Who are you?" she cried out.

"That is not important, Miss Aston."

"You speak English! Oh, thank God! Are you a policeman come to release me?"

"No, Miss Aston, I not a policeman. I have captured you."

"Captured me!"

"Yes, Miss Aston! You are now my property. And you are now in the Middle East!"

"What!"

"Yes! And cast your mind back a few months. Surely you must realise that the rich Arabs you so scathingly treated in your programme would pay almost anything to get their hands on you!"

"Bah! Arabs! How I despise those rich womanising bastards! Anyway I'm a free Englishwoman! They can't do anything to me!"

"Unfortunately for you, Miss Aston, they certainly can under Arab law - once they've bought you from me!"

"Arab Law! Who cares a hoot about some bloody wog Arab Law!"

"You will, my dear Miss Aston! For you are now in an Arab country and you're going to be sold to a wealthy Arab."

"But - but why -"

Hassan laughed, not a pleasant sound. "To put you into his harem, of course."

"His harem! But this is the twentieth century, for Heaven's sake."

"Yes, and in Arabia the harem system is still very alive. Many harems have attractive European women in them - and the more unwilling they are, the more desirable they become."

"Oh no!" sobbed Amanda. "But I'm British and surely the British Ambassador..."

"Will never even know of your presence here. And as for being British, just remember that for so long the British were the hated ruling power in many Arab countries. The idea of having an Englishwoman, especially a well known feminist, locked up in one's harem would be particularly piquant. Of course, in your case it is really more a question of seeking revenge on an outspoken, I would say a very rashly outspoken, Englishwoman!"

"Oh no!"

"Oh yes! You are a very valuable investment. So you are now going to start rehearsing and practising for your sale. I want to get the best possible price for you."

"No! No! It can't be true, it simply can't," cried Amanda. Then she shook her head and pulled herself together. No one was going to treat her like this! "Well I certainly won't do anything to help you. I won't! You horrible creep! You can go and jump in the lake for all I care. So there! I'm off."

She turned towards the door.

"Miss Aston!" The voice was commanding. Amanda stopped. "On the contrary, you will do exactly what I say".

Then things seemed to move very fast. Hassan gave an order in Arabic to one of the little black boys. The boy raised his electric cattle goad and touched her with it - and she screamed.

Hassan gave another order in Arabic. The second boy suddenly seized Amanda's wrists and held them firmly behind her back. Hassan rose from his desks and came over to Amanda. He raised his hand and slowly slapped her across the face, hard, twice.

"Oh! No, please!" cried the now struggling Amanda.

"Silence!" shouted Hassan, raising his voice for the first time. Then he bent forward and expertly and quickly unbuttoned her negligee. He threw it back, baring her body from her neck to her ankles. Then he also gripped her wrists and nodded at the first boy, the one holding the dreadful goad.

The boy pressed the switch and, touching Amanda's skin, slowly drew it across Amanda's heaving breasts.

Amanda was screaming and wriggling at the pain of the shocks. She jumped back away from the terrible thing, but she was held tightly. Slowly they pushed her back, screaming, towards the goad.

But the black boy had maliciously switched off the goad. He slowly began to draw it down across her belly. Relieved, she felt nothing except the touch of the cold metal. Then he suddenly switched it on again, making her scream and jump. The goad was now drawn down slowly to the most sensitive part of her body. Her screams and wriggles became those of a maniac.

Then the goad was withdrawn and her hands released. Sobbing, she covered her face with her hands.

"You must do everything I tell you to do," came Hassan's quiet voice. "At once! You have no choice in the matter. Do you understand, Miss Aston?"

Amanda nodded dumbly, her head still buried in her hands. Never again, she resolved, would she ever be so silly. She would do whatever this awful man wanted her to do.

"Now listen carefully. I'm going to have you trained to show yourself off properly at your auction - to the crack of my whip. But that will be merely for effect. You will know, and I will know, that if you do not perform properly, if you make the slightest mistake, if you do show off your body as you will be taught, if you do not smile, if you are bad tempered or if you simply slouch about, then you will feel the goad, down between your legs again - but this time for longer, much longer."

"Oh God!"

"Do you understand, Miss Aston?" Momentarily he touched her intimately. "Just remember the goad will be placed here - and held here."

"No!"

"Very well, but just remember!"

A few minutes later, Amanda was back in her room with the door locked again from the outside. Her training would begin in half an hour, Hassan had told her. Helpless and overcome with the emotion engendered by her interview with Hassan, she flung herself weeping onto the bed. Her life in England, her family, her friends, her feminist writing, her broadcasts, all now seemed very distant and hazy. What was real, terrifyingly real, was the dreadful goad!

7 - INSPECTED!

Another week had gone by, a week of shame-making rehearsals.

Now she was standing naked on a table on the stage of the display room with her wrists fastened above her head to either end of a bar hanging from the ceiling, so that her belly would be at eye level. In this way it would be easy to reach down to inspect her intimacies or up to feel her now firmer and enlarged breasts and longer nipples, or to examine her teeth, or to walk round behind her to judge her back and waist and to assess the firmness of her buttocks.

Her knees were slightly bent and her ankles fastened wide apart to provide easy access to her beauty lips.

A pot of slippery oil was placed between her outstretched legs to make it easier to feel up her from both in front and behind - something to which these experienced judges of soft female flesh attached great importance if they were to advise their Masters properly.

And she was blindfolded.

Standing helpless on the table, unable to see what was going on, she was horrified to hear heavy footsteps approaching and then to feel hands, many hands, touching and probing, probing deeply inside her. Ashamed and humiliated, she was astonished to hear the high falsetto voices as the black eunuchs laughingly exchanged views on the body they were so intimately examining on behalf of their Masters.

But then, as if that was not enough, she felt herself being deliberately aroused by experienced fingers playing with her beauty bud, rubbing her nipples and stroking her body lips. Her body began to respond. She could feel frantic twinges of fire leaping from her breasts down to her womb and back. Her breasts felt larger than ever. There were approving comments as her blushes spread from her cheeks to her neck and and breasts.

Tied as she was there was nothing she could do to prevent nature from taking its course, a course that the watching black eunuchs wanted to see so as to be sure that she could be made to be highly responsive in her Master's bed.

As she began to approach her inevitable climax she felt, to her horror, additional fingers probing to feel her wetness and so satisfy themselves about the genuineness of her arousal.

Then there was sudden silence as all the fingers except one were removed. Writhing, crying out, tugging frantically at the straps that held her, she was expertly brought to a frantic climax.

Then her blindfold was removed, and, overcome with shame, she screamed as she saw that she was surrounded by a group of very black negroes, many of whom were busy scribbling in notebooks. One of them, a huge brute of man, was still stroking her intimately. He must be the one who had brought her so unwillingly to that devastating climax. He lifted up her chin to look in her eyes, and she gasped as she saw his brutal-looking face with the distinctive tribal scars and cold calculating eyes.

The party of black eunuchs left her and started to gather round another table on which was standing the blindfolded and naked figure of the young English daughter. She watched in horror as each eunuch checked for himself her undoubted virginity, before they methodically proceeded to do to her what they had just done to her - and then moved on to her mother.

8 - SOLD!

Ten white women, all beautifully dressed and made-up, stood nervously and silently in a line, under the eyes of little black boys, in the preparation room next to the auction and display room.

Each woman was mentally running through the routines that they had been taught. Their hands were at last free of the restricting gloves. Amanda gripped the hand of the English mother standing next to her. She felt her squeeze back.

In her other hand she held a white card with an Arabic number written prominently on it. This would be used to help identification during the forthcoming parade.

Amanda had been told that a dozen or more Arabs had come, or sent their black eunuchs, to bid specifically for her. A similar number, frightened off by her likely price, were more interested in the other women. She knew that her opening price would be much higher than that of the other women, higher even than that for the two English women who were being sold for that rare and much sought after commodity: a beautiful mother and daughter.

She realised now that all this was due to her notoriety in the Arab world, and was terrified of the thought of the revenge that her future Master might take on her.

Through the open door of the preparation room they could hear voices coming from the big room next door. Amanda shivered as she realised that they were the voices of the men to whom she was about to be displayed. She could hear the falsetto voices of the black eunuchs and the deeper voices of members of Arabian ruling families and other wealthy Middle Eastern gentlemen.

A bell tinkled. The voices died away. Amanda shivered and clutched the hand of her friend more tightly. She knew from the rehearsals that the curtains of the little stage next door would now be drawn back and the lights in the small auditorium would be dimmed, leaving only the catwalk leading out from the stage brilliantly lit, together with a spot light trained on the entrance onto the stage from the preparation room.

The bell tinkled for a second time. One of the small black boys nodded at Amanda. How she hated being ordered about by them! He raised his goad. It was enough. Amanda let go of the Englishwoman's hand, and straightened herself. Then, as she had rehearsed so many times, she, the most valuable piece of merchandise at the sale, proudly led the women out onto the stage and down onto the catwalk, one hand nonchalantly placed on her hip, the other displaying the numbered card, and her buttocks and shoulders swinging in the exaggerated walk of a top class model.

As she did so she was acutely aware of the way her now enlarged breasts, unrestrained by any bra, bounced under the silken material of her well cut Parisian cocktail party dress, and of the way her newly elongated nipples pressed against it.

The line of lovely women slowly walked down the catwalk, pirouetting periodically. Hassan, in an auctioneers rostrum on one side, described them one by one in Arabic. But all this was all merely a preliminary warming up exercise to arouse the interest of the buyers and to show them what was shortly going to be on offer.

Because of the way the bright lights were trained on the catwalk, Amanda could scarcely make out the faces of the watching audience. She turned and walked back up the catwalk, continuing to pirouette, smiling at the other young women as they passed, and towards the invisible watchers, before turning back down the catwalk again.

After a couple of minutes the bell tinkled again, and the women all left the catwalk.

Amanda was breathing heavily under the emotional strain of what she had just been through. She hastened to change out of her cocktail party dress and into a beautiful copy of a long Edwardian taffeta dress with a little bustle, long black gloves and a big black picture hat, for Hassan had decided to have her dressed for her sale as an English lady of the turn of the century.

She was greatly relieved to see the two black boys smiling at her as they helped her dress. She knew that if she had made the slightest mistake, on the catwalk, or if Hassan had felt that she had not done her utmost to look pleasing, their goads would be brought into action again.

The bell rang again and one of the women she did not know was sent onto the stage. She could hear Hassan's voice extolling the virtues of the unfortunate creature. She heard the woman's footsteps on the catwalk. Then she heard the rustle of her dress as it dropped to her feet.

Amanda shivered as she heard the crack of a whip. Again she heard Hassan's voice and heard the bidding start and gradually, punctuated by more cracks of the whip, become more eager and urgent.

Then the hammer fell, and a moment later the sobbing and now naked woman was hustled through the preparation room to the despatch room next door.

Then it was Amanda's turn. As her auction would be the high spot of the sale, it was important to dispose of her early on, so that unsuccessful bidders could make up for their disappointment (and use their money!) by buying one or more of the other women on display.

Her knees felt weak, but the frequent practices proved their worth as she went through her performance in a daze. Once again she started to strut up and down the catwalk. She heard Hassan describing her and calling for opening bids. Then the two little black boys ran in and unfastened her dress. The bids were just starting when, blushing with shame, she stepped carefully out of the long dress. Just wearing her long cotton under skirt, stockings, high heel shoes and the gloves and hat, she set off down the catwalk again, her bare breasts bouncing more than ever, and her painted nipples gleaming under the spotlights.

Hassan put her through an erotic display intended to show how this once proud feminist could be trained to perform to please her Master. As she reached the end of the catwalk, Amanda heard what she was expecting - the crack of Hassan's whip. Instantly, just as she had been taught, she froze with her head up and her hands clasped behind her neck, her firm breasts thrust out.

Then, after a full minute of taking bids, Hassan cracked his whip again. Keeping her back straight and her hands still clasped behind her neck, she parted her legs and bent forward so that her breasts hung down, tipped by long nipples. It was a pretty and revealing sight, and having to hold this awkward posture showed off well her state of training and her fear of the whip.

At last it cracked again, flicking her buttocks. She straightened up and swung her arms high, keeping her fingers straight and raising her knees level with her hips as she marched back towards the stage. As she did so, the bidding rose to a crescendo.

Now the lights were turned up to help Hassan control the bidding, and out of the corner of her eye Amanda saw the terrifying face of the black eunuch who had so shamed her that morning. He was actively bidding for her! Dear God, she prayed fervently, don't let that swine buy me!

Then she noticed a familiar figure sitting splendidly alone on a sofa dressed in a spotless white Arab robe and white keffiyah headdress. He calmly raised one finger and Hassan quickly acknowledged his bid. As he did so, Amanda recognised him: Prince Rashid, one of the men she had interviewed so scathingly!

Prince Rashid! My God! Her racing thoughts were cut short as she reached the stage and was grabbed by the young boys. They turned her round to face the bidders. Then slowly they lowered her under skirt, baring her slim waist, her flat belly, her powdered and hairless but rouged mound and the painted beauty lips. She was now a highly erotic sight and stark naked from her knees to her neck. The gloves, hat and shoes merely heightening the effect.

Hassan nodded with approval as the boys held her hands behind her back.

Then the whip cracked once again. The black boys let her go. One raised his goad. It was enough. She started down the catwalk again, this time very slowly turning round so that all the bidders could see every aspect of her body, every soft line and curve.

Again the whip cracked, flicking her buttocks, this time meeting bare flesh. She dropped to her knees, facing the bidders on one side of the catwalk, and clasped her hands behind her neck. The whip cracked again and she parted her legs wide and raised herself up so that her body was now in a straight vertical line from her widely parted knees on the floor up to her neck. Again she blushed as she realised what the bidders could see.

Again the whip cracked down on her. Now she lowered her head to the floor, her hair flung forward, her arms stretched out straight before her as if in supplication, her legs still parted and her scarlet painted intimacies displayed to the men sitting behind her.

The bidding rose. Blushing she repeated the whole process, this time facing the other way.

The young boys ran up, put a collar round her neck and snapped on a lead. Then they led her, crawling on all fours, slowly along the catwalk and back again.

She was being auctioned like a prize animal.

PART II: CONCUBINE

9 - THE GOLDEN CAGE

On the boat, days went past like a dream. Never had Amanda felt so happy, so relaxed, so fulfilled. And so in love! It was so unexpected! She was in love, madly in love, in love as she had never been before, with the most romantic, the most exciting, the most satisfying, the most courteous and the most charming man she had ever met: Prince Rashid.

She felt strangely excited as she lay on the comfortable deck mattress, almost touching his strong hard muscular body. She touched his hands. Once again she expressed her gratitude for what she saw as a rescue. Once again he dismissed it as nothing, a little money, of no consequence.

"The company of such a beautiful Englishwoman is all the reward that I need." He handed her a glass of deliciously ice-cold champagne. "To England - and your return to civilisation!"

England! Civilisation! She too longed for them again, of course, but somehow she had been thinking about London less and less. The relaxing life on the yacht was already pushing it out of her thoughts. Instead she was feeling more and more attracted to the strong and influential man who had saved her from some horrible fate. How could she ever repay him? She began to long for his touch, for his hands, but he kept his distance, treating her with great respect - disappointingly so.

Not until the third day did he seduce her, did she eagerly surrender to him, finding him a dream, experienced and expert but at the same time commanding and dominant. He raised her to peaks of arousal and pleasure that she had not previously experienced, so that she hoped it would be a long long time before he returned her to England.

Indeed, the cruise was like a honeymoon, a honeymoon that she came to pray would never end.

But end it did, as all things do. Now Amanda sat alone in the back of one of the large cars that had met the yacht early that morning.

The windows were tinted black. No one would be able to see who was in the car. Even the window between the back of the car and the silent black chauffeur was tinted black.

Her car followed that of the Prince. Escorted by police outriders on motor cycles, they drove from the private jetty on the outskirts of the capital to the palace, sitting proudly on a promontory jutting out into the sparkling blue sea.

The windows of the Prince's car were not tinted and people waved in a friendly fashion to the well liked Prince. They never gave a second glance to the following car with its opaque windows. Such cars, used to transport the women of the rich and powerful, were commonplace.

The cars drove through an imposing gateway guarded by armed sentries. The beautifully proportioned palace was suddenly revealed, gleaming white. Marble steps led up to an imposing entrance with, on either side, a covered passageway sheltered from the sun by high Moorish style arches. Above, the windows were protected from the sun and from the eyes of strangers by Arabesque stone tracery that made it impossible even to guess what lay beyond.

It was a secret world she was entering and Amanda shivered with apprehension as the gates closed behind her. But she quickly dismissed her concern as absurd. She was the honoured guest of her adored Prince and no harm could come to her!

The Prince's car swept up to the entrance step and uniformed guards and numerous attendants ran down to bow him from the car and welcome him back. Then, to her surprise, her own car drove past the main entrance, turned a corner, and stopped before a small door. The door of the car was opened by the chauffeur and a veiled woman beckoned her through the small door into the building.

Amanda followed up some narrow stairs that led to a passage which in turn led to a large iron-studded door, in front of which armed guards kept watch. They challenged the woman and then, apparently satisfied, unlocked the door. Amanda followed and the door was slammed shut behind her.

A few yards beyond the door, Amanda and her guide were confronted by a beautifully worked gold painted grille which was also locked. It was decorated with a star and two scimitars - the same crest of the Prince that she had seen embroidered on the gorgeous underwear in the yacht - some of which she was still wearing.

The woman pressed a bell and a large black man waddled up to the grille. He was naked to the waist, his large belly hanging over brightly coloured red baggy trousers, gathered in at the ankle. On his head was a large white turban. He held a short embroidered leather dog whip like a badge of office, and tucked into a voluminous silk cummerbund round his waist was another whip, black and short-handled with a rolled up leather thong some six feet long - the sort used to crack when training animals.

Could this be the kennel of the Prince's hunting dogs? And was this fat ogre the kennel man in charge?

The woman said something and pointed at Amanda. The big black man laughed and unlocked the grille. They were now on the upper floor of a beautiful modern interior courtyard, rather like the covered inside atrium of some departmental stores. The courtyard was not open to the sky but roofed over in an attractive arched Arab style. It felt wonderfully cool after the heat outside - evidently it was all air conditioned.

Near her, on this upper floor, were four beautiful pavilions or suites of rooms, each with its own balcony looking down into the courtyard. In the centre, looking down onto the ground and first floors, and across at the adjoining four pavilions, was a single imposing balcony decorated with with a large crest - once again the star and two scimitars of the Prince's arms.

A handsome winding staircase led down to the beautiful marble floor of the courtyard. Half way down, the curving staircase linked into a mezzanine floor with a dozen or so rather smaller suites, still very attractive. Each was different and each had its own balcony looking down onto the ground floor - again rather like the lower boxes at an opera house.

Over the ground floor of the courtyard was a gold painted iron work tracery, rather like the grille door. It was like the roof of an aviary, a golden aviary designed to hold a variety of beautiful birds.

The only way out was up the winding staircase. But access to this staircase was barred at the bottom by another gold painted grille. This again was decorated with a large star and two scimitars, as if to remind anyone on the ground floor of the omnipotent power of the Prince.

But in this was no aviary, for under the gold painted iron tracery were sofas and cushions, and amongst them fountains, green shrubs, and pools with goldfish darting among the shadows of water lilies.

Amanda gave an excited little shiver. The ground floor seemed more like a golden cage.

The suites and their balconies took up three sides of the courtyard, again like the boxes that surrounded the stalls in an old fashioned theatre. The fourth side was made of glass and beyond the glass was more thick arabesque stone tracery that kept the hot sun off the glass and gave the courtyard a light and airy aspect whilst enabling people inside to see out easily - but they could not be seen from the outside.

She was surprised to see, beyond the arabesque stone tracery, an intricate design of iron bars - to keep people out, or to keep people in?

Through the glass and through the Arabesque tracery and iron bars, Amanda could see the brilliantly blue sea.

Looking down, she saw another gold painted grille, this time in the glass wall of the ground floor golden cage. It led out into a small but well kept tropical garden that sloped down towards the sea - and towards an enveloping wall that would guard the garden from the eyes of anyone approaching the palace from the seaward side.

But there were iron spikes on the top of the wall, curved over towards the garden as if to prevent anyone trying to get out over the wall.

The woman led Amanda down the twisting staircase towards the ground floor. Still gazing around her in astonishment, Amanda felt that this strangely built courtyard, with its spectacular views, was one of the most beautiful things she had ever seen.

In the front of the garden, just beyond the gold painted grille in the glass wall, was a large swimming pool surrounded by a high gold painted iron fence, again surmounted by spikes.

Now she saw that a thirty or more young white and olive skinned women lay around the pool on reclining couches!

As Amanda watched two of them got into the pool and started to splash each other like little girls. There were no men amongst them - which was just as well, she thought, for the women all seemed to be naked.

Then she was shocked to see that watching the women was a black youth, naked to the waist, dressed like the fat negro whom she had seen earlier - bright red flowing trousers, gathered at the ankles, and a white turban.

The two girls started to splash each other more violently and she saw the black youth pull the short handled black whip from his cummerbund and crack it in the air. The two girls instantly stopped splashing and nervously lowered their heads.

Amanda could hardly take her eyes off this extraordinary example of strict discipline.

Then, still open mouthed with amazement, she came to the bottom of the winding stair and was suddenly confronted by the closed golden grille, this one guarded by two more black youths in red Turkish trousers and white turbans. They too were holding beautifully embroidered leather dog whips and had short handled black leather whips tucked into their silken cummerbund.

Once again the woman said something to the two young negroes. The negroes looked at Amanda, grinned broadly and unlocked the grille, locking it again carefully behind her.

It all seemed like a Hollywood set for a film about the Arabian Nights.

But it was real. These rather frightening black guards were certainly very real - and so were the women out by the pool. A sudden feeling of jealousy swept over Amanda. Surely they were not anything to do with the Prince, her Prince? He had never mentioned other women to her, and she had never questioned him.

With a sudden shock Amanda saw a very pretty and obviously Levantine girl coming towards her across the marble floor. The shock was caused by her dress, for she simply wore a pair of mauve transparent harem trousers gathered at the ankles and held up by a wide and beautifully embroidered belt that left her navel bare. She had little embroidered Turkish slippers with the pointed toes curled up. Over her shoulders was a short bolero made of stiff mauve material, too small to do up in front and only half covering her otherwise naked breasts.

She also wore a little embroidered Turkish cap and her beautiful long dark hair hung down her back in two braids threaded with pearls. Her sparkling eyes were made up with mauve eye shadow that matched the colour of her clothing. She was very beautiful, with a perfect if slightly voluptuous figure. She looked at Amanda, with a kind if rather sad smile.

"Welcome! I have been told by Princess Naima to look after you and show you around," she said. "Please excuse my English - I have not been able to use it very much for several years." She laughed prettily. "It is a little, how do you say, a little rusty!"

"Nonsense!" Amanda smiled patronisingly. "It is very good. Where did you learn it?"

"I am Christian girl from the Lebanon. My parents were rich and sent me to school in London for a year. I was eighteen. That was before His Highness chose me to become one of his concubines." She paused. "Just like you!"

Amanda looked at her in open mouthed astonishment.

"What!"

"Like you," she repeated. "You are now a concubine too."

"Oh no I am not!" replied Amanda angrily. "The Prince is my lover!"

The girl smiled pityingly.

"Do not deceive yourself! You are a concubine like the rest of us. Just one of the Prince's many concubines, locked up in his harem. Like me. I don't even have a name now. Here I'm just 'Mauve' and I always have to wear mauve harem dress so that he doesn't have to bother to remember my real name. I even have to wear a mauve ribbon round my neck in his bed so that he can identify me more easily!"

"Oh no, that can't be true!" Amanda cried out.

"It is," replied the girl called Mauve. "And you're going to be just Sky

Blue. He chose the colour, and hence your name, himself."

"You're mad! The Prince loves me, he rescued me. He's sending me back to London. He's just invited me to stay in his palace for a few days before I go back to England."

"Then he has deceived you!"

"Rubbish! There's some mistake, some misunderstanding. I'll go and see the Prince straight away. He'll soon put a stop to this silly nonsense."

"Please, please be sensible. You can't get to the Prince, you can't even go up the staircase without permission."

"What are you talking about?" cried Amanda in a fury. "I've never heard such nonsense! I tell you I'm a guest here, and free to come and go as I like. Look!"

She strode to the bottom of the winding staircase and tried to fling open the grille.

Angrily she turned to the young negroes guarding it.

"Unlock this grille at once!" she demanded imperiously.

They just laughed. Furious, Amanda tried to snatch the key hanging from one of their waists.

Instantly there was a flash of steel. Her way was barred by two scimitars, held by the now menacing looking young negroes.

Amanda gasped and stepped back. She remembered her previous thoughts about the Arabian Nights. It all seemed to be coming horribly true.

The girl in mauve put her hand comfortingly on Amanda's shoulder.

"You see! There is no escape from the Prince's harem. You must simply accept that you are now just one of Prince Rashid's concubines."

"My God! What a cruel deceiving bastard he is! And I thought he was such a kind and loving man."

"Well, he is - by his own lights. And the silly thing is that my sister and I - well, we both still love him. I think we learnt to love him more than ever as our Master."

"Your Master?"

"Yes, and now your Master too, your beloved Master."

"Beloved Master! That swine who tricked me? I hate him!"

"And so did my sister and I - at first. But then you'll find yourself more in love with him than ever."

"Never!"

"Oh yes, you will! You will never see another man again - except these black eunuchs and they don't count. But look out for their whips - they can really sting, I can tell you!"

She paused for a moment.

"You'll never see another man!" she repeated. "So all the time you'll find yourself thinking more and more about our handsome Master, about his his strong hands, his voice, his body, his..."

"Oh!"

"You'll soon become so jealous of the other women in the harem that you'll happily scratch their eyes out - as they would yours!"

The girl gave a sob.

"We are even locked up in the dormitory when the gardeners come to do the harem garden, or clean the swimming pool. And the harem is cleaned every day by women servants and they bring us our food, under the supervision of the black eunuchs - so we don't even see the harem cooks! We are not even allowed to see a male animal - no dogs or tom cats! And the black eunuchs make sure we only see special harem magazines and books that don't show any photographs of men or even mention men."

"What about television?" Amanda pointed to a big television set in the corner of the room.

"They only allow us to watch specially made childrens' programmes and videos which never show a man - and which have been specially approved by the Mullahs for showing to women."

"Oh God!"

"The black eunuchs also keep us ignorant of what is going on in the outside world. We're never allowed to see a newspaper, or see or hear a news programme, or talk about politics, or read a serious book. They think these might distract us from just thinking about the Prince all day. So they treat us like children."

Again Mauve paused.

"I suppose it's a little like being a nun, sublimating all her thoughts and desires towards God. For us, the Prince is God!"

Amanda had listened with mounting astonishment. "For us, the Prince is God!" she found herself repeating slowly.

"Yes! And don't forget that here you must always call him Master or Your Highness, no matter what you may have called him on the yacht. In his presence you will always be half naked. Never sit, never speak unless he speaks to you first, never ask him to release you from his harem, always tell him how happy you are here and that all you want to do is to please and serve him, always ... oh, there are so many rules, but you'll learn them all in time. The slightest mistake and you'll get a whipping!"

Amanda's head was reeling from the emotional shock. Was this the Prince's revenge, she suddenly wondered. To pretend to free her, and then to lock her up in his harem? To make her fall in love with him, and then use her as a concubine? To seduce her like a moon struck school girl, and then turn her over to his cruel black eunuchs?

Mauve's hand shook Amanda out of her reverie.

"Come on! Cheer up! You must get changed quickly into your harem clothes."

"Harem clothes?"

"Yes, we are not allowed to wear European clothes. The eunuchs say it would give us ideas above our station! We're only allowed to wear this skimpy harem dress. The odalisques are allowed to wear caftans - the lucky things. But only the Prince's wives are allowed to wear European clothes - they can order all their clothes straight from Paris!"

"Goodness!" exclaimed Amanda.

"And they can wear a bra! We can't - our breasts have to be on display all the time."

Amanda glanced at Mauve's open bolero and at the bare nipples peeping round their edge. How humiliating to be kept like that. How unfair that the wives were excused it.

"Well," said Mauve as if reading her thoughts, "you must remember that all three of the wives were very grand Princesses in their own right before they married the Prince."

"Three! He has three wives? And all these other women too?"

"Yes, of course. He's a rich man. And as for wives, every Moslem is allowed four. We all dream of becoming the fourth!"

She looked around anxiously.

"We must stop gossiping, or they'll be angry. I'm only supposed to be briefing you on harem life. Come on, I'll show you round."

10 - CONCUBINES AND ODALISQUES

Mauve led Amanda through an open archway at the side of the courtyard into another large room containing some thirty little couches. There were cupboards all round the room.

"This is the dormitory."

Amanda's head was already reeling. It all seemed unbelievable - a nightmare from which she would soon wake up.

At least, she kept telling herself, perhaps she hadn't been quite such a fool in falling in love with the Prince. After all, he had taken great trouble to get her into his harem, and in the yacht had behaved with what she still felt was genuine passion. Perhaps he was not just seeking his revenge but was genuinely attracted to her as well.

Should she even look on it as compliment that this rich and powerful man had decided to put her into his harem? Might she even find it exciting - surely it would not really be for very long...

Her thoughts were interrupted by Mauve.

"This is your bed - next to me and my sister. And here she is!"

A very pretty girl came into the dormitory, dressed like Mauve but in scarlet - bright scarlet trousers through which her long white legs gleamed in the half light, a scarlet bolero that scarcely reached her nipples. On her head she wore a little red Turkish cap below which hung her long straight hair, black and braided. She was slightly taller than Mauve, with larger breasts, and looked slightly older, but the family resemblance was strong.

On her feet were scarlet slippers with turned-up tips to which was attached tiny bells that rang with her every movement, making it impossible for her to move about quietly. Amanda had noticed that Mauve wore a similar pair of mauve slippers. Would she have to wear blue ones?

The newcomer walked towards them, smiling, her feet tinkling. Amanda suddenly realised that she was pregnant, her bare tummy curving up prettily above the embroidered belt slung across her hips.

"Sky Blue, this is my sister, Scarlet. She only speaks a little English. She was studying chemistry at the University at Beirut. Now perhaps she is carrying a little son for the Prince!"

"What!" exclaimed Amanda jealously. And then, finding herself feeling rather sorry for her, added: "How awful for you."

The tall girl smiled. She shook her head.

"No! Not awful!" She spoke rather broken English with a pretty accent. "I not poor thing. Great privilege to present Master with son! I hope have son and be odalisque, no longer be concubine. Then I will teach this Mauve, my sister, her place!"

Amanda looked blank.

"We concubines," explained Mauve, "all long to become odalisques. Odalisques each have their own small suite of rooms on the first floor. And they have a much easier life - nearly as easy as the Prince's wives. And although they're not allowed to wear European clothes like the wives, they can wear caftans and high heeled shoes - and a bra! And no slippers with bells, like us."

"Well, why do concubines have bells on their slippers?"

"So that the black eunuchs can always hear us, of course! We are not allowed any privacy for fear we..." Mauve giggled in an embarrassed way. "Lest we are naughty!"

Amanda still looked blank.

"And the Master decides which of the concubines are to be promoted to odalisque," said Mauve. "It's a great honour, for he visits his wives and odalisques in their rooms, in their little pavilions at night - and sleeps each night with one of them. He only uses concubines for his siestas and evening recreation. So to become an odalisque you must be very beautiful and very pleasing in bed. But before you can even be chosen as an odalisque you must first be chosen to try and bear the Prince a boy. That's why my sister hopes her baby will be a boy."

"And if it is a daughter?"

"Then my sister will not be eligible to become an odalisque."

"Oh!" cried Amanda shocked.

"You see, the Princess Naima, the Master's first wife, she is also the harem Mistress, she sees that the black eunuchs keep us on the pill."

"Princess Naima? What has it got to do with her?"

"Everything!" replied Mauve. "She is the Mistress of the Harem. In some harems there is a eunuch in charge but here the Prince prefers to leave it to his first wife. The various Trainers, senior black eunuchs in charge of groups of girls, are responsible to her."

"Goodness!" said Amanda amazed at how the harem was apparently so well organised.

"Anyway," went on Mauve, "two years ago, Princess Naima decided to allow me to try and bear the Prince a son. Then one afternoon he chose me. It was the right time of the month. I conceived. The Prince was pleased. He likes one or two girls in the harem to be in what you call an Interesting

Condition. Every day, the eunuchs would parade me naked in front of him. He would feel me. It was very exciting - and wonderful to see him every day ... especially when they gave me special pills to bring on my milk. Many Arab men also like that - and so does the Prince!"

Amanda was listening open mouthed, not certain whether to be shocked or intrigued.

Mauve looked suddenly sad.

"But the baby was a girl. And I will not be allowed another chance."

A tear ran down her cheek. "She's such a pretty little girl. What a waste! But if my sister now succeeds in becoming an odalisque, then I'll be able to go and visit her in her room. The Prince likes the idea of having sisters in his bed!"

"Oh!" gasped Amanda, both mystified and shocked. And this was the man she thought she loved!

"Do not be shocked. He never sends for one concubine anyway. Always two. Or three. And he only sleeps with us when he has his siesta in the afternoon. You'll never spend the night with him again, and you'll never again be alone in his bed - not unless you become an odalisque."

"My God!" said Amanda. It was all too much. She sat down on the bed and sobbed.

"Stop!" said Scarlet firmly. "You stop crying. This is a happy harem. We are all well treated. We not often punished. We all love our Master."

"Yes," added Mauve. "You are lucky you were bought by him. He's handsome and virile. He's kind. Not like some. There are such stories about a certain Sheik, for example, Turki he is called ... well, anyway, just think what it would have been like if you had been bought by one of the other Arabs you insulted on your programme. He might have been really cruel!"

"My programme? How do you know about that?"

"Oh, the wives are allowed television and radio in their rooms and they saw the programmes. They were very angry when they saw you ridicule their husband. Especially Princess Leisha, the second wife. She, too, went to school for a time in England. But the other girls there teased her about being an Arab and now she resents white women. Watch out for her. She can have your thrashed by her personal black eunuch, Faithful. He can really hurt with the cane!"

"A cane? You mean they cane grown women?"

"Oh yes!" Mauve nodded, rather ruefully. "It's an old harem custom. Here the black eunuchs in charge of the concubines carry whips - and use them! But the Prince's wives can order the concubines to be caned - caned by their own black eunuchs!"

"My God! It's all too awful!"

"No, not really. We don't get the cane all that often in this harem. You'll soon be happy here... now you must hurry and change, or my sister and I will get into trouble. Please hurry! I don't want to be beaten. And you don't want to be responsible for getting her caned. So please help us get these clothes off you. Then I have to take them up to Princess Naima - and take you too. She'll want to see that you're now properly dressed as a concubine before the Prince makes his midday choice later this morning - his first for a fortnight, thanks to you and your lovely cruise with him on his yacht."

Amanda sat up. She dried her tears. She took control of herself.

"What do you mean, midday choice?"

"After the midday prayer call, the Prince comes on to the latticed balcony in the centre of the top floor, outside his bedroom, and looks down at us. We all have to stand there whilst he looks us over, but we can't see him behind the lattice. Sometimes, he tells the eunuchs to make us walk about or even run round the courtyard. But first you must salaam to him."

"Salaam?" queried Amanda.

"Yes, you know, prostrate yourself to him. Just stand next to me and my sister and copy us. It will be a pretty sight: Scarlet, Sky Blue and Mauve. Then, he will tell his pages which women he wants for his siesta later in the day, and meanwhile return to his office in the male part of the palace. He'll have lunch with his male friends and assistants, while the women he has chosen are being prepared for his bed - and not allowed any lunch! Now come on, Sky Blue, take off your dress, or the Princess will have me flogged!"

Appalled at all she had heard, Amanda let the two young women undress her. They fingered the superb material of her smartly cut dress lovingly and with regret. They admired Amanda's white body. Scarlet said something in Arabic to Mauve who laughed.

"She says you've got child bearing hips," Mauve explained.

By now, they had dressed Amanda in her Sky Blue trousers, her humiliating tinkling slippers, her bolero and her cap. They had let her hair down and they made up her eyes with blue eyeshadow. They took her to a long mirror. Amanda caught her breath, half in horror, half in admiration. The figure looking back at her in the mirror was an astonishingly provoking and attractive looking Eastern houri.

The transparent trousers suited her long legs admirably, though she was horrified at how much her beauty lips were revealed - hairless, since her time with the slave dealer. Her enlarged breasts and nipples peeped round her stiff but scanty bolero. Her hair hung down her back in two bejewelled braids. Her eyes seemed huge and dazzling. She looked dramatically different now, but very like the other concubines, except for her very fair skin and blonde hair.

It was indeed a new Amanda who was standing there, dressed as an Arab Prince's concubine, dressed to provoke and please her Master. She felt embarrassed at the display of her blatant nudity, of her blatant sexuality. But she could not also help feeling how exciting it would be to stand half naked in her harem dress alongside the white robed Prince.

She turned to Mauve. "What's the point of it all if he sees so little of us?"

"Don't you see? It's the feeling that he owns us all that is so exciting for him. We all belong to him. We are his possessions and are not allowed to see any other man. He may only enjoy each of us sexually occasionally. But, they say, he enjoys coming secretly into that latticed balcony several times a day and seeing us half naked and locked up in his harem. It's something that Arab men feel very strongly about. We never know when he's behind the screen watching us."

Mauve laughed.

"These rich Arab Sheiks get more pleasure from the feeling of owning a harem of beautiful identically dressed women than from anything else."

Back in the main downstairs room, Amanda, or Sky Blue as she now was, found herself looking up at the balcony with its large crest. She could not help smiling up at it eagerly. Was she already trying to attract the Prince's attention? Despite everything, was her body longing to be in his arms again? Even if her head told her he was a cruel and cunning man who had quite outmanoeuvred her? Did that not make him all the more exciting?

Was it imagination, or was there a vague shadow moving behind the screen in the centre of the balcony? She could not help tossing her head coquettishly.

11 - THE PRINCE'S TERRIFYING FIRST WIFE

Mauve took Amanda by the hand to the young black eunuch guarding the foot of the stairs. She said something to him. He had a special intercom connected to each of the wives and odalisque's pavilions. He dialled the pavilion of the Prince's first wife and spoke briefly.

Two other young black eunuchs, also wearing only trousers and a turban, came out onto the Princess' balcony. They were carrying silver tipped canes. They looked down at Mauve and Sky Blue, then ran down the staircase and said something to the black eunuch at the foot of the stairs. The golden grille was unlocked. Then gripping Mauve and Sky Blue by the arm, they led them up the staircase.

They were led into the pretty pavilion of the Princess Naima. The waiting room was beautifully decorated like a French drawing room. There were French prints on the wall, French wallpaper, some very valuable Louis XVI furniture, French satin curtains, chairs covered in velvet and gold leaf, and a huge chandelier.

Amanda went as if to sit down, but Mauve gestured to her desperately not to do so. Concubines did not sit down in the rooms of a wife, particularly those of the all powerful first wife!

The other eunuch came back, but the two women were left standing awkwardly in the waiting room in silence for over five minutes, watched by the Princess's two personal eunuchs who were whispering together. Amanda was to learn later that their names were Harmony and Melody and that they were much feared by the concubines.

The Princess knew well the psychological importance of keeping young women waiting when she sent for them, but finally a bell tinkled and Harmony waved the two women into the Princess's drawing room.

This room was decorated like a typical English country house with flowered chintz on the comfortable sofas and arm chairs, and with matching chintz curtains. Amanda had no time to look around, for Mauve had dropped to her knees in front of a large desk behind which was sitting a very attractive and well groomed woman in her forties.

She was wearing a well cut French lightweight suit, with a matching scarf tied at the side of her neck. She looked brisk, efficient and very self confident, in glowering contrast to the two half naked and nervous young women now kneeling in front of her, their heads modestly bowed - for Amanda had had the good sense to copy Mauve's actions.

There was silence in the room. Through the open window that looked down into the courtyard below, Amanda could hear the gentle tinkling of the fountains.

"Stand up, Sky Blue!" The voice of Princess Naima was soft but firm. She spoke English fluently but with an Arab accent. Awkwardly Amanda rose to her feet. Mauve remained kneeling, her head still bowed.

Amanda stood there awkwardly, ashamed of her half nakedness in front of this elegantly dressed and self possessed woman. She put her hands over her breasts.

"Hands to your sides!" ordered the Princess harshly. "Now turn round and go and stand in the corner, facing the wall!"

Amanda did as she was told, acutely conscious of the transparency of her new silken harem trousers.

"Now, hands behind your neck. Keep your head up and your eyes fixed on the wall."

Amanda was humiliated at being treated like this by another woman, a woman who had made her stand in the corner like a naughty child. But, she realised, the fact that she was not facing the Princess made her listen all the more carefully.

"Now, listen to this. You are now merely one of the many concubines of His Highness Prince Rashid. I am his first wife, and the ruler of his harem. You will address me as Your Highness, and do the same to the Prince's other two wives. You will address the odalisques as Miss. You will address all the black eunuchs as Sir, even if they are young boys. You are not to speak to me, or to the other wives, unless you are first spoken to. If you wish to speak to us then you must do so through our personal black eunuchs, not forgetting to call them Sir. The same rules apply when you are in the presence of your Master. Remember your only name in the harem is Sky Blue. You left behind all other names when you entered it. If you remember these simple rules, and the others which Mauve will teach you, then you will be happy here, happy loving your Master and happy knowing that he is fond of you as one of his concubines, and that, one day you hope, you may be allowed to show him a swelling little belly."

The Princess paused.

"In a moment, I shall ask if you understand. You will then turn to my personal black eunuch, Harmony, and say to him: 'Please, Sir, tell Her Highness that Sky Blue understands' Do you understand?"

There was a silent pause.

Then, embarrassed and awkwardly, Amanda turned towards the Princess's black eunuch.

"Please, Sir," she murmured hesitantly, "tell Her Highness that Sky Blue understands."

She heard the falsetto voice of Harmony speaking to the Princess in Arabic, and the Princess addressed her again.

"You must speak up properly, girl. I warn you, I don't like muttering concubines, and I don't like sullen ones. Now face the wall again."

Somehow Amanda managed to control her anger at being treated like a naughty child.

"As a concubine you will be expected to satisfy your Master. You will be allocated to one of the black eunuchs who will be responsible for your training. If I have reports from your trainer, or from any of the other black eunuchs, that you are being lazy and inattentive, then I may have you also punished by my own black eunuchs. Don't expect any mercy from me, after the way you tried to make the Prince look foolish on television. Do you understand? Answer me directly."

"Yes, Madame," answered Amanda, overcome by this terrifying woman.

"Good! Well, your Master has told me that he intends to teach you a lesson by making you bear him a black slave, fathered by a one of his Black Guards."

Amanda's heart beat fast, as she faced the wall. My God, she thought. She wanted to turn round and protest, but she did not dare do so. She felt strangely over-awed by this Princess.

"But not just yet. In the meantime you are to report every day to your trainer, and in front of him you are to swallow whatever pills he gives you. He may give you contraceptive pills or he may give you fertility pills. You will not ask him which he is giving you. It is none of your business."

Still facing the wall, Amanda gasped.

"You will also report to him three times a day to have your temperature recorded and also your periods. You will be allowed to write a letter once a week to your Master, the Prince. Several different girls write each day, and you will write on Mondays. If you are called to his bed during his siesta, you may also write to him immediately afterwards. These letters will normally be the only opportunity to tell him of your secret thoughts and desires, or to confess any mistakes or malpractices, so you should compose your letters with care. Your letters are to be sent unsealed to me in the first place, and I will send them to him with my comments."

Amanda was shocked. She did not know whether to be more shocked about her forthcoming sex lessons, or about the news that she was to be made pregnant as part of the Prince's revenge, or about the embarrassing details of birth control in the harem, or that her letters to her adored Prince were to be read by this rather terrifying woman.

"Come on, Sky Blue! Do you understand, speak up!"

"Yes," whispered Amanda.

"You silly girl!" shouted the Princess angrily. "I've already told you not to address me directly unless I give you permission."

"Please, Sir, tell Her Highness that Sky Blue understands," Amanda found herself saying to the eunuch in a firm voice that did not accurately portray her real nervousness and fear.

"Now turn round and kneel with Mauve," ordered the frightening Princess Naima. Amanda turned. Nervously she started to walk back towards Mauve.

"Stop! Hold out your left hand!" The Princess was looking very severe. "Who gave you that ring you are wearing? You may speak to me directly. Was it a man?"

"Yes, Your Highness." Amanda looked down at her hand almost proudly. It was a ring that had been given to her by her last boyfriend, Hugh. It was her one link to her previous life in England.

"Concubines are not allowed to have anything given to them by a man other than their Master," said the Princess angrily. "You are here to devote yourself only to your Master, and to think only of him. Your thoughts must not be diverted by anything that might remind you of your previous life, or of any other man."

"But the Prince never said... "

"To you he is His Highness, and don't you forget it," interrupted the Princess.

"His Highness never objected to me wearing the ring when I was on the yacht. Indeed, he said he was going to send me back to London," said Amanda in a strident tone.

"Don't be impertinent to me, young lady, or I'll have my eunuchs thrash you! What the Prince may say to a guest on his yacht, and what happens when the same woman becomes a concubine in his harem, are two quite separate things. You must abandon any idea of leading your former life in Europe again. You must forget it. You belong to the Prince now. Now take off that ring and give it to me at once!"

"No, please, Your Highness! It's all I have left to remind me of my home, of Hugh..."

"And that is exactly why you must take it off at once. The only man in your life now is your Master and your home is here in this harem."

"Oh please, Your Highness," Amanda begged almost in tears.

"Sky Blue, I have been very patient with you. I have made allowances for the fact that you are new to Arab ways and to this harem, but I will not put up with your disobedience any longer."

The Princess said something in Arabic to her young black eunuchs. They came over and gripped Amanda by the arms. Holding her tightly they took her, struggling, into the Princess's private punishment room, a room in which she maintained discipline in the harem. The door from the Princess's room was left open. They led Amanda up to a wooden stocks that stood in the middle of the room. It was nearly four feet high. There were holes in it to take a woman's head as she was made to bend over, and, on either side, holes for her wrists. The top of the stocks was hinged at one side and could be locked down into place.

Amanda was horrified when she saw the stocks. She started to cry out. But the black eunuchs paid no attention, they made her stand close to the stocks and locked her into them, upright but helpless.

Harmony went round and gripped the tips of the fingers of one of her hands, bending it backwards painfully. Melody went to a cupboard and took out a long whippy cane.

They were going to cane her on the palms of her hands, like a naughty schoolgirl! It fact, it was a variation of the old Turkish harem punishment of the bastinado, though this was applied to the soles of the feet of recalcitrant young woman.

Not a word was said, but suddenly the Princess seated at her desk next door, and Mauve kneeling in front of her desk, heard the swish of a cane and a scream of pain from Amanda. It was repeated twice. Then there was a pause as her other hand was now stretched out for the cane. They could hear Amanda begging and imploring them to stop. Then came another three strokes and another three shrieks.

Moments later they brought a tearful Amanda back through the door, her hands gripped tightly under her armpits to help ease the awful pain.

The Princess held out her hand. Quickly Amanda started to pull the ring off her finger and handed it to the Princess.

"Kneel next to Mauve," said the Princess.

Amanda knelt on the floor in front of the Princess's desk. She bowed her head, like Mauve. There was a long silence. The pain in her hands was beginning to ease off. She could hear Mauve breathing hard as if, she too, was in fear of something.

"Mauve! I blame you for not spotting the ring. You should have brought it to me. You will have double the number of strokes as Sky Blue. Let that be a lesson to you both."

The Princess spoke again in Arabic to the two black eunuchs. They reached down and lifted up Mauve. Amanda saw that she was white with fear but she did not dare speak. They took her next door, this time leaving Amanda kneeling on the floor. And this time, it was Amanda who heard the whistling of the cane and the cries of poor Mauve. She found herself counting the six strokes.

Then they were both kneeling again side by side in front of the Princess.

"Dismissed! You may both go back now down to the concubines quarters. Remember to behave yourself, Sky Blue! I don't want to have to send for you again."

12 - THE MASTER!

It was half an hour later.

Mauve, still rubbing her hands under her armpits to ease the pain of her humiliating caning, had been explaining more of the harem rules to Amanda and introducing her to the other concubines. They had all been made to look very alike with identical skimpy harem dresses, identical make-up and bejewelled long braided hair - only the colours of the outfits were different. Most of the Arab girls spoke only a little English, but as the Turkish, Persian and Indian girls only spoke very little Arabic, English was the second language in the harem.

Suddenly a bell rang. Immediately there was the noise of whips being cracked by the black eunuchs.

"Hurry! Hurry!" Hurry!"

There was pandemonium as the girls rushed to the bathroom next to the dormitory.

"What's happening?" asked Amanda, as Mauve pulled her there too.

"The Prince is coming! He must be so keen to see his harem again that he's advanced the time for the normal midday inspection. Quick! Brush your hair! Make yourself look as a pretty as possible. Hurry! Is my lipstick alright? And my hair? Hurry! We must get back."

Mauve now rushed back into the main harem room and pulled Amanda so that she was standing between herself and Scarlet in the line of concubines. Some thirty beautiful young women, from various Middle and Far Eastern countries, were being lined up for their Master's inspection by a young black eunuch.

They had to form a perfectly straight row with their toes just touching a red line painted on the floor. Amanda saw that the women were all looking up eagerly at the lattice work on the central balcony that dominated the harem courtyard.

Two young boys appeared on the balcony in front of the latticed grille. They were dressed identically in long pink robes and wore distinctive tall white conical hats. Their fine long blond hair hung down to their shoulders, set in page boy style. Tucked under their arms, they carried, like a badge of office, a long leather covered swagger stick - rather like a riding whip. Their lips were painted scarlet, their chubby cheeks were rouged and their eyes were carefully made up and gleaming as they looked down onto the assembled young women.

"The Prince's page boys, Pleasure and Patience," whispered Mauve.

"But they are white!" whispered back the astonished Amanda.

"Yes, white eunuch boys," murmured Scarlet.

"White eunuchs?"

"Yes! They were two Dutch boys," explained Mauve out of the corner of her mouth, "who ran away from home and stowed away in a ship going to the East. They were found and handed over to the ship's agents in Port Said to be sent home. But instead, he sold them to some slavers who specialise in supplying young black eunuchs to the harems of wealthy Arabs. They were castrated, like black eunuchs, and sold to the Prince as page boys."

"What! White boys castrated to be eunuchs!"

"There's always a demand for them in this part of the world. I believe that later they will be trained as his private secretaries. White eunuchs have a reputation among Arabs as being very loyal to their masters - just like neutered dogs stop running away from theirs. But they are also much more vicious. They can really hurt!"

Astonished at what she had just heard, Amanda looked up at the two pretty page boys, who were now standing facing each other at either end of the balcony. She saw that one of them gave a signal to the black eunuch who had been busy lining up the women. Immediately his whip cracked.

"Silence!" he ordered, "Stand at attention! Hands behind necks and elbows back!"

It was a position that drew the edges of the girls' bolero's back, showing off to perfection the hang of each beautiful breast.

Amanda blushed as she followed the other girls, realising that the Prince must now be looking down at them from behind the grill in the centre of the balcony. How humiliating - but also how exciting!

The Prince smiled as he looked down at his concubines for the first time since his return. Pride of ownership surged through him and stirred his loins.

Quite apart from the pleasures they provided for his bed, watching them unseen from behind his grill provided hours of enjoyment as they went about their highly disciplined life under the control and supervision of their black eunuch trainers.

They really did look in splendid fettle. All of them seemed to have the fullness and firmness of breast allied to slenderness of waist that he found so arousing.

He noticed Scarlet's condition was becoming increasingly apparent. Nor was it only her belly that was swelling up prettily, for, as he noticed with delight, her breasts, which before had been too small for his taste, were also showing signs of being well capable of carrying out the future role that he had envisaged for her in his personal service.

Interesting Conditions, as they were always called, formed an essential part of owning a large harem, and a very enjoyable part too, as their name implied. In Arabian eyes such a girl was in her natural state and her condition only served to increase her beauty and desirability.

The Prince's black trainers took as much pride and care over one of their charges in an Interesting Condition, as in the West, or indeed in Arabia, a stud groom might of a valuable mare in foal. He expected his stud groom to report to him, as the mare's owner, her progress and condition, and to invite him to see her. So, too, here in his harem he expected the trainer of a girl in an Interesting Condition to report to him details of the girl's progress and condition, and to parade the blushing young woman daily, naked, for his inspection.

He noticed the blonde Amanda, now dressed in her revealing sky blue harem trousers and open bolero, standing between Mauve and Scarlet. The sight of the famous Amanda Aston, now ranged for his inspection amongst his concubines, greatly pleased him. Revenge was indeed sweet!

He could imagine only too well what she must have gone through in the last two hours: the shock of having to dress herself so revealingly as a concubine and to be now merely called by her colour; the shock of learning about harem life; the pain of her first thrashing by his first wife's black eunuchs; the shock of being told that he intended to use her to bear him a black slave child and that she would not see London again; and the terrible shock of realising that she was now just one of the many women he owned.

Yes, indeed, his revenge for the way that she had insulted him in England was very sweet - and was far from over yet!

Indeed looking at her breasts, he wondered how they, too, might be improved by having her put into an Interesting Condition. Choosing the right stallion from his Black Guards to cover her, and then watching her being mounted whilst hooded so that she never saw her mate, and then seeing her fears, and doubtless tears, as her belly grew, would indeed be another delightful form of revenge.

The other white page boy, Pleasure, now made a signal to the watching black eunuch. Immediately the young negro's whip cracked again, making Amanda give a little shiver of sheer fear.

"Salaam!" he ordered.

Immediately like well drilled dolls, the women all fell to their knees and prostrated themselves on their knees before their Master, still in perfect formation with their chins touching the red line, their naked breasts pressed to the cold marble floor, their hair flung forward and their arms stretched out straight in front of them. They made a perfect picture of abject female submissiveness.

Princess Naima now came out onto her balcony alongside that of the Prince, to enjoy the scene and to make sure that all the concubines, and especially the new girl, Sky Blue, were behaving with sufficient subservience.

Several of the odalisques, beautifully dressed in long embroidered caftans that flattered their figures, also came out onto their balconies, partly to show themselves off to the Prince after his long absence, and partly to enjoy the humiliating scene in which they themselves had had to take part every day until their promotion from being mere concubines.

Mauve had tugged Amanda down when they all prostrated themselves before the Prince, and now, putting her head sideways for a moment, she whispered: "For God's sake get right down on your knees and stretch your arms out straight in front of you. And keep you eyes down! Those awful white eunuch boys are always on the look out for a woman to report for what they call 'lack of respect' - and so are the black eunuchs down here."

Scared by what Mauve said, and with the palms of her hands still burning from the cane, Amanda knelt down humbly before the man she was now being forced to recognise as her Master.

Yet despite her anger she could not help being affected by the sheer sensuousness of the harem, and by the presence of thirty other half naked and beautiful women, all kneeling adoringly before one man and watched over by eunuchs. She, an active and sophisticated woman of the West, was beginning to react passively and humbly to the cunning harem system in the same way that other captured white women had done for centuries.

Then, apparently unusually, the Prince stepped from behind the grill onto the balcony. He looked down on his assembled concubines. There was a gasp of admiration from the line of beautiful women as, keeping their heads lowered, they discretely peeked up adoringly at their strong and dominant looking Master.

The Prince looked tanned, virile and handsome. He was dressed in a spotless white Arab dress, covered by a black transparent silk cloak, heavily embroidered with gold. On his head he wore a white Keffiyah headdress with the golden cords of a Prince.

One of the Prince's page boys, Patience, stepped forward and clapped his hands.

"We all love our Master!" the women chorused in Arabic, keeping their heads dutifully down. "We all love our Master!"

The Prince looked down on the now uniformly prostrate women. It was a delightful and colourful sight, with each woman dressed in a different colour. Each was showing her Master her gleaming white or coffee coloured back, naked from her short bolero to the belt slung low on her hips. Each woman's soft buttocks showed provocatively through her transparent trousers. Each woman's hair was flung forward onto the marble floor between her outstretched hands.

Only one woman's hair was blonde - that of Amanda, or rather Sky Blue, as he had already mentally begun to call her. Her very white skin contrasted excitingly with the olive or slightly dusky colouring of the other women.

He could see that she was trembling with emotion as she knelt between Mauve and Scarlet. She must, he thought with a smile, be biting her lips to keep herself silent, trying not to protest loudly and clearly at the way in which he was choosing his bed companions for his forthcoming siesta.

He would, in fact, have probably enjoyed taking her to bed that afternoon more than any of the other concubines. But he was determined that she must learn her new place. What better way to make the point than to choose for his siesta Amanda's two new friends, Mauve and Scarlet, the two Lebanese sisters he had taken into his harem several years before. They had become very accomplished and loving concubines, and performed well together. The fact that Scarlet had finally been allowed the rare privilege of trying to produce a son did not in any way put him off, just as he had not been put off Mauve when she, too, had been been allowed to try. On the contrary!

He would not, of course, want to have a half European son by Amanda, but having her, an outspoken feminist, forced to carry a half caste black child, and to provide him with sustenance, would be an amusing part of his revenge - as well as being a good introduction to harem life. Indeed, breeding coloured slaves from the more attractive captured women had been a traditional form of revenge for centuries among the bedouin tribal chieftains from whom he was closely descended.

The Prince looked down again at the line of silent prostrate women. Mauve and Scarlet would make very satisfactory bed companions for his siesta. He decided, however, to defer a final decision until all his concubines had been put through their paces.

"Up!" he murmured to one of his white page boys.

The young Dutch eunuch, Pleasure, again clapped is hands twice. The women knelt up, clasping their hands behind their necks to show off their breasts, now pushing past their open boleros.

"Walk," he murmured.

"Walk!" called out Pleasure in a half falsetto voice, first in Arabic and then in English.

The women rose to their feet, and, still keeping their hands clasped behind their necks, began to circle round the room in front of the Prince. Each was glancing up silently and imploringly at the masterful and handsome figure of the man who was looking down at them.

Amanda found herself also glancing up at him. He looked so strong and so commanding. She felt herself becoming weak with longing for him, for his arms, for his touch, for his manhood. She caught his eye for a moment and she thought he had smiled at her before turning to the next woman. She saw him say something to the white page boys.

"Run!" they shouted out together.

The black eunuch cracked his whip and, hands still clasped behind their necks, the women began obediently trotting round the room, raising their knees high in the air in an erotic prancing step.

Each woman was trying to outdo her rivals in showing off her swaying body, her swinging breasts and her undulating buttocks, and each was trying to flutter her eyelashes up at her master as she ran.

After another minute one of the page boys clapped his hands and the panting women formed up again into a line facing the Prince, their half naked breasts falling and rising quickly with the exertion of running. The Prince slowly cast his eye down the line, resting for a moment on each woman. When he looked sternly at Amanda she found herself blushing proudly - obviously he was going to choose her!

He said something to the white boys standing on either side of him. "Mauve and Scarlet," they chorused in Arabic. And then in English. "Mauve and Scarlet."

The Prince smiled as he saw Amanda's face twist with an expression of jealousy and fury.

The women now assembled for a light lunch, sitting subserviently on their heels around a low table. It was a position that would take Amanda some time to get used to.

Mauve and Scarlet had been taken off to make themselves more beautiful for the Prince's bed. They were not allowed any lunch and would not be allowed to eat anything until after they had pleased their master.

Then a red light came on outside the Prince's master bedroom on the upper floor of the courtyard. It was the sign that he was there, awaiting the arrival of the chosen concubines. A similar red light would be switched on each evening outside the bedroom of the wife or odalisque he was honouring with his presence for the night.

Immediately Mauve and Scarlet appeared, dressed in pretty satin nightdresses, each of the appropriate colour. They had been beautifully made up. To help their Master distinguish between them when naked each wore an appropriately coloured ribbon in her hair and another round her throat.

The other concubines, all desperately jealous of the two chosen ones, formed up in two lines at the foot of the staircase, which was, as ever, guarded by two black eunuchs. The girls formed an arcade, each holding up the end of a curved rod bedecked with fresh flowers.

The Prince's white page boys, still wearing the tall white hats that marked them as eunuchs, came down the staircase to conduct the chosen concubines to their Master's bed. Mauve and Scarlet, holding hands, slowly made their way under the flowered arches held up over their heads by their companions who started to sing together the Arabic refrain:

'Please our Master with your bodies,
Make our Master happy,
Tell our Master that we also love him,
Tell him that we wish him joy with you!'

The grille at the foot of the stairs was locked behind the two sisters. Amanda could not help feeling madly frustrated and jealous as she watched the two young women being led up the staircase by the white eunuchs to the Prince's bedroom. A pretty Indian girl dressed in yellow came up and touched her hand.

"We are all also feeling jealous," she said quietly in English. She had had a good education in Bombay before being abducted while on holiday by Baluchi bandits. "Harems are based on love and jealousy. Love for the Master, jealousy for the other women. The Master has not sent for me to share his siesta for a whole month." She sighed. "Now is siesta time for us too. We must go to the dormitory."

Amanda wanted to talk, but she put her fingers to her lips and pointed to the young black eunuch following them into the dormitory.

Now all the women lay down on their couches. The black eunuch drew the shutters across the window leaving the dormitory in a half light. Then he drew back the curtains that hid a picture and switched on a spotlight that shone across the dormitory lighting up a large portrait of the Prince.

Amanda gasped, for it portrayed the Prince standing erect and naked under a long half open Arab robe. The muscles of his hard body glistened. His expression was one of dominance. The eyes were penetrating. In one hand was a riding switch which he seemed to be tapping against the palm of his other hand. At his feet two women knelt. Only their naked backs and buttocks were visible. One had a white skin, the other was coffee coloured, both looking up adoringly.

Amanda shivered. It was one of the most erotic pictures she had ever seen. She could not help but associate herself with the two naked women. The picture made her shiver, but shiver deliciously with a mixture of dread and delicious anticipation. It also made her think, as it was intended to do, of the two women, Mauve and Scarlet, who were even at this very minute in the Prince's bed. Her imagination ran riot. Why two of them? The idea of two women in a man's bed shocked her deeply, but it seemed to be accepted as normal in the harem.

As Amanda lay on her couch she could not take her eyes off the picture. It seemed to symbolise the dominance of the handsome Prince over his women, a dominance that she had just seen so emphatically and unequivocally demonstrated in the ceremony of choosing his siesta companions.

It was a picture that would haunt her frustrated dreams at night and her fantasies by day - just as it did those of all the other equally frustrated concubines. It would be the last thing she would see before dropping off to sleep and the first thing that she would look for when she woke.

Suddenly, as she lay there, she saw a little red light start to flash slowly below the portrait.

"It is the signal from the Prince's white eunuch boys," whispered the friendly Indian girl, "that the Master is beginning to approach his climax."

There were little groans of disappointment from the other women. Then the young black eunuch clapped his hands and called out something in Arabic.

"On your backs!" he repeated in English. "Hands clasped behind your necks, knees together!"

As the red flashes became faster, Amanda, like the other women, could feel herself becoming wet with frustrated arousal, as she wondered what was going on in the Prince's bed. Would he be thrusting deeply down into one of the women? What would the other be doing? Licking him from behind? Or would they both be lying alongside him, each using one of their hands to squeeze his nipples whilst with the other they brought his manhood to a climax?

"Raise bellies!" called out the young black eunuch, as the red light turned from a flashing on to a much stronger bright light - a clear indication Amanda realised that the Prince was reaching his climax.

"Bellies up higher! Knees up! Keep your heads back!"

Like the other panting and frustrated women in the harem dormitory, Amanda found herself straining to raise her belly up, as if offering herself to her Master. Her thighs were wet with excitement. To ease her frustration she longed to touch herself. She just had to!

"Keep hands clasped behind necks!" shouted the young black eunuch as if anticipating Amanda's now frantic desire for relief and those, of course, of all the other young women, their eyes on the portrait and on the now steady light below it.

"Keep hands still clasped behind necks!" again warned the young black eunuch.

Amanda felt desperately frustrated and humiliated. There was a strong smell of arousal in the harem dormitory. How could her Prince, her wonderful lover, have spurned her so? She resolved to do her utmost to attract his attention and to be chosen to please him.

She may have been a sophisticated Western career girl, but already the sensuous and artificial atmosphere of the harem was having its effect.

13 - SKY BLUE IS ALLOCATED A TRAINER

"The black eunuchs are fighting amongst themselves to have you allocated to them," said Mauve the next day. "They're all pressing the Princess Naima to allocate Sky Blue to be trained by them!"

"You make it sound as if we were valuable racehorses belonging to a rich owner," said Amanda.

"Well, it is rather like that," replied Mauve seriously.

"Oh my God!"

"The Harem Mistress, who is Princess Naima, the Prince's first wife, allocates a trainer to each girl. The trainer overseers her lessons in pleasing the Prince in his bed and makes sure that she is always looking beautiful. He is responsible for her health, he keeps the record of her natural functions, of her monthly cycle, of when she was chosen by the Master, and of what happened when she was. He even watches over her progress if she's in an Interesting Condition. A girl can have no secrets from her trainer!"

"Oh!" gasped Amanda. "And these trainers - they all want me to be given to them?"

"Oh yes, they think you will do well and the trainer gets a hundred Dhirams every time she's chosen and another hundred if the Prince marks her as the best girl. That can soon add up to a tidy sum - especially for an ignorant black from a simple African village - not that they are ignorant when it comes to handling their charges. On the contrary, they know exactly what makes a girl catch the Prince's eye, and just what he likes in bed.."

"And if I don't please the Prince?"

"Then he'll be the one who gives you the cane - for losing him money!"

"Oh!"

"It's all part of the harem system. Some of the trainers are terribly cruel. Poor Scarlet is always getting beaten by her's. "

Mauve paused.

"I hear that you're going to be allocated to Yunis. He's that young one over there."

Amanda recognised a young black eunuch who she had seen thrashing one of the girls for some minor fault, and trembled.

"I also hear that he's already negotiating with the other black trainers for an eventual marriage for you - as they call it!

"A marriage!" gasped Amanda

"Yes! You know how strict all the eunuchs are about not allowing us to play with ourselves. or with each other?

"Yes, it's all so embarrassing!"

"And frustrating?" asked Mauve with a smile.

"Yes," admitted Amanda, blushing.

"Don't worry!" smiled Mauve. "We're all equally frustrated. It's part of the harem system to make us all the keener to catch the Prince's eye - and earn more money for our trainers!"

"Yes, but what's that got to do with this marriage business? I thought the Prince was only married to his official wives?"

"Oh this sort of marriage isn't to the Prince! It's a so-called marriage to another concubine - arranged by the two girls' trainers. Although we aren't allowed to play with each other in private, the Prince often likes to watch two or more girls putting on a performance together. And if he's pleased he'll give the eunuchs a generous tip. So two eunuchs may get together, decide that their charges would look good doing it together in front of the Prince, agree to share any tips, and start to train their girls together."

"But how awful!" cried the genuinely shocked Amanda, thinking back to her own lesbian affairs. "The girls may not be attracted to each other!"

"That has nothing to do with it. They'll just use the whip on your backside until you put on a show of really passionate love! Why, once Scarlet and I were put together. The Prince loved the idea of it being two sisters. We hated the idea, but the whip won in the end, as it always does."

She looked at Amanda gravely.

"Once the trainers have come to an agreement, then you'll be made to walk hand in hand with your chosen bride in the harem garden - under supervision of course - and even sleep in the same bed as her - but with the hands of both of you kept chastely in view on top of the bedclothes. So you'll be kept doubly frustrated. Your only hope of any sexual release will be if the Prince chooses you to do a show."

"Oh no!" murmured Amanda.

"I expect Yunis will strike a hard bargain with the other trainers about you," added Mauve. "With your blonde hair, you're expected to be in great demand. So Yunis will want at least two thirds of what the two of you earn for himself. I know he's trying to make a deal with my trainer!"

"Oh!" gasped Amanda again, wondering what it would be like to be made to perform a sexual act with the beautiful Mauve in front of the Prince.

"But first he'll want to train you to please the Prince!"

So it was that the strict young Yunis now took over full responsibility for

Amanda's training and punishment. He was short and rather fat. He rarely smiled and clearly had no qualms about dealing with women. Indeed he was already the Trainer of several other concubines and, like them, Amanda soon found herself dreading his quick temper - and his whippy little dog whip.

Above all, she was appalled at this nasty young black having a financial interest in the Prince choosing her - and in her pleasing the Prince. It was rather like being a tart in the hands of a strict and nasty pimp.

Yunis now dominated every minute of her life.

When the bell rang in the morning she and Yunis's two other girls, one a vivacious Egyptian and the other a lovely little creature from Thailand, all had to run into the main harem room where Yunis would be waiting, dog whip in hand.

There, they had to line up in front of him and hold up the front of their short little nightdresses, and part their legs, so that as they kept their heads up, and their eyes fixed on the wall in front of them, Yunis could go through the formality of checking for any signs of misbehaviour during the night. Other groups of girls would be doing the same in front of their trainers.

It was only a formality because with a black eunuch patrolling the dormitory all night to check that each girl's hands were above the the bedclothes, there was no real opportunity to misbehave. Nevertheless the daily morning check did have a strong psychological effect on the girls, as Amanda soon realised. It was indeed a harem tradition going back hundreds of years.

Then they had to run into the bathroom, hang up their nightdresses and, now naked, line up in front of a bowl, marked with Yunis's name, and get themselves ready to perform. Once again other small groups of naked girls were similarly lining up in front of other bowls marked with the names of other trainers.

When Yunis came into the bathroom, each of his girls would, in turn, have to step forward, stand astride the bowl, and, at a tap of his dog whip, perform quickly and accurately.

Once again, Amanda found that this humiliating health check, carried out in front of a grinning black eunuch, who was noting down the results in a notebook, had a strong psychological effect in driving home her new lowly status as a strictly controlled and disciplined concubine of the Prince.

It was Yunis who then bathed, washed and dried each of the girls, for they were not allowed to touch their bodies - their bodies belonged to the Prince. Yunis supervised them as they brushed their hair, made up their faces, painted their nipples and body lips, and put on their skimpy harem dress.

Then it was time for breakfast. Here, as with other meals, each girl's food was chosen and ordered for by her Trainer, depending on whether he felt she should be slimmer or plumper. In Amanda's case she was only allowed yoghurt and fruit. Jealously she watched another girl being made to gobble down huge quantities of fattening food as her trainer stood over her, whip raised. Clearly, he liked to keep her hugely fat - as an occasional change of scenery for the Prince. It was, indeed, one that earned him a generous extra tip from the Prince, when intrigued he would try out her huge gorgeously soft body.

Every day Amanda had lessons, very explicit lessons, in ways of satisfying and giving pleasure to the Prince. She was never alone for these lessons - sometimes she was with one of Yunis's other girls and sometimes with both of them. Sometimes it was with girls of another Trainer, so that both Trainers, watching their girls closely, could compare notes on whether it might be profitable for them to 'marry' their respective girls.

She was appalled to be told that the Prince invariably used at least two girls at once and would mark each girl's performance out of ten and that the one with the lowest marks would be thrashed afterwards.

Yunis marked her performance every day, caning her at the end of each lesson more or less severely depending on how she had done.

She had to practice techniques and positions that she had never even dreamt about before. A life-size rubber male doll played an important role in these sessions. Using the doll she had to learn such techniques as using her hands and tongue from behind it, or underneath, to give her Master extra pleasure as he took another woman. She also had to learn to recognise Arabic words of command and to obey them instantly in conjunction with whatever girls she was being made to perform with.

It was highly embarrassing to be taught and made to practice all this by a highly critical young black eunuch. It was even more embarrassing when the Prince's personal white page-boys, Pleasure and Patience, also came to see and criticise her performance. She was horrified to learn that they were often in attendance on the Prince when his concubines were pleasuring him.

She was even more horrified when she learnt that these boys used their swagger sticks at the slightest sign of recalcitrance by a woman in his bed, and to drive her to greater efforts.

These two young white boys, therefore, had great experience of just what a woman should do to please Prince Rashid in his bed, and were not backward in criticising Amanda's performances to Yunis - criticisms that earned her several strokes of the cane from her grinning young black eunuch trainer.

14 - IN HER MASTER'S BED

One morning, after the women had lined up beneath the Prince's balcony, the white page boys had called out: "Mauve and Sky Blue!"

In a wild, delirious dream, Amanda spent an hour, under Yunis's delighted supervision, making herself look as irresistible as possible.

Then she put on the lovely long blue satin nightdress that Yunis gave her. It was the first time that she had been allowed to wear such a garment.

In no time, it seemed, she and Mauve were getting ready to walk hand in hand under the pretty flowered arches held up by her companions as they jealously sang their little song. How many times, driven almost mad with jealousy and frustration, had she held up one of the arches over her companions, and sung the words of the song. She looked around contemptuously at the other young women. Now it was her turn! She'd show them how the Prince really adored her!

Then just before they passed under the arches, one of the Prince's pageboys called her over.

In his hands was a leather dog collar with a long chain lead fastened to it. Deftly he locked it round her neck and and led her by the lead towards the now open golden grille. She saw that no such collar and lead had been placed round Mauve's neck. Evidently it was considered that she had been too long in the harem to attempt to escape!

She saw that the other young women, holding up the little arches, were now grinning at each other as they pointed at her collar and chain. She was alarmed to notice that Yunis, who had been smiling happily whilst he washed her and supervised her toilet, now looked angry.

The white page-boys led her and Mauve into the anteroom to the Prince's bedroom. Amanda's heart was pounding with excitement and anticipation - especially when she saw the red light come on over the door to the bedroom. It was, she knew, the signal that the Prince was now in his bed and awaiting his chosen concubines.

Amanda had been trained to crawl into the Prince's bed from the bottom, under the bedclothes. But she had not understood the purpose of the collar and chain that the Prince had ordered to be put on her. Mauve was looking at it and smiling in the same rather superior way as the other women had done back in the harem.

The two white eunuch boys led them into that holy of holies the Prince's bedroom. It was half in darkness, but she saw a huge European four poster bed with curtains drawn around it. A reading light had been switched on inside the curtains. The two women were led to the foot of the bed. The white eunuch boys unfastened the straps of their nightdresses and let them fall to the floor.

In the half light, Amanda saw that one of the white eunuch boys was pointing at the floor. Immediately Mauve knelt down and bowed her head. Amanda followed suit. She could feel the loop of her chain running down her back.

There was a long silence, then a page of a book was turned, followed by a chuckle. It was too much! Here she was, almost mad with desire and anticipation, kneeling at the bed of her lover, her Master - and he was simply amusing himself reading a book!

Five long minutes passed. Still kneeling at the foot of the bed, Amanda was going crazy. Then from within the curtains came a snap of the fingers. Pleasure lifted up the end of the quilt. His companion, Patience, gripped both the women by the neck and thrust their heads down underneath the bedclothes.

Amanda was now in the dark. She could smell the male aroma of the Prince. It was something that she had missed badly during the last few weeks. At last she was going to feel his hands again! But nothing happened! Instead, once again there was a long pause.

Then the book was slammed shut and put down on the bedside table. Amanda felt the sharp tap of one of the white page-boy's canes on her naked buttocks. It was the signal for both women to start crawling slowly and humbly up the bed.

Suddenly she felt the Prince's legs on either side of her. Oh, the excitement! Slowly the two young women inched their way up under the bedclothes. Amanda could hear Mauve kissing the outside of his leg. But she was kissing the inside! Soon she was between his knees.

Again she felt the chain running down her back. It seemed to be getting tighter. Something was wrong. But then it seemed to go slack and soon she was between his thighs.

Her face touched his already erect manhood. How she remembered it from the yacht! Then suddenly she was held back by the chain. She tried to lift her head up higher, to show her gorgeously made-up face and eyes to the Prince, and to greet him again as her lover - but to no avail. She was held firmly down with her head still under the bedclothes and level with the Prince's loins.

She felt so frustrated as, meanwhile, Mauve continued to crawl up the bed, making loving noises as her head parted the bedclothes and became level with the Prince's. Amanda heard the Prince embracing Mauve, kissing her violently, stroking her breasts, murmuring the name Mauve. Furiously jealous, she heard Mauve give a gasp of pleasure and excitement. Then she felt Mauve put her hand down to touch the Prince's throbbing manhood - the same manhood she was reaching out for with her tongue.

It was horrible! As the Prince moved about the bed, so the page-boys shortened or lengthened her chain to keep her down - and, more to the point, out of sight.

She did not dare call out, for she knew that to speak to the Prince without permission would bring down dire punishment onto her head. Instead she frantically used her tongue and the tips of her fingers on the Prince's body, in the way that she had been taught and made to practice over and over again. It was her tongue and fingers that were giving the Prince most of his thrills, but it was Mauve who was the recipient of his attentions.

Helpless, she had to watch, under the bedclothes, as Mauve now slid down the bed again and took the Prince's manhood deep into her mouth.

Disgusted, Amanda took her head away and started to inch her way down the bed again. Let Mauve get on with it! But instantly she felt the Prince's hand gripping her hair and pulling her back. Very well! Eagerly she tried to reach his manhood with her tongue and to use it to push away Mauve's mouth. But once again she was held back by the white eunuchs, and had to satisfy herself with tongueing him lower down, whilst the Prince, gripping her by the hair, held her firmly in place.

She could feel the Prince's body tensing. She heard him cry out, as she remembered him do just before climaxing. It was too awful. But she could not move. A sharp tap on her buttocks made her strive to use her tongue for its maximum effect.

Minutes passed as the groaning Prince became more and more aroused by the double pleasure that he was receiving. Then suddenly he gripped her head more tightly as he reached an ecstatic climax in the mouth of Mauve.

The Prince's body relaxed, He let go of Amanda's hair, but the chain still held her down - invisible and anonymous. Instead he reached down for Mauve's hair and pulled her up level with himself. He took her into his arms and fell asleep on her breasts.

Mauve, still basically unsatisfied, but proud that she had been allowed to give her beloved Master so much pleasure, did not dare to fall asleep. Her duty was to let her breasts act as a cushion for her Master and to keep quite still, not disturb his dreams.

As for Amanda, she was left, still hidden under the bedclothes, utterly frustrated and disappointed.

The Prince woke half an hour later. Amanda heard him kiss Mauve and murmur his thanks. Then she felt him put his hand down and pat her own head, as if she were a pet dog. Angry though she was, Amanda could not help being grateful for this gesture. Greatly daring she held his hand, and kissed it silently and reverently.

Then the Prince got out of bed. Still crouching hidden under the bedclothes, she heard him being washed and dressed by the two page-boys. Then, escorted by them, he returned, not as usual to his office in the male part of the palace, but secretly to the screened part of his balcony looking down into the harem.

Minutes later the two page-boys returned, dressed the women in their nightdresses, and took them back down to the ground floor of the harem. The other concubines, released from the dormitory, were now crowding around the golden grille as it was temporarily opened to let Mauve and Amanda through.

But standing in front of the women, at the foot of the staircase, was Amanda's black keeper, Yunis, together with Mauve's keeper. They eyed the white boys quizzically. As Patience handed Yunis the chain fastened to her collar, she heard him say something. Yunis looked furious and the other women laughed at Amanda.

Mauve's Keeper, however, was rubbing his hands with delight as he proudly put a tick against her name on the board and put a ring round it to show that the Prince had judged her to have given him the most pleasure. Mauve had earned him a hefty tip!

No such tick, however, was placed against the name of Sky Blue. Her score remained nil. Evidently being chained down out of sight at the bottom of her Master's bed, did not count.

Amanda could sense the derision and contempt of her companions. It was so unfair for the Prince to have treated her so cruelly! She burst into tears as Yunis angrily turned to her.

"No tip for me from Prince! Six strokes! Now! Bend over!"

Moments later the harem rang with the sound of the cane on bare flesh and Amanda's cries - and the laughs of the other concubines.

The same sequence of events happened the next day. though this time it was not Mauve who enjoyed her Master's full attention, but Yellow, the pretty Indian girl.

Once again Amanda was held back, held down between her Master's legs by the combination of her chain and the Prince's strong hand. The pleasure she provided was even greater than on the previous day, but it was still given silently and completely anonymously. She never saw her Master's face and he never spoke a word to her as she crouched hidden and frustrated under the bedclothes, held back by her chain, so humiliatingly held by the two white boys.

And so it went on for for another five days, with a variety of different companions, each being taken in a different way , whilst Amanda remained held down by her chain and hidden beneath the bedclothes. Her score on the board remained a humiliating Nil, and every day, on her return, the harem resounded to her cries as an increasingly angry Yunis gave her an increasing number of strokes from his cane.

Poor Amanda was desperate, desperate with frustration, desperate with shame, desperate every day in the knowledge that Yunis would thrash her even harder.

There seemed nothing she could do about it. Thoughts of her Master filled her mind every moment of the day. She longed for one real touch, one loving look, from the man whom she now regarded as her beloved Master.

How he must be enjoying his revenge for the way that she had insulted him!

PART III - PERSONAL MAID SERVANT

15 - THE PRINCESS LEISHA

One day the Princess, accompanied by her personal young black eunuch, Faithful, came down to swim in the pool.

Amanda, forgetting that if a wife appeared the pool must be cleared by everyone else, called out: "Come on in! The water's lovely!"

The Princess was livid. She screamed with rage and stamped her foot as Mauve came rushing over to the pool and prostrated herself in front of the Princess.

"Sky Blue! Sky Blue!" Mauve called. "Out, out, immediately! This is Princess Leisha!"

Suddenly realising the enormity of what she had done, Amanda got out of the pool, naked as all the concubines were when they swam. She stood dripping before the Princess, who was wearing an attractive beach coat. The Princess shouted something in Arabic at Mauve. Then suddenly she turned, smacked Amanda's face, threw her beach coat to her black attendant, and dived neatly into the now empty pool - an attractive figure in a stunning well cut one piece swimming costume.

Mauve nudged Amanda.

"I've to take you up to her apartment to await her return. I'm awfully afraid she intends to have you beaten."

"Oh no! But surely the Prince wouldn't allow that!"

"The Prince never interferes with internal harem discipline - nor with his wives' rights. Hurry! I must take you up there now, just as you are."

A minute later, Amanda found herself kneeling humbly on all fours, naked and wet, on a priceless Persian carpet in the middle of the Princess's drawing room. The room showed the influence of an English education and might have been in a flat in Belgravia, instead of in a palace in the Arabian desert.

Mauve left Amanda kneeling there, prostrated on the carpet, her forehead touching it, her hair flung forward, and her hands flat on the carpet on either side of her head, trembling with fear.

When the Princess came back, she ignored the prostrated figure of Amanda. She stood in the middle of the room as her eunuch took off her beach coat and then slipped down her bathing dress. The Princess stepped out of it and now stood proudly in front of Amanda.

"Raise your head, Sky Blue!"

Amanda saw that the Princess had a very beautiful body. To her surprise, she also saw that, unlike herself and the other concubines, she had retained a little sliver of her body hair - another privilege of being a wife!

The Princess put on a loose silken housecoat. She nodded to her eunuch, who produced a long thin cane. He handed it to the Princess, who was now sitting in a large chair.

"Get up, Sky Blue!" she said in good English, "and come and stand in front of me."

Nervously and embarrassed by her nakedness, Amanda rose to her feet and then ran obediently across the room to the Princess, anxious to get into her good books.

"Head up!" ordered the Princess. "Hands behind your neck! Look up! Tongue out!"

It was the humiliating first position of Inspection that Amanda had so often been made to assume in her lessons.

The Princess lifted up the cane. She started to trace the line of Amanda's enlarged breasts, tickling her stretched nipples in turn. Then she thrust the tip painfully into Amanda's throat.

"I told you to get your head up!"

Poor Amanda strained to raise her chin even more. Her eyes were now on the ceiling.

"So this," she heard the Princess say, "is the famous Amanda Aston who thought she was so clever that she could get away with trying to make a fool of my husband on the television!"

"Yes, Your Highness!" the trembling Amanda cried out, not daring to move her eyes away from the ceiling. "I mean, no, Your Highness!"

"You're quite a pretty little girl."

Amanda hated being called a little girl by a woman of her own age. But she did not dare to say a word. The tip of the cane moved down Amanda's body slowly. Above her knees it stopped and moved from side to side. Ashamed, Amanda recognised the signal - blushing she parted her knees and bent them, and thrust forward her belly in the second part of the Inspection position.

"Yes, quite a pretty little girl."

The cane moved up slowly. Amanda blushed even more.

"Oh!" she gasped.
"And a responsive little girl too!"
The cane moved up to Amanda's chin again. She strained her head back even more.
"I hear His Highness is giving you a hard time, huh? Keeping you nicely frustrated, eh? Well you deserve it, don't you? Don't you!"
"Yes, Your Highness!" whispered Amanda with a sob.
"What do you deserve, girl? Say it!"
"To be kept frustrated by the Master!" Amanda cried.
"Yes! But don't forget that a harem is a world of women." The Princess's voice was now soft and alluring. "You'll find that not everything depends on the Master. I could easily find excuses to have you brought up here frequently to be beaten!"
The voice was even softer and more alluring now. The tip of the cane had returned to between Amanda's legs.
"Would you like that, little girl?"
"No, Your Highness!" The tickling of the tip of the cane was insistent. "I mean, yes Your Highness."
"Good, little girl, good! You see I always think that this harem is a little like the girls' school I went to in England. At the top there is the Headmistress, the first wife, Princess Naima. Then there are the Assistant Mistresses, the other wives, Princess Fatima and myself. Then there are the prefects, who have certain privileges, the odalisques. And then there are all the other girls, the concubines - like you. Do you follow me?"
"Yes, Your Highness."
"And, of course, there is the school governor, the Prince. But he doesn't really concern himself with what goes on behind the scenes. The Governor is not concerned, for example if one of the girls has a crush on one of the mistresses. Did you have a crush on one of your mistresses when you were at school, Sky Blue?"
"Yes, Your Highness," replied Amanda blushing again.
"Was she as beautiful as I am?"
The Princess stood up, put down the cane, threw her housecoat back over her shoulders and bared herself to Amanda's gaze. Amanda lowered her eyes. The Princess was indeed beautiful.
"Was she as beautiful as me?"
"No, Your Highness. You are a very beautiful woman."
"More beautiful than you?
"Yes, Your Highness," replied Amanda humbly.
"And attractive?"
"Of course, Your Highness."

"Attractive to you, Sky Blue?"

"I - I -" stammered Amanda, her mind racing.

"Well, Sky Blue?" The Princess picked up the cane again. "Well?"

"Yes, Your Highness!"

"And perhaps here in this harem, deprived of the sight and company of men - who knows, Sky Blue, who knows?"

The Princess put her hand on Amanda's cheek and smiled.

"Perhaps a school mistress might have a favourite amongst the pupils - a favourite who is allowed to visit the mistress's room; a favourite who is allowed to wash the mistress in the bath, dress her and become her maid servant; a favourite who is allowed to keep the mistress company at night, sleeping on the floor in the mistress's bedroom and perhaps even being allowed to creep into the mistress's bed; a pretty young favourite whom the governor might even be delighted to find in attendance on the mistress when he comes to visit her!"

Amanda's head was reeling as she took in what the Princess was saying.

"Would you like to be my favourite, Sky Blue? Or would you rather just have a beating every day from my eunuch? I can always find reasons for that! Which is it to be, Sky Blue?" She flexed the cane between her two hands. "Well?"

Amanda, shocked and yet fascinated at what she had heard, and equally terrified by the Princess's threats, did not know what to say.

"Well, while you think about it, I think we should let Faithful beat you. You deserve it and he's going to be so disappointed otherwise! Think of it as a little foretaste of what might be happening every day, if you don't become my favourite! Or if you do, and misbehave!"

She tossed the cane to the eunuch, and said something to him in Arabic. Amanda could hardly believe what she was hearing. She was going to be beaten so that a black eunuch wouldn't feel disappointed!

"I like to see a well striped backside! So bend over that chair, buttocks up, on your toes! Put your hands over the top, so that I can hold them tight. Now, Faithful!"

The young black raised his cane and brought it down across Amanda's naked bottom. Amanda screamed with the pain. The Princess's eyes were gleaming.

Amanda wriggled and writhed. She longed to rub her bottom to ease the pain, but her hands were held by the Princess. Moments later the eunuch gave her another stroke. Again she screamed and again the Princess held her tight.

"Now," said the Princess, "if you ask for it nicely, and say you want to be my little girl, then you'll only be given one more stroke - otherwise it will be a round dozen!"

Never had Amanda felt so humiliated as she forced herself to say the words.

"Please Your Highness, may I have one more stroke - and may I be your little girl?"

"And you deserve the stroke, don't you?"

Amanda sobbed. It was all too much.

"Say it!"

"I deserve the stroke!" Amanda whispered.

"Good! But first you must thank Faithful for the first two strokes! Now go and kneel down and kiss his feet. Right down! That's better. Thank him nicely."

"Thank you, Sir, for beating me!"

"Which you richly deserved!"

"Which I richly deserved."

"Good! Now go and bend over again - and this time it'll be a really hard stroke and then you're going to thank Faithful again."

Amanda gave a terrible scream, a scream that was heard almost all over the harem. The Princess was smiling happily as she gripped Amanda's hands and then kicked her away to crawl sobbing to the black eunuchs's feet.

The Princess smiled. The Prince might have acquired this girl for his harem that he could have his revenge on her but, by making this educated Englishwoman her servant girl, she too was going to have her revenge - for all the humiliations she had experienced at school in England.

The Princess held out her arms. The eunuch put down the cane.

Hesitantly Amanda came up to the Princess. She could feel the Princess's breasts thrusting against her own. The Princess reached forward and holding her head, kissed her violently, thrusting her tongue into Amanda's mouth.

"Lick me!" she ordered in a hoarse whisper.

Amanda reached up and humbly licked her under the chin.

The Princess thrust her naked leg between Amanda's. Instinctively Amanda tried to push her away, but then she suddenly felt the eunuch holding her arms behind her back. She was helpless as the Princess, still kissing her, ran one hand slowly down her body. She was held quite unable to move until the Princess's lowered hand began to feel the distinctive signs of her arousal. Then the Princess pushed the shamed and blushing Amanda away.

"Yes, I can see that you'll do very nicely. Now, not a word to anyone for the moment - not until I've had a chance to speak to the Prince. Yunis is going to be very disappointed at losing control of you and we don't want him spoiling things, do we?"

16 - THE PRINCE GIVES A PARTY

At breakfast next morning, all the girls were excited, chattering away to each other more than usual.

"The Prince is having one of his harem parties!" explained Mauve. "It's just like a party in London or Paris!"

"What! Here in this harem?" exclaimed Amanda incredulously. "But what about men - are they invited, too?"

"No, no,," replied Mauve sadly, "there will be no outside guests, but the normal harem rules will be relaxed. He may even take just one concubine back to bed for the night!"

"Indeed!" exclaimed Amanda beginning to become interested.

"There will be dancing, music, delicious food and drinks... But I must warn you that concubines aren't allowed to drink - only the wives and odalisques. The Master says it would be against his religion to allow concubines to start drinking."

"And," added Scarlet, "the wives put on their smartest Parisian evening dresses and the odalisques their most beautiful caftans. And their jewellery! It's gorgeous!"

"And what do we wear?" Amanda asked eagerly. The thought of being wearing civilised clothes again was very exciting. Perhaps one of those lovely evening dresses she had worn in the yacht!

"We are allowed some rather lovely silk cloaks," replied Mauve, "but underneath them just our harem dress. But, it's all so romantic! The Prince will wear a white dinner jacket and a silk turban - just like an Indian maharaja, and dance with us to his favourite romantic tunes."

"But he can't dance with all of us!" objected Amanda.

"No," replied Mauve, "but the wives and odalisques also ask us to dance, and so do the Prince's white eunuch pageboys, also dressed in dinner jackets and behaving as if they were real men."

"What! You mean those awful cruel bastards, Patience and Pleasure!"

"Shush, Sky Blue," warned Mauve. "You'd get us all into serious trouble! Just remember that this a harem, where eunuchs reign supreme. Just enjoy the party. I doubt if there'll be a midday parade today. The Prince will want to have his siesta alone - saving himself for tonight!"

The concubines made a strikingly beautiful and colourful sight as they stood in the spacious ground floor courtyard of the harem, waiting for the party to begin.

The women, Amanda amongst them, her long blonde hair gleaming distinctively, were all beautifully groomed. Their black trainers had seen to that! Over their revealing harem dress, they each wore over their shoulders a short little silk cloak of the same colour as their harem trousers. The very shortness of the cloaks only served to set off their look of near nakedness. a look which was further accentuated by little gold caps perched on their heads, below which their hair hung down their backs - for concubines were not allowed to put their hair up or cut it short.

After a time, the odalisques started to come down the staircase to join them, each wearing a lovely long silken georgette caftan, covered in sequins, and which trailed along the ground. They were all beautifully made up, their eyes sparkling, their hair cut and set in a variety of styles.

Then the youngest of the wives, the Princess Fatima, slowly came down attended by her personal black eunuch. She made a magnificent sight in a huge crinoline dress and diamond necklace that made her look quite delightful. There was a gasp of envy from the other women - all so long deprived of the right to wear Western dresses - and, in the case of the concubines, forbidden to own any jewellery.

Even Amanda caught her breath when, moments later, Princess Leisha came down the staircase, followed by Faithful. She was wearing a beautiful Dior evening suit - tight black satin trousers that showed off to perfection her almost boyish figure, a frilly white silk shirt, a tight fitting long black silk coat and a bow tie.

It was as if she was trying to distance herself from the other women, all dressed in a soft and ultra-feminine way. The significance of her dress was not lost on Amanda - especially in view of what had happened the previous evening.

The Princess flashed a glance at Amanda from under her heavily painted eyelids, and Amanda found herself bowing deeply towards this impressive figure - and blushing as she did so.

Then came the first wife, Princess Naima, wearing a clinging creation in gold lamé, made especially for her in Rome during a recent visit, exuding an air of calm but firm authority. Her piercing eyes darted here and there amongst the women, checking that all were suitably dressed and suitably beautiful.

Behind her came her two personal black eunuchs, Harmony and Melody, wearing robes of gold lamé to match that of their Mistress.

Try as she might, Amanda simply could not bring herself to meet their eyes - nor those of Princess Naima. They were all too frightening, too terrifying. Amanda was reminded of Princess Leisha's description of her as being like the strict Headmistress of a girls school.

There was a sudden silence. The women all looked up expectantly at the the Prince's own balcony. His two white pageboys came into sight, this time wearing short white sharkskin evening spencers, tight black dinner jacket trousers and big floppy pink bow ties that made Amanda smile - they were so appropriately pansy-looking for eunuch boys!

The two boys, clearly enjoying the authority their Master gave them, held up their hands for silence.

Then the Prince appeared.

He was looking breath-takingly handsome in a white dinner jacket that showed off his virile figure, with a white silk turban on his head. He smiled as he looked down onto the glamorous sight below him.

Thirty women curtseyed to him in perfect unison. They were all his! His to do with, or dispose of, as he liked! He thought of the sensual pleasure that all these women provided - or perhaps, even more excitingly in the case of Sky Blue, could be made to provide, as he came down the stairs.

"Charming, my dears, quite charming!" he said in Arabic and then in English.

Then his pageboys started to introduce him formally, first to his wives, the Princess Naima, the Princess Leisha and the Princess Fatima.

Each stepped forward and again curtseyed gracefully, to be greeted by an individual little compliment that made each of them blush with pleasure.

Then it was the turn of the odalisques: the Rose odalisque, the Tulip odalisque, the Hibiscus Odalisque ... for although on promotion to odalisque each was allowed to give up her concubine's name as a mere colour, each had then been given the name of a flower, which she had to have embroidered on all her caftans, her underclothes and her nightdresses, so that the Prince still need not have to remember their names.

Soon it was the turn of the concubines: Pink, Orange, Magenta, Emerald Green, Scarlet - her little belly swelling prettily - Mauve, Grey, Sea Green, Chestnut, Beige... - and finally the newest of them all, Sky Blue.

"Sky Blue! How nice to see you again and how ravishing you're looking this evening."

Amanda curtseyed deeply. Her heart was pounding under her cut away bolero and short revealing cloak as he reached forward to raise her up. This was the touch of the man she had been so longing for ever since her arrival in the harem two weeks before.

Then a wave of anger swept over her, for this was also the man who had so built up her hopes of freedom, of a return to civilisation, to her friends and to her career.

She raised her head to look up at a him with a gesture of defiance and disdain. Her eyes flashed with fury. Yunis stepped forward to seize her, and indeed she seemed about to throw herself at the Prince, about to start scratching and clawing his eyes out, cursing him for being a sadistic swine, when he gently put his hand under her chin and quickly and effortlessly raised her to her feet.

"I can see that our delightful holiday together on my yacht, and then your stay in my palace, has really transformed you into one of the most desirable women I have ever known."

The compliment took her breath away, but only for a moment. The sheer impudence and arrogance of the man! Desirable indeed! And yet kept hidden away under the bed clothes as if she was an ugly duckling! She was about to explode with anger and resentment, when once again he anticipated her.

"I do hope that you are being well looked after whilst you are staying here as my guest."

A guest! A prisoner more like, Amanda wanted to scream. But, once again before she could say anything, he turned to Princess Leisha.

"My dear, do please keep an eye on our delightful and highly intelligent guest. I met her in England, you know."

"Of course, Your Highness," replied Princess Leisha coolly, without so much as batting an eyelid. "We are already friends. Leave her to me, I am sure that she will be very happy here!"

The Prince then touched Amanda's hair caressingly. He touched her cheek gently, the back of his hand running down her neck. It was the first time he had touched her, other than to grip her hair to hold her still under the bedclothes, since she had left the yacht. She gave a sob. But it was not a sob of despair or sadness, rather it was one of renewed adoration. She raised her own hand and silently gripped his, the tears running down her cheeks.

"There's nothing to cry about," he murmured softly, resuming the same affectionate tone of voice that he had so often used to her onboard the yacht. "Now dry your tears. This is a happy occasion."

She could not take her eyes off him. The contrast between his well cut evening dress and her own near nudity overwhelmed her. Love and hatred alternatively filled her agitated mind. This charming, well travelled, urbane, and civilised man - how could he have subjected her, and indeed all these other women, to a life of captivity under the constant and cruel supervision of strict black eunuchs?

"Patience and Pleasure!" he called out. He had chosen the names of his pageboys personally. Their own Dutch names were now forgotten. "A little champagne and caviar for my charming guests!"

They came forward, carrying big silver trays, offering them first to the Prince.

"No, no! Serve the ladies first!"

Eagerly, Amanda reached for a glass of champagne. It was the first drink since she had left the yacht. So much had happened since then. She needed it!

Suddenly Mauve nudged her. She remembered! The champagne was only for her Master and his wives and odalisques - not for the mere concubines. Biting her lips, she took a glass of orange juice.

The Prince was in excellent form, laughing and joking with his women, mainly in English, for only a minority understood Arabic. He was telling them stories of his last visits to Europe and to Egypt, and about other members of the ruling family here in Shamur.

The women, wives, odalisques and concubines alike, were flirting with him outrageously, each trying to out-do the others in catching his attention, fluttering their eye-lashes at him provocatively, trying to make him laugh, touching his hands momentarily and brushing their breasts accidently against him.

Amanda found herself madly jealous, even of her friends Mauve and Scarlet. She too began to make herself amusing, attractive, irresistible.

Music filled the harem, soft, romantic love music: Night and Day, Oh Solo Mio, J'attendrai... The door into the garden was flung open. Coloured lights had been hung from the trees above a little patio. It was a most romantic scene.

The Prince asked his first wife to dance. She smiled happily, and they made a perfect picture, dancing cheek to cheek. Some of the odalisques asked their favourites amongst the concubines to dance. The two pretty white pageboys each asked a concubine to dance. Suddenly Amanda felt her hands being gripped.

"Come, Sky Blue!" whispered Princess Leisha hoarsely.

She led Amanda to the far corner of the floor. She held her as a man would - something she had learned at her English school. She pushed Amanda gently back as she led her, dancing in the warm night air, down towards the pool. There was hardly any light in that part of the harem garden, except for the stars, which as usual in the desert were strangely bright.

The Princess did not say a word. Amanda was too embarrassed even to whisper a word of protest. The Princess pushed down Amanda's protesting hands and held them tightly behind her back. Then she danced cheek to cheek with the graceful Englishwoman.

After a few minutes, Amanda tried to break away.

"Keep still and relax," murmured the Princess, "or do you want me to call over Faithful and tell him to give you the rest of the ten strokes!"

Horrified, Amanda stopped struggling. The Princess rubbed her breasts against Amanda's and soon Amanda was fighting desperately to keep control of her aroused emotions.

"Now, darling," whispered the Princess, "I must go and dance with the Prince."

She led the silent Amanda back into the harem and slipped into the arms of the Prince.

17 - A NIGHT OF LOVE

"Sky Blue!" came the strange falsetto voice. It was Patience. "His Highness requests the pleasure of this dance."

He led her over to where the Prince was laughing and chatting to several of his women. He turned, put down his glass of champagne and led her out onto the dance floor.

She felt his strong arms around her. She looked up at him. She could not help it, but it was, she knew, a look of sheer adoration. It was the same look that she had seen so often on the faces of his other women. Suddenly her feeling of joy and excitement was dashed by the thought that perhaps he had noticed the way the Princess had held her when they had danced together.

The Prince had indeed noticed it all. He had been expecting something like it. It did not worry him particularly. It was a normal part of harem life. It would make both Sky Blue and Princess Leisha more responsive in his bed! Of course he could not countenance any such goings on between concubines, and his black eunuchs made sure that they did not - except as part of an exhibition they were training two girls to perform before the Prince. But for a wife, or even occasionally an odalisque, to have a favourite amongst the concubines was quite harmless.

Amanda jumped as the Prince turned and snapped his fingers. She remembered how this same imperious snap of his fingers, in his bed, was so often the signal to the waiting white eunuch boys to lift up the bedclothes and to apply their dog whips to her buttocks to drive her into applying her tongue yet more zealously.

But this time it was the signal for the two boys to come running over to him. He said something to them. Amanda saw them run out of the room. Moments later they returned and clapped their hands for silence.

"Your Highness, Your Highnesses, Ladies, Concubines - we have a little entertainment for you."

The Prince sat down on a low sofa. The women sat down on the floor around him. He beckoned Amanda and Princess Leisha to come and sit at his feet as the lights dimmed.

Amanda felt a hand on her breasts. She gave a quick intake of breath. She saw the Prince's other hand thrust into Princess Leisha's jacket. She felt his finger and thumb on one of her nipples, rolling it gently. Automatically she put her hands to her bosom, pressing her Master's hand to her breast in a sudden ecstasy of delight and love. Then she saw that the Princess had done the same.

The music of a fast Eastern rhythm filled the room. Two of the concubines, well known Egyptian belly dancers until they were acquired by the Prince, came forward, undulating their almost naked bodies in a violent mime of passionate love making.

Two of the watching women, greatly daring, stood up and came behind the sofa. One bent down to tickle the Prince's ear with her tongue. The other began to kiss and massage his neck. Amanda saw that the Princess had meanwhile reached up with one hand towards the Prince's groin. Then another young woman came and knelt quietly between his knees, her back to the dancers, her head bowed over the Prince.

It was the first time that Amanda had ever taken part in such an orgy of sensual delight - especially one that was entirely aimed at pleasing one man.

At last the dancing stopped and the lights were turned up. Delicious food was brought in, and each woman tried to tempt the Prince with morsels held between her lips, or offered him champagne from a glass she held to her own mouth, or teased him with sweetmeats that they held entrancingly between their breasts.

The dancing was repeated and the lights lowered again. The Prince slipped the Princess's coat and blouse off her shoulders, leaving her painted nipples bare. He also slipped Amanda's silken cloak off her shoulders and pulled back her bolero. Other women also bared their breasts for his delight.

Soon almost all the women were virtually naked as they slipped in and out of the Prince's arms in a veritable orgy of pleasure.

Amanda sat to one side, watching open mouthed and feeling jealous and out of it all. Suddenly one of the pretty pageboys, beckoned her. She saw it was Pleasure.

"Sky Blue!" he ordered. "Go upstairs and wait for the Prince in his bedroom."

Then he went to the Princess and whispered the same order, but in a more respectful tone.

The Princess stood up, gathering her discarded clothes, looked around proudly and took Amanda by the hand. They went upstairs together followed by the white eunuch boy. They were no longer a Princess and a mere concubine. They were two beautiful women, thrilled at having been chosen by their Master.

Under the eye of the white eunuch boy, they both climbed naked into the Prince's huge bed. To Amanda's delight and surprise, nothing was said about crawling up from the bottom, nor were the collar and chain produced.

The page put his fingers to his lips to order silence, and the two women lay on opposite sides of the bed, each imagining what was going to happen.

Suddenly, the Prince strode into the room. He glanced at the two now frightened women, flung his clothes at the eunuch boy and then, to Amanda's surprise, ordered him from the room. Princess Leisha might put up with a lot of things from her husband but, he knew, having her love-making witnessed by a pageboy was not one of them. Then he threw himself onto the bed, each hand reaching out for one of his favourite women, each of whom was reaching up for him, raising her body towards him in a gesture of desire...

It was a satiated and deeply satisfied Amanda who staggered down the stairs the following morning behind her escorting white eunuch, the Prince's pageboy, Pleasure.

Oh what a night of love it had been! The Prince had repeatedly and alternatively penetrated first the Princess and then herself, raising both of them to a pitch of excitement, and then watching them playing with each other and with him as they both reached a series of deeply satisfying climaxes.

Finally the Prince had erupted deep into the Princess, whilst Amanda had licked from below in the way that she had so often been made to when chained down in his bed. But this time, there was no chain and she had found herself enjoying assuming a subservient role.

Now she saw with a strange feeling of pride that, opposite her name on the board, was the figure 1. She was even more proud when she saw Pleasure add after her name the words 'Lent to the Service of the Princess Leisha.'

She expected cross words and scowls from Yunis, but he was all smiles as he helped Pleasure collect her few possessions. He knew that he would soon be collecting a large tip from the Princess, who had effectively bought Amanda from him.

Simultaneously, an equally satiated and satisfied Princess Leisha was being escorted back to her own suite by her personal black eunuch, Faithful, who had run a special hot foam bath for his mistress.

Meanwhile an invigorated Prince was lying back in his own hot bath whilst Patience, his other white pageboy, stood waiting with a large towel. He had, he reflected, been quite right: Sky Blue and the Princess Leisha made a very good pair, even if it was rather unorthodox to mix a royal Princess and a white concubine together.

He could imagine what the Princess's family would have to say if they ever heard about it!

It was partly to stifle any such complaints that he had agreed to the

Princess's request to have Amanda allocated to her personal service as a maidservant. This would, in any case, heighten his revenge. It would also make his regular visits to the Princess's bed even more interesting - and perhaps more frequent!

Similar thoughts were soon to run through the Princess's brain as she lay in her bath. She was admiring the trim white slim figure of Amanda, dressed in just her scanty blue concubine's harem dress as she stood alongside the black skinned Felicity who was showing her how to hold a large towel in readiness for her Mistress. Through her transparent trousers, the girl's hairless beauty lips and mound gleamed entrancingly, making an exciting contrast to the well trimmed hair that she, as one of the Prince's wives, still retained.

Indeed keeping her Mistress's body hair well trimmed was just one of the many little tasks that Sky Blue would have to learn to do, and to do perfectly, in her new role as the Princess's white ladies maid - and personal concubine.

Looking at them both, the Princess toyed with the idea of dressing the girl in the same red baggy trousers and open waistcoat as the black eunuch boy. They would after all be doing many of the same tasks. Friends who came to visit her, the wives of other Prince's and Sheiks, would find it highly amusing to see her two servants both dressed identically, with only the girl's half exposed breasts disclosing her true sex.

But no! Quite apart from giving pleasure to her new Mistress, the other main reason for the English girl being transferred to her own service was to tempt the Prince into visiting her more often. The girl must be kept looking as femininely beautiful and ravishing as possible!

18 - AMANDA GETS HER NEW ORDERS

"Now, Sky Blue," came the incisive voice of the Princess, "there are certain rules for you to obey, now that the Prince has agreed that you should become my maid servant. I don't want last night's events giving you any ideas above your station."

"Oh!" exclaimed Amanda. It had all been so exciting, but now the harsh reality of being a mere maid servant struck home.

"Stand up properly! At Attention! I don't like girls who slouch. Head up! Shoulders back! Hands to your side. Look straight ahead! That's better. Now just remember in future to stand like that when I send for you - or I'll have Faithful deal with you, and you know what that means!"

Amanda did indeed. Six strokes of the cane from the Princess's young black eunuch!

He was indeed now standing on one side of her. On her other side stood Yunis who had come to hand over responsibility for Amanda to Felicity - and to receive a generous tip from the Princess.

Indeed, the Princess now turned to Yunis and handed him an envelope.

"Thank you Yunis. You've done a good job breaking Sky Blue into harem life. I think you'll find this more than compensates you for your trouble. Kindly hand over her record book to Faithful."

Yunis bowed to the Princess and handed a little red book to the other black eunuch. Amanda blushed with embarrassment. The book contained, she knew, a record of all her bodily functions, her monthly cycle, her punishments and the dates when she had been sent for by the Prince. Now the Princess's own personal black eunuch would be responsible for keeping it up to date and showing it to the Princess for her to initial. It was so humiliating!

Yunis left the room. Amanda had now formally left the concubines part of the harem and entered the service of the Princess.

"For a start you are to continue to wear your sky blue harem dress."

"Oh, no!" wailed Amanda. "It's so humiliating."

"Yes, and that's probably one of the reasons why the Prince finds it exciting and arousing. And from now on your sole purpose in life is to excite and arouse the Prince so that the pleasure he gives me is all the greater. I think your English race horse breeders have a word for it - a Teaser, a filly who is used to excite and arouse a stallion before he covers a mare. Well that's what you are now going to be - my Teaser!"

"Oh no!" gasped Amanda, the reality of her new role striking home.

"Yes, and moreover I shall also use you to excite and arouse me before the Prince arrives - so that I am ready for him."

"Oh!" was all that Amanda could now say.

"And if you don't carry out these two tasks with enthusiasm and dedication Faithful's cane will be waiting for you. Won't it, Faithful?

The white of the black youth's eyes gleamed. His English was not very good, but he had understood the gist of what was being said and especially the word Cane. He nodded eagerly, gripping his long whippy cane, the badge of his office. It would indeed be a pleasure to cane this lovely Englishwoman.

"Twenty strokes! And if I tire of your attentions, then I shall have you sent back to the concubines quarters in disgrace."

"No, no, Your Highness!" sobbed Amanda realising that this would mean that she would no longer be frequently seeing the Prince, the man she loved. She would do anything for that. And, anyway, twenty strokes! My God!

"No Mistress, I'll do as you say."

"And a good Teaser for the Prince?"

"Yes," sobbed Amanda.

"And a nice loving little girl friend for me?"

Scared stiff, Amanda nodded eagerly.

"Now the second rule is that you will be under the orders of Faithful, as my personal black eunuch. You will call him Sir and treat him with the same respect that you learnt to treat your trainer in the concubine's quarters. I have told him that he may punish you with up to three strokes a day for any sign of laziness, or dumb insolence. Understand?"

"Yes," murmured Amanda feeling utterly crushed.

"Speak up!" screamed the Princess. "I'm not going to have you muttering to yourself!"

"Yes, Your Highness," Amanda almost shouted.

"That's better! Faithful will be responsible for ensuring that you keep yourself pure. and don't try and misbehave. He's been told to tell me if he even suspects that you have been trying to be naughty. You're going to concentrate on keeping yourself pure for me - and for the Prince. So don't think that being taken out of the concubine's quarters, means that you'll be able to start playing with yourself. Do you know what we do in this part of the world with girls who misbehave?"

Amanda shook her head.

"They have their little beauty buds snipped off, so that they can't give themselves any pleasure! You wouldn't like that Sky Blue, would you?"

Horrified, Amanda fell on her knees in front of the Princess and, clasping her round the ankles, abjectly looked up at her beseechingly.

"Oh, no, please don't ever do that to me, please!"

"Then just make sure that Faithful doesn't ever catch you at it, behind my back! And he will also be responsible for keeping your monthly cycle recorded in the book that Yunis handed over to him, together with your daily weight - I'm not going to have you tucking into food at my expense and becoming a fat slob! He'll decide what you will be given to eat each day".

The Princess paused.

"And I'll have him thrash the living daylights out of you if I ever find you trying to look out of my secret little window that looks down into the male part of the Prince's palace, or if I ever catch you reading one of my novels or looking at my television set. Just remember that you are not allowed to see, hear or read about other men!"

Amanda's heart fell.

"And as for your duties, you will sleep on the floor in my bedroom, ready to come and please me if I snap my fingers at any time of the night, or to please the Prince if he stays the night with me. You will accompany me to the bathroom and the loo - and the Prince, too, if he is present."

The Prince! Amanda's heart leapt. She would adore to perform the most intimate task for him! She must be a masochist. Certainly she was happier now than ever before. Being in the complete power of the strong minded Prince, and of his equally strong minded second wife seemed to satisfy some deep seated need.

19 - THE PRINCE'S MAJLIS

It was several days after the party and the Prince was about to start his regular Majlis which he held in the cool of the evening. He went over to a low sofa surrounded by several other similar ones and sat down. He rang a bell and his two white page boys began to usher in half a dozen grave faced, bearded men, dressed in long white immaculate robes and headdresses, just like the Prince himself.

They greeted the Prince with respect and waited until he graciously gestured to them to sit down on other sofas, keeping the spare seat on his own sofa free. After some minutes of general conversation, the Prince beckoned one of his visitors to come and join him on his sofa and explain his request or complaint.

The Majlis had commenced in the age old Arab way.

Whilst the other men chatted discreetly to each other, the Prince and the Arab sitting on his sofa would join in quiet earnest conversation whilst the Prince's male secretary, standing behind him, took notes of any required action.

The Secretary would discreetly cough when each man's time was up, and he would rise and bow to the Prince. The Secretary would then discreetly beckon another of the men to come and join the Prince on his sofa.

Often, in exchange for the Prince's support, a favourite daughter might be offered for his harem. It was a useful and traditional way of binding a man to his service. For the family of the girl, it would be a great honour, and something the father would boast about to his friends.

Few such offers would be accepted.

First, one of the Prince's black eunuchs would make a discreet visit to see the girl. He would then report back to the Princess Naima.

If the report was favourable, then she herself would go and see the girl, to judge if she was sufficiently beautiful and intelligent to attract the Prince, and sufficiently docile to fit into harem life as a concubine, or if high spirited, which the Prince liked, whether she would eventually settle down to the discipline imposed by the black eunuchs.

Usually the girl had no idea that her father had offered her to the Prince. Often she herself might have her eye on a young man of her own age, or being well educated had set her heart on taking up one of the few careers open to a woman in the Arab world: perhaps teaching or nursing.

However, none of this was judged to be an impediment to her entering the Prince's harem. As a woman her views were of no account by comparison to the great honour that would accrue to her family - and the Prince would enjoy her all the more.

The white page boys periodically offered tiny fresh cups of Turkish coffee, murmuring in their high pitched falsetto voices. They played a key part in the discreet, but impressive, display of power and wealth.

But there was more to come.

Traditionally a Bedouin tribal chieftain would, at the end of his Majlis, offer his visitors milk from his prize camels. But camel milk, whilst still being highly appreciated, was rarely served in these days of large limousines and private aircraft.

After his last private conversation was over, the Prince nodded to his Secretary who left the room. Conversation became more general and the Prince gestured to one of the page boys.

Silently, the pretty youth went to a curious looking large wooden cabinet, standing to one side against the wall on the other side of which was the harem.

The Prince's visitors were too well mannered to turn and watch, and instead carried on talking.

The cabinet had had a false front added, with several beautiful carved doors and slides. It had been strengthened with ornamental iron bars on the front and sides as if to prevent anything from trying to break out of the cabinet.

On each of the sides of the cabinet was a small lattice-work grill, as if intended to provide air and ventilation.

The eunuch boy unlocked two little doors half way down the front of the cabinet and opened them, revealing a small almost open space with, at the back, the original plain front to the cabinet.

Two little silver cups hung down on chains from the top of the small open space.

But it was the original front of the cabinet, at the back of the open space, that would have caught the eye of one of the visitors if he had bothered to turn his head. But he would not have been surprised, for the Prince's wealth and hospitality were legendary - as were the number of his women.

There, just above the two little hanging silver cups, and thrust through two circles in the wood at the back of the otherwise space, were two breasts, surmounted by a prominent dark red nipple!

Only a regular small rise and fall of the quivering breasts showed that the breasts were not plastic or cleverly carved ivory, but belonged to a living woman.

Above and below the two holes, through which the breasts were thrust, were two strong looking brass buckles. These were attached to soft leather straps which passed through the back of the open space.

The upper strap was obviously designed to go round the neck of the woman hidden behind the solid wood at the back of the open space, and the other round her waist, both combining to hold her upper body pressed tight up against the holes.

A faint moan came from the upper part of the cabinet as the page boy began to stroke the nipples to bring on the milk. Soon they were firmly erect.

The Prince's visitors were, of course, too well mannered to show that they had heard a female trying to cry out. Arab men did not discuss or pay any attention to each other's women. What a man did with his women in the privacy of his home was his business, no matter how he might be envied for the number of his women, or admired for the strict discipline he maintained. The visitors simply carried on their discussions as if nothing had happened.

The page boy closed the upper doors of the cabinet, shutting the two breasts off from view.

He pulled out a little stool and sat down in front of the strange cabinet. He slid back a small shutter in the cabinet, a foot or so below the open space containing a woman's breasts.

Now disclosed was another small open space. Lying on the wooden bottom of this space was long soft ostrich feather.

At the wooden back of the space, covering another hole cut in the real front of the cabinet, was a curtain.

The page boy reached into this second open space and gently pulled back the little curtain.

Again the visitors would not have been surprised to see that on display was a hairless female mound surmounting two pretty beauty lips, beautifully decorated in henna and outlined in black kohl.

Below the curtain on either side of the wooden back to the space were two solid looking brass buckles, each also attached to soft leather straps, like the ones above and below the exposed breasts, higher up in the cabinet.

This time the straps were clearly intended to keep a hidden woman's thighs closely pressed against the front of the cabinet, as still mainly hidden she knelt up against it.

The effect was to hold her steady with her beauty lips well and truly exposed.

Unseen at the back of the cabinet was a large door which opened into the harem where it was locked.

Every evening, before the start of the Majlis, the black eunuchs would thrust a folded handkerchief into the mouth of a woman in a suitable state and then seal her mouth tightly shut with a wide strip of sticking plaster.

Now very effectively gagged, she was made to climb up into the cabinet, and then kneel down with her legs apart facing the false front of the cabinet with her breast pushed through the cut away holes. The straps would then be fastened and her hands would be tied behind her neck so that with her elbows kept back by the false front of the cabinet, her breasts and beauty lips were thrust forward.

The bars across the false front and sides of the cabinet were to prevent this ingenious piece of furniture being used as a way of escaping from the harem.

The eunuch boy now picked up the ostrich feather. Carefully parting the exposed hairless beauty lips he slowly drew the ostrich feather several times through the lips. After a time he was rewarded by the sight of the white lower belly beginning to quiver with induced excitement.

He then put down the now moist feather, and parting the beauty lips with one hand, with the middle finger of the other found the beauty bud. It was nicely swollen!

The experienced page boy now judged that the woman would let down her milk easily. Taking his hands away he closed the little curtain at the back of the space, then closed the shutter at the front of the cabinet.

It had all been delicately and fastidiously done - this parody of the way in the old days a difficult she-camel was induced to let down her milk.

Now the page boy stood up again and re-opened the two little doors. The two breasts seemed to be even more swollen and the nipples even more prominently erect.

He unhooked one silver cup and expertly squeezed milk from one breast into it. As he increased the pressure, so the milk began to jet into it.

When the cup was full, he turned, went over to the Prince and offered it to him. The Prince with a courteous gesture told him to offer it first to his guests, each of whom took a sip of the deliciously sweet liquid.

One of them complimented the Prince on his substitute for camel's milk - a compliment which the Prince acknowledged with a proud smile. Both of them knew exactly from where the milk had come, but both were too polite to mention it.

Then the page boy went back and filled the silver cup from the other breast. This time the Prince himself took a sip. Indeed it was delicious. He must remember to see for himself which of his women was the source.

Twice more the boy went back and refilled the cups. By now the breasts were empty and, hanging up the cups again, he closed the small twin doors of the cabinet.

It was the signal for the end of the Majlis.

The visitors rose and bowed to the Prince and were ushered out, each well satisfied with the way that he had been received and listened to by the popular Prince - even if he had not quite got all that he wanted. Each felt highly complimented by having been offered milk from the Prince's very private harem. It would indeed be something to talk about in future!

The Prince walked over to the cabinet.

He opened the twin doors. The shape of the quivering breasts seemed faintly familiar, but he wasn't sure.

He switched on a light switch at the side of the cabinet and then slid open another shutter on its front - this time several inches higher than the twin doors.

There blinking in the sudden blindingly bright light shining in her eyes, which prevented her from seeing the Prince standing outside the cabinet, was the very prettily made up face of Scarlet.

Surprised, the Prince remembered that he had asked the Princess Naima to arrange to have Scarlet's milk brought on early. The miracles of modern medicine! Even Scarlet herself had not known the purpose of the pills that her trainer had made her take.

She had, it was true, felt her breasts become increasingly heavy but she had thought that this was merely part of her pregnancy.

Smiling, the Prince switched off the bright light and slid the shutter closed. Yes, Scarlet had proved a very good milk slave. He would send for her more often - for his own use.

His thoughts returned to Amanda. How amusing it would be to have her in the cabinet. The milk of his tormenter offered to his Majlis!

20 - AMANDA IS JUDGED TO BE READY

The Princess had kept Amanda running off her feet for some some time now, fetching and carrying, ironing her many clothes, attending on her when she went to the bath, to the loo or to the harem swimming pool, and sleeping on the floor of her bedroom at night and during her siesta.

Several times each night, as well as during her siesta, Amanda would be awoken by a sudden flick of her Mistress's fingers. That would be the signal for her to crawl to the foot of her bed, gently lift up the covers, and carefully insinuate her way up between the Princess's legs, just as she had earlier been made to do in the Prince's bed, and apply her tongue and fingers to her Mistress's pleasure.

The Prince, during his afternoon siestas had often summoned his white eunuch page boys to lift up the bottom of the bed clothes and apply their swagger sticks to her now exposed bare buttocks to drive her to greater efforts. Now, during her siestas, the Princess would call upon her young black eunuch, Faithful, in the same way.

The Princess's nipples were still almost virginally small and she felt that as a contrast it would be amusing, for the Prince, for Amanda's to be drawn out again and made yet more prominent. The Princess therefore carefully supervised Faithful, as several times a day, having tied Amanda's hands behind her back so that she could not interfere, he fastened two little spring grips onto Amanda's nipples.

Then, for some ten minutes he would gently pull and pull on the nipples, whilst poor Amanda clenched her teeth and tried not to cry out in protest. Then to prevent the now enlarged nipples from becoming small again, he would oil them and bind them with cotton twine.

The Princess was also the secret possessor of something that was strictly forbidden in the harem: a modern vibrator. She taught Amanda how to use it to raise her Mistress to even greater heights of lust and excitement, whilst swearing her to secrecy.

As Faithful stood over Amanda, his cane ready, not only did she have to learn to keep the vibrator moving over her Mistress's most sensitive parts, but also to hold it in her own mouth, and move it in and out buried deep inside the Princess's beauty lips. She was thus able to give the Princess further pleasure with her hands - either on her nipples or her beauty bud.

As well as this double physical satisfaction, the Princess also had the occasional additional pleasure of feeling the girl's mouth against her beauty lips every time she gently thrust the little vibrator in again.

Then one day the Princess told Amanda that she was to attend on her when she came to the balcony of her apartment when the Prince carried out his daily midday inspection of his women. This would be the signal to the Prince that Sky Blue was now sufficiently trained and disciplined.

Amanda had to dress the Princess in a lovely, and exciting dress in orange organza that had just arrived from Paris. It showed off to perfection her long legs, her small waist and her voluptuous bosom.

She herself, half naked in her simple harem dress, her humiliatingly enlarged nipples thrusting the edges of her bolero apart, made a perfect foil for the Princess as she stepped onto her balcony.

Standing humbly behind her Mistress, Amanda discreetly surveyed a scene that previously she had only seen from below. She now saw that the Prince's balcony with its trellis-work screen on the front, allowing him to look down into the harem without being seen, was in fact open at the sides so that he could be seen by his wives, each standing proudly in her own adjoining balcony.

Amanda suddenly caught her breath, for just then the Prince, as always looking unbelievably slim, virile and handsome, stepped onto his balcony.

Still hidden from his odalisques and concubines by the trellis screen, he ceremoniously bowed to his first wife, standing in her balcony to the right of his own one.

Then he turned to his second wife standing, for the first time for several days, in her balcony to the left of his. Her presence was a clear signal of her availability and his eyes gleamed as he took in the gorgeouse figure of the Princess, who was making a little Eastern gesture of obeisance with the palms of her hands pressed together just beneath her lowered brow.

His eyes gleamed further as he saw her half naked figure, partly dressed in blue, standing discreetly behind, her distinctive long blonde hair half covering her bowed face as she too made the same gesture of obeisance.

The Prince turned to survey his odalisques, the mothers of his sons, as each prettily displayed herself in a variety of beautiful caftans on their much smaller balconies.

Amanda saw the Princess gasp jealously as the Prince pointed out one of the odalisques to his white pageboys, one of whom made a note on a little pad he carried.

Then the white pageboys stepped to the side of the Prince's balcony and clapped their hands. It was the start of the ceremony that Amanda remembered so well with a mixture of shame and excitement. She saw Mauve look up at her with an amused look. Had she noticed her newly enlarged nipples?

She saw that the black eunuch on duty was her former trainer, Yunis. He now had several large rings on his fingers.

Then in obedience to the crack of Yunis's whip, the girls clasped their hands behind the necks, pulling back their open boleros and displaying their naked breasts.

The whip cracked again, and the girls fell kneeling with their heads to the marble floor, and called out in unison their love for their Master.

The whip cracked again, this time repeatedly and the girls started to prance round the room, clasping their hands behind their necks, their well displayed breasts bouncing prettily in time and their knees rising high in the air.

Scarcely had the Princess, still accompanied by Amanda, returned to her apartment, when there was a knock on the door. Faithful opened it. There stood one of the Prince's white pageboys. He handed Faithful a letter, whispered something with a smile and left.

Excitedly, as if expecting it, the Princess snatched the letter and opened it.

"He's coming! After his dinner tomorrow night! He's spending tonight with that odalisque, the one he pointed out to his pageboy, damn her! But to be in good form for me, he's cancelling tomorrow's harem inspection parade and will not be taking any concubines to bed for his siesta in the afternoon - just one of the milk girls, Scarlet, for a little light refreshment. Oh, how lovely!"

Amanda found herself becoming as excited as the Princess!

"And he's sending me some of his supper tonight," added the Princess proudly. Local custom decreed that a man did not eat with his women. Moreover for him and his male guests, the cooks provided delicious food, whereas the women in the harem, even wives, were largely kept on fruit and yoghurt. Not only was it much cheaper but the Prince liked his women to be slender.

So the despatch to a particular woman of a little food from the Prince's plate was not only a great honour, but also a special treat.

Amanda could not help licking her lips. How she longed to taste real food again! But she knew that it would never occur to the Princess to share with a her.

"Now listen, Sky Blue, if you collaborate fully with me in making this a night for the Prince to remember, and if he goes away swearing to return again shortly, then the next day I'll allow you to reach a climax. But if he is disappointed, then it will be twenty strokes of Faithful's cane!"

21 - THE TEASER

When the Prince, immaculately dressed as ever in white robes, was ushered into the Princess's apartments the following evening, he was obsequiously welcomed at the doorstep by a bowing Amanda whose harem dress was even more erotic than ever.

Amanda felt overwhelmed. The anticipation and build up had driven both women almost mad with excitement. Oh how she had been longing for this moment!

Her little cap, her bolero and her tinkling shoes were unchanged, but her sky blue trousers had been completely cut away in front, displaying beauty lips that had been carefully painted blue. From the edges of her bolero peeked blue nipples.

Then when she turned, she showed that her trousers had also been cut away over the cheeks of her pert little bottom, displaying the clear red marks of three separate and recent strokes of the cane. She felt ashamed at the contrast between her own revealing dress and this gorgeously robed man. And yet she also felt wildly excited in the presence of the man she adored, the only man she had seen for so long.

The Prince appeared to ignore Amanda, but in reality he had taken everything about her in. It was a sight that, combined with her beautifully brushed honey coloured hair, made the Prince feel instantly aroused. Amanda's role as her Mistress's teaser had indeed started!

Not daring to say a word, she ushered the Prince into the Princess's drawing room.

The Princess was dressed in a severe long black evening dress that only hinted at the delights of her body. Under it, Amanda knew, she wore just a black satin waspie corselet that left her breasts and beauty lips bare.

Her eyes sparkled and she exuded a sense of sensuousness - brought on not only by anticipation of her tryst with the Prince, but also by Amanda's now well-trained tongue. When the Prince had knocked on the door, she had been standing with her feet apart, whilst Amanda had been kneeling under her billowing skirt, her mouth clamped to the imperious Princess's beauty lips and her naked little bottom protruding prettily from beneath the Princess's dress.

Standing behind Amanda had been the grinning figure of Faithful, his long whippy cane raised, ready to be applied to Amanda's soft buttocks whenever the Princess with a wave of her fingers indicated that Amanda's tongue was tiring.

It was a scene that had lasted for a little time, before being interrupted by the knocking on the door. The three stripes now showing on Amanda's little bottom had been inflicted during it.

Although the Princess had been careful not to reach a climax she was now thoroughly aroused. As the Prince's white eunuch attendants knocked on the door she just had time to remind Amanda that she was merely a teaser, not permitted to climax herself...

Faithful discreetly left the room, and Amanda stood silently in the corner, head raised, hands clasped behind her neck and eyes fixed on the wall in front of her, whilst the Prince and Princess greeted each other affectionately. How she, too, longed to be greeted affectionately by the Prince. She could hear them kissing. The Princess was determined not to waste time in idle talk. If only, thought Amanda, if only...

A snap of the Princess's fingers woke her out of reverie.

The Prince and Princess were now sitting down happily alongside one another on a sofa. Hastily Amanda picked up a plate of caviar and biscuits and took them across to the sofa.

As she did so she was acutely aware of her exposed and painted beauty lips. Then in accordance with Arab custom, she offered the plate first to the Prince and then to the Princess.

Then, as she had been carefully rehearsed to do, she returned with a little cushion in her hand. She placed it at the feet of the seated Prince, who was busily flirting with the Princess.

She knelt down on the cushion and lifted up the Prince's robe slightly and pulled it over her head. She recognised his masculine smell. Oh how she adored him! For a moment she hesitated, but if she did not please the Prince, then the Princess would indeed have her thrashed to within an inch of her life.

She raised her head and hands under the Prince's robe and found his manhood. It was already erect. She lowered her mouth in a servile gesture and, also exciting the Prince with her hands, began to suck.

Soon she heard the sound of the Princess's silken dress being slipped down over her shoulders... Of course she was jealous, but what could she do? It was still quite early in the game that she had rehearsed with the Princess.

She felt the hand of the Princess gripping the Prince's manhood through his robe.

"Darling," she heard her say, speaking in English, "the girl doesn't seem to be very good. Perhaps I ought to punish her?"

Fearful of what was now to happen, and yet, despite herself, madly excited at the prospect of it, Amanda withdrew from under the Prince's robe and stood up facing him.

Once again her hands were clasped behind her neck and her eyes fixed on the wall behind the sofa. Her belly was level with the Prince's eyes.

She could hardly restrain herself as she felt the Prince's hands touch her henna decorated mound. Then he reached up and felt her enlarged nipples. How suitable she would be, he was thinking, in the milking cabinet - and carrying a large black child would firm up her breasts splendidly!

"Kneel!" ordered the Princess. "Head to the floor! Buttocks up!"

She was now kneeling sideways onto the Prince. She heard the Princess hand him a little dog whip.

"Beat her!" she urged.

Amanda screamed as the whip caught her across the lower buttocks.

She heard a rustle as the Princess again reached to feel the Prince's manhood through his robe.

"That's better!" she heard her say. "Now beat her properly! Get up, girl and bend over that chair!"

With a sob, Amanda jumped up and ran over to the chair. She bent over one of the arms as they followed her slowly across the room. Out of the corner of her eye, she saw that the Prince was still gripping the dog whip.

"Up on your toes!" ordered the Prince.

Three times the whip came down and three times Amanda screamed in genuine pain.

"Now let's see if she's any better," said the Princess.

As the Prince stood proudly over her, Amanda knelt at his feet, and put her head under his robe once more. Yes, his manhood was even more erect! She resumed her duties. She heard the Princess come up to the Prince and kiss him passionately. They both ignored the girl hidden under his robes. She had served her purpose!

"Oh, darling! You're so strong!" murmured the Princess. "Come to bed..."

Half an hour later, Amanda, now naked, was kneeling behind the equally naked Prince, who in turn was kneeling between the outstretched legs of the Princess who was lying on a couple of bolsters.

Once again Amanda's tongue was active - giving intense extra pleasure to the man she loved whilst he enjoyed her Mistress who was moaning with the pleasure of feeling him inside her.

She had to grip her Master's muscular thighs to keep her tongue in place as he thrust in and out.

She kept asking herself why she was demeaning herself in this way, whilst getting no physical pleasure herself. It was not only fear of the whip, though her Mistress's threats were never far from her thoughts. No, there was, she knew, another reason. She really enjoyed contributing to the overall pleasure her Master was receiving. Such a situation might perhaps be inconceivable in the West, but she was in the East - and shut up in the highly sensual and artificial atmosphere of a large harem.

Earlier on, as her Master lay on his side facing the Princess, she had, as she had been taught to do, reached round to squeeze alternatively his and her nipples, giving them both intense pleasure. Then as they had played and aroused each other further, she had dropped down in the bed, to apply her tongue to where it was now rooted.

Then the Princess had encouraged him to turn towards Amanda, to arouse himself by holding her enlarged nipples, and playing with her beauty lips.

Then, excited beyond all bounds, she had felt his manhood pressing against her beauty lips. Amanda was now at the very pinnacle of excitement. Eagerly she had found herself parting her legs for her Master.

Then suddenly she had been brought down to earth by a warning cough from the Princess. Aghast at the extent to which she had allowed herself to be carried away, she remembered the Princess's warning. Hastily she had slid away from the Prince who had turned back to the welcoming soft arms of the now rested Princess.

Finally, when her tongue felt utterly exhausted she felt the Prince reach his climax. She felt his manhood jetting into her Mistress, an action that triggered the Princess's own violent climax.

"Lick us clean!" the Princess called out after she came to her senses again. "Both of us!"

Starting with the Prince she did just that - finding a strange mental pleasure in humbling herself before him and then before her.

It was a scene that was repeated in the early hours of the night...

It was not until next morning, long after the Prince had left them, that the Princess remembered her promise.

"Very well, Sky Blue, you may now play with yourself." Still lying in bed, she tossed the little vibrator to Amanda who stood by the side of the bed in her abbreviated harem dress, looking groomed and ready to help her Mistress with her bath.

"Go on, girl, excite yourself!" the Princess ordered. "And don't pretend you don't know how to."

"No, please Your Highness, not, not..." Amanda stammered embarrassed beyond belief.

"Not what, girl? You just do as you're told - or I'll call in Faithful to do it to you. Go on! I want to watch it!"

Shamefacedly Amanda picked up the vibrator. She turned it on and slowly placed it between her legs. Soon she felt it achieving its inevitable result. The Princess's eyes gleamed and her hand slipped below the bedclothes.

"Go on!" she called out hoarsely. "I want to see you wriggle! And stand up properly while you do it. Head up and eyes fixed straight ahead."

Amanda was soon indeed wriggling wildly. She tried to think of the Prince, that the vibrator was his hand, his manhood.

Kept frustrated ever since she had been tricked into the harem, she was soon ready.

With a sudden shriek of excitement and shame she collapsed onto the floor, whilst the Princess also reached yet another climax.

22 - A SHOCK FOR AMANDA

It was whilst the Prince was away on one of his trips that the Princess disclosed a plan that really horrified Amanda, and made her desperate to get away from the harem, even though it meant leaving her beloved Prince.

"His Highness wants you in milk," the Princess said casually, as if it were a minor matter. "He plans to have you covered by one of his black servants when he gets back."

Now Amanda stood in the cool of the evening by the side of the swimming pool in which Princess Leisha was enjoying a cooling swim.

She looked across the harem garden and down into the dip which permitted a glimpse over the wall of the calm sea that was lit up by sunset, dark red but brilliant - the sunset of the desert.

At the bottom of the garden, near the sea, there was a wall with an electrified fence, so that even if by some miracle a woman did manage to get out of the harem she still could not get out of the palace grounds - and anyway even if she did where would she go?

The port and airport of Shamur were closely controlled. No woman was ever allowed to leave the country without her husband or father's written permission and a passport. No foreign embassy would ever dare risk having oil supplies to their parent country cut off by shielding a runaway concubine from a royal harem. No foreign company would risk its very profitable local operations closed down.

Suddenly a slight dark figure, probably one of the Arab serving women, appeared from nowhere. Without a word she thrust a tiny piece of paper into Amanda's hand and ran off into the gathering darkness that surrounded the pool.

There was writing on the paper. It must be something secret, but there was nowhere to hide it in her scanty harem dress.

The Princess was still swimming up and down the well lit pool. Amanda screwed the piece of paper up in her hand and then, walking slowly and nonchalantly, went towards one of the harem garden lanterns.

No one seemed to be looking at her, not even the ubiquitous black eunuchs. She smoothed the paper and glanced down. She gasped at what was written in a strange handwriting:

DEAR MISS AMANDA ASTON

IF YOU EVER WANT TO BE FREE AGAIN, BE BY THE THIRD LANTERN IN THE GARDEN ON THE LEFT OF THE SWIMMING POOL AS SOON AS IT IS DARK TOMORROW NIGHT. DON'T TELL ANYONE. JUST DO AS YOU ARE TOLD. MEANWHILE DESTROY THIS NOTE

A FRIEND

23 - ESCAPE?

Each passing hour seemed to last for ever.

Was she really going to escape? But how? And which of her friends had organised it? And how had they discovered where she was?

Amanda was now terrified lest the Princess might at the last moment tell Faithful to give her some task that would prevent her from attending on her when she took her evening swim - or that she might change her mind and not swim that evening.

And might it all be a trap? Her thoughts became more and more agitated as the evening began.

Trying to look normal, she ran along behind the Princess to the now deserted swimming pool. Her heart was beating fast under her open bolero as she helped the Princess to undress.

It was already beginning to get dark as the Princess started to swim vigorously up and down. The pool was now lit up by bright lights, whilst the garden was only partly lit by colourful lanterns.

Soon the trees and shrubs were looking indistinct. The quick twilight of the tropics was over. Amanda sauntered over to the third lantern on the left.

She saw a negress come down a path, sweeping away the leaves.

Suddenly all the lights went out. Amanda's heart leapt. Power cuts were almost unknown in the palace.

Her arm was suddenly gripped. She almost jumped out her skin. It was the woman who had been sweeping. Without a word, she pulled Amanda at a run across the lawn, down the garden, down towards the harem garden wall, down towards the sea. As she ran, Amanda heard the Princess calling her from the swimming pool and ran even faster.

Vaguely she made out a small heavily barred door in the wall that she had never noticed before. It must be the one used by the gardeners when they came to do the garden in the early morning before the women awoke.

The negress knocked on the door. A peculiar knock. The door opened gently and softly. The woman pushed Amanda through the doorway and then quickly closed it behind her.

For a moment Amanda thought she was alone. Then she heard the noise of keys in locks. A man's figure loomed up out of the darkness and, again without a word, gripped her arm.

He ran with her along a little path by the sea. She was out of breath, but he kept pulling her along. He pointed up at the watch towers on the palace wall and at the lights that normally lit up the approaches to the wall. Clearly he was saying that if the lights came on whilst they were still there, then they would be seen.

He hustled her across a piece of wasteland. Soon she made out a car. She could hear its engine running, but it showed no lights. A door was opened and she was pushed in. The car drove off.

Not until the car was well clear did the driver switch on the headlights. As he did so she saw other lights coming on again. The power failure had been corrected. Clearly it had been artificially induced for her escape.

The car drove fast, away from the town, away from the palace, away from the sea, and out into the desert. After ten minutes they stopped. The door was opened and a man flung a long all-enveloping black tcharchef over her. She now looked just like any Arab woman. She was led out. The tcharchef was adjusted over her. She could see through a small lace grill in front of her eyes.

She was led across the sand. In the darkness she heard the car driving off. Suddenly she saw the outlines of a helicopter...

PART IV - THE ISLAND

24 - A FRIGHTENING ARRIVAL

The helicopter had flown over trackless desert and scrub and a brilliant blue shark infested sea. Now it hovered over a small flat island that was only a few miles across.

To a casual observer this island looked dull and uninteresting. However on the far side, away from the shipping lanes, and up a long creek, was a modern white building. It looked rather like a yacht club, with flagpoles, a jetty with fast speed boats moored to it. Painted over the entrance of the building was a rather distinctively designed crest of two palm trees.

Behind this was a helicopter landing pad which was marked with the same crest of two palm trees. A dozen smart looking helicopters were parked near the landing pad. There was also a long quay to which some twenty strange craft were moored stern on. Long and slender, and lightly built, they were open except for a raised poop, which was covered to give protection from the hot sun, and a low pointed bow.

Also scattered around the island were some twenty well separated sets of white painted stone buildings, the sort of stables used to house horses in a hot climate, with next to them cool bungalows for grooms.

Some way behind the white painted club house with its green well watered lawns, its shaded tables and chairs, and its large blue swimming pool, was what might be taken for a cattle or horse market: rows of neatly painted pens surrounding a shaded auction ring, and facing it living quarters for servants and the barracks of the inevitable guards.

There was activity: several cattle trucks and horse boxes were bumping their way across the island on the rough tracks that converged on this market from the various sets of buildings to the creek.

Amanda was in a state of great excitement as the helicopter descended. Its engine died away. She was about to taste freedom at last!
Then her nightmare began.

Almost before she had time to realise what was going on, she was gripped by strong black hands, her enveloping black shroud was ripped off and with it her blue harem dress. She found herself crouching naked on her knees in a small cage with her hands gripping the bars. A blanket was thrown over the cage blotting out everything. Through the bars at the bottom of her cage she saw that it was being placed on a trolley.

Her cries for help were greeted with laughter as the trolley was pushed across the landing pad and into a shed. The cage was lifted up and put down onto the sandy ground and the blanket removed. She had a momentarily vision of other similar cages, of other caged and naked women, and of burly laughing negroes naked to the waist and wearing a sort of uniform of baggy red trousers and a red turban.

The mere sight of the black men made her tremble.

In England she had been proud of saying that she had no racist feelings. Indeed many of her journalist colleagues had been coloured. They had been intelligent and educated men.

But here in Arabia it was different, very different, and so were the ignorant and brutal black men employed by the wealthy Arabs to take charge of their women. Now, after all the humiliation of being intimately controlled and constantly supervised by the black eunuchs in charge of Prince Rashid's harem, she was scared of black men. Indeed, as she had learned in the harem, it was a natural deep-felt fear in white and Arab women that rich Middle Eastern men had taken advantage of for centuries - by employing black eunuchs to supervise and subject their women.

Two burly negroes came up to the cage. They were grinning at her. The fact that these black men, with their deep voices, didn't seem to be eunuchs, frightened her even more.

With them was an Arab, holding a piece of paper on which some Arabic numerals had been written. He looked at the piece of paper and at some numbers prominently engraved on the front of a metal collar handed to him by an assistant. She saw that the collar had strong looking rings welded onto the front and back and that a length of stout chain hung down from the back ring.

The Arab looked at the piece of paper and at some numbers prominently engraved on the front of the collar. Then he nodded to the negroes, who reached down and unlocked the top of her cage.

One of the black men put his boot down on her neck to hold her down while the other one gripped her hair to hold her head still. The Arab reached down and closed the collar round her neck. It was hinged and the negro keeping her down with his boot now held together the ringed ends opposite to the hinge. The Arab inserted a lead pellet into these two rings. Then using an instrument that looked like a large pair of pliers, he squeezed the lead pellet until the ends were riveted together.

Then one of the negroes fastened her collar chain to the bars at the bottom of the cage and pulled her right arm through the bars of the cage, whilst the other held her still with his boot.

"No!" she screamed.

The second negro reached down and smacked her sharply across the cheek, shouting out a word of command in Arabic. Obviously it was an order to keep silence. Smarting from the shock of having her face smacked, she obeyed.

Then, out of the corner of her eye, she saw the Arab bend down and pick up another instrument. She felt it touch her forearm. Nervously she tried to pull her arm away, but it was firmly held.

She could not now see her arm, but she felt it being wiped with something wet. Then the Arab picked up another instrument and there was a buzzing noise followed by a pricking sensation as if a little needle was being repeatedly jabbed into her skin...

Suddenly the instrument was withdrawn. The Arab took a last look at the numbers he had tattooed onto her skin and the number engraved on her new collar. They were the same! Satisfied he left.

The negro standing over her lifted up his boot, and slammed shut the top of her cage, carefully locking it. The other threw the blanket over her cage again.

Once again she was in darkness. She heard the sound of weeping, the sound of a woman weeping.

Then she realised that it was herself.

25 - IN THE PENS

An hour later the blanket over Amanda's cage was again pulled off by the two burly negroes.

This time one of them bent down and unlocked her collar chain from the bottom of the cage, whilst the second unlocked the top of the cage itself. Then, gripping her tightly, they fastened her hands behind her back.

The second big negro now lifted her up right out of the cage and set her down, still holding her up for a moment, as she tottered unsteadily on her feet, after being confined to the small cage.

Then they led her by the chain fastened to her collar to a door which was decorated with a crest of two palm trees. They opened the door and led her out into the open.

To her horror, Amanda saw that half a dozen naked women were standing in two lines of straw lined pens. Some looked Chinese or Filipino, others Indian, but they looked strangely inhuman as their mouths were held wide open by a chain fastened behind their necks. They also had shiny metal collars like hers, with Arabic numbers prominently engraved on the front on either side of a central ring, together with the emblem of two palm trees.

She was brutally pushed into a pen and a strap passed round her waist to hold her belly tightly up against the bars. Then the ring on the front of her collar was clipped to one of the bars, holding her up even more tightly against the bars.

The pens were like the cattle pens in a market, though the gaps between the bars were too small for a woman to slip out between them, and wire netting over the top of each pen would prevent her from climbing out.

However, there was little chance of that, for not only were their arms fastened behind their backs, but they too were held up against the front bars of their pens by a clip onto the ring at the front of their collars and by a strap round their waists.

On the the front of each pen was a white plastic shield decorated with the same crest of two palm trees, underneath which Arabic writing and numerals had been written with a maker pen.

Now a light chain was pushed through her mouth and round her cheeks, holding her mouth wide open like the other women. It too was fastened

113

behind her neck, gagging her very effectively.

The negroes stood back and looked at her. She had the impression that they were taking particular pleasure in humiliating her as a white woman - and perhaps as a hated Christian.

They now started to measure her bosom and waist, seeming delighted with the way her breasts had been enlarged and her nipples elongated. And they kept pointing to the difference between her full bosom and small waist, which had been kept trim by her regime with Prince Rashid.

They wrote the figures on the white plastic shield hanging from the front of her pen, and then went off leaving her standing there unable to move or speak.

After some minutes the two negroes returned with an Arab-looking man dressed like a doctor in a white robe with a stethoscope round his neck. He was holding a writing pad with a long form printed in Arabic. One of the negroes was wheeling a trolley containing medical equipment and a printer to which several wire leads were attached. It also held a portable weighing machine.

They stopped at Amanda's pen. She tried to back away but, of course, she was held tightly up against the bars of her pen. The doctor reached through the bars with his stethoscope and started to sound out her heart, making notes on the printed form as he did so. Then he took her blood pressure and again made notes on the printed form.

He then ran his hands over her body, feeling first her arm and shoulder muscles carefully and then her breasts and finally her stomach and thighs.

Then he turned to one of the negroes and pointed at her intimacies. The negro gestured roughly to Amanda to part her legs and bend her knees. When she hesitated he picked up something that looked like an electric cattle goad, and with it touched the inside of her thighs. Amanda saw him flick a switch in the handle and immediately she felt a sharp shock on her thigh. The pain made her jump, but the strap round her waist and the clip on her collar held her tight.

The negro repeated his gesture. This time she parted her legs and bent her knees immediately. Anything rather than be given another shock!

She felt the doctor parting her beauty lips, as if searching for her beauty bud. She gave a sudden jerk as he found it. She saw him nod and note something down on the form. My God, thought Amanda, was he checking whether she had been circumcised? She had heard about that cruel Middle Eastern custom - indeed she had broadcast about it.

Then he felt up inside her. She tried to call out in protest, but her gag kept her quite quiet.

Then the doctor said something in Arabic, and the negro produced a bottle.

He gestured menacingly with the electric goad. His meaning was only too clear and, highly embarrassed, Amanda was made to give a specimen which the doctor started to test immediately. He was testing whether she was pregnant! Again the doctor made a note on the form.

Then he started to stick the ends of the wire leads onto different parts of Amanda's body, and switched on the printer. Amanda recognised that a cardiograph of her heart was being taken.

The doctor looked closely at the print out, and wrote something on the form whilst the negroes removed the wires.

Then the other negro lifted the portable weighing machine off the trolley and put it on the ground by Amanda's feet. The negro with the goad gestured to her to stand on it. Quickly she did so, her eyes on the terrifying goad. The doctor bent down and read off her weight, making her step on and off the weighing machine several times so as to be sure. Finally he wrote down a number on his form and signed it. He handed the form to one of the negroes, who stuck it onto the white plastic shield hanging from the front of Amanda's pen.

A few minutes later a younger negro, holding a comb and hairbrush, came to Amanda's pen and started to brush her hair and smarten her up.

After a few minutes the young man left her and started to work on the woman in the next pen. Amanda looked at her companions in misery. One was a pretty, slender, Italian-looking girl, and next to her was a strongly built Indian girl and then a Scandinavian-looking blonde young woman. Further along on the opposite side the passageway were the pens of two very pretty Siamese-looking girls who were gazing around with a terrified air.

All had been shorn and their beauty lips were well displayed - like her own, for she had been kept carefully depilated in Prince Rashid's harem.

Then three other young women were marched in. Two were Chinese and the other European. They were put into pens right opposite Amanda's and she saw that they had not yet been shorn.

Amanda watched as they were strapped to the bars at the front of their pens, and put into shiny metal collars whose side chains held them rigidly still.

Then the gagging chains were fastened round their necks. As the chain was pushed between the lips of the European woman, Amanda heard her cry out.

The young negro who had combed and brushed Amanda's hair came back along the passageway, carrying a stool and some electric clippers, and sat down on the little stool so that his face was now level with the intimacies of the blushing Englishwoman.

Amanda watched as he ran his clippers over the woman's mound, removing all the hair. Then, using a goad to make her part her legs, he carefully removed all the hair around her beauty lips. Soon both she and the Chinese girls had the same little girl look as Amanda and all the other women - as the doctor noted as he proceeded to examine them and sign their certificates.

A few minutes later two other new arrivals were brought in and subjected to the same treatment and examination. The negroes seemed particularly pleased by their already muscular bodies. Although, of course, Amanda had way of knowing it, they were Israeli girls who had been working in a Kibbutz, from which they had recently been kidnapped by Arab terrorists who had earned themselves a nice sum from the despised but fit Jewish girls.

Down between the two lines of pens came some twenty immaculately dressed Arab gentlemen. They were all wearing long white spotless and freshly starched Arab dress and Arab headgear. Some also wore the gold embroidered black transparent over-robe of the wealthy ruling families.

Many had short pointed beards. Many were wearing large opaque sun glasses that hid their eyes and the expression of cruelty and lust in their faces as they eyed the trembling women chained in the pens.

Walking deferentially behind each of these ruthless and powerful men were their whipmasters, cruel looking men, each proud to be in charge of his master's women on this strange island.

Some of the whipmasters only wore a cotton sarong around their shining black muscular bodies - black because in Arabia, as Amanda had learned in the harem, negroes were traditionally used to supervise and discipline the women of the rich.

Amanda shuddered as she saw that all the whipmasters carried, like a badge of office, a short handled whip with a black leather thong that was curled up in their hands. The tip of the thongs were knotted.

Some of these whipmasters were eagerly reaching through the bars of the pens to feel shoulder muscles and thighs, as well as breasts and waists, before whispering into the ears of their masters who were busy looking at the details of the women written on the plastic shields hanging from the front of each pen. They were, Amanda thought, rather like stud grooms at a horse sale, some interested in buying, others in selling.

The black whipmaster in charge of the Italian-looking girl unfastened her gagging chain, and the strap round her waist and the clip on her collar. Then, leaving her hands fastened behind her back, he proceeded to show off her agility by throwing lumps of sugar into the air, making the poor girl jump up to catch them in her mouth, like a performing dog. Clearly it was a trick that she had been trained to do.

Impressed, another of the black whipmasters, a huge fat bald headed man, felt her muscles, carefully weighed her breasts with his hands and made her turn round so that he could feel her hindquarters and up her backside.

Then, cleaning his hands on the straw of her pen, he turned her round again and, bending down, parted her beauty lips.

When he was satisfied, the big negro went back to where his master, immaculate in white and black Arab robes, was standing, unrecognised by Amanda, his eyes hidden by dark glasses.

But Sheik Turki was really more interested in watching the humiliation of Amanda. She had attracted considerable attention - not only for her English nationality and her beauty, but also for her large bosom and small waist.

Numerous Arab and negro whipmasters had felt her all over - and up inside her. She was blushing with shame. She felt that she had never been so humiliated. Sheik Turki's eyes glinted with pleasure behind his sun glasses as he watched her evident feeling of shame.

Selling her and then buying her back might cost him a little, but he didn't mind that - it was merely the beginning of his revenge!

26 - SOLD!

An hour later, one by one, the women were taken by the negroes, and tied by their collar chains to a line of rings set in the wall outside the auction ring.

By this time the wealthy Arabs and their whipmaster advisers had finished their inspection. They sat on comfortable chairs looking down into the ring itself, and it was these men, laughing and talking amongst themselves, that Amanda first saw when she was taken into the auction ring - the first woman to be sold.

Under her naked feet, Amanda could feel sand on the floor of the ring - so that if a woman disgraced herself under the stress of being sold, it could all be quickly raked over.

In the middle of the ring was a post with a long horizontal arm attached to it. Naked in front of all these well dressed men, Amanda allowed herself to be led up to it. The arm was neck height, and on the end was a ring to which a woman's collar chain could be attached.

She stood trembling in the pit-like area, surrounded by a high round wooden wall, above which were seated staring men. Her hands were still chained behind her back, and her collar chain was fastened to the bar. She longed to cry out, to protest, to beg for her release, but the other chain was still fastened tightly between her teeth, gagging her.

The auctioneer, standing in his rostrum to the side of the ring, pressed a switch, and the arm started to revolve round the post, making Amanda break into a run. Soon her breasts were bouncing prettily.

But what the immaculately dressed Arabs and their mainly black whipmasters really wanted to judge was the stamina of a young woman and how she would stand up to physical stress.

The auctioneer pressed another button and the rotating arm increased its speed, making Amanda strain to keep up. Soon she was sweating freely and her breasts were flapping wildly from side to side, as she was made to run faster and faster.

Sheik Turki enjoyed the spectacle whilst he sat comfortably, sipping a cool refreshing drink, his whipmaster, Osman, seated behind him.

The auctioneer began.

"Number 731. A new girl. European. Weight 56 kilos. Well breasted and slim. May I have an opening bid?"

The bidding started briskly. Christian women were quite rare in the auction ring.

Unable to understand Arabic, and forced to concentrate on her footing as she raced round behind the rotating arm, Amanda had little idea of what was going on. But when suddenly the awful arm stopped going round, and her collar chains were unfastened.

One of the black whipmasters came into the room in which women who had been sold were kept chained up by their collar chains. He was a large frightening looking man. She learned his name was Osman.

He looked carefully at the numbers on Amanda's arm and then signed a receipt for her which he handed to an official looking Arab.

The Arab went and collected a pair of manacles, connected by a heavy chain about a foot long. He weighed the manacles in front of Osman and looked at him enquiringly. Osman nodded his agreement: they were of the regulation weight.

Then the Arab motioned to Osman to unfasten Amanda's wrists from behind her back. Amanda sighed with relief as her arms were freed, and rubbed her wrists. Astonished she now saw for the first time the mark of two palm trees that had been prominently tattooed in black onto her very white forearm. She saw that they were followed by Arabic numerals.

Before she could think more about it, Osman gripped her wrists again, holding them in front of her body this time, and the Arab slipped a manacle onto each: she was appalled at the weight of the short chain now linking her wrists.

Now the Arab inserted a wire containing a special seal into the flanges holding the manacles closed and drove a lead pellet down into them with a special tool like a pair of pliers. Not only were the manacles now locked round her wrists but they were officially sealed as well - as a precaution against a keen whipmaster from seeking an advantage over his rivals by replacing them with a lighter pair of manacles.

Amanda longed to cover her intimacies with her now half free hands, but Osman made her hold her arms up with the chain over her neck and behind her head. Because of the weight of the chain, Amanda found that that it was a strain holding this position but, eyeing Osman's whip, did not dare to try and move her hands. It was a position that she would be frequently ordered to assume in future.

Then Osman unfastened the chain gag and handed it back to the official-looking Arab. Delighted Amanda eased her mouth. But her feeling of relief was short lived for the chain was quickly replaced by a muzzle of Osman's own design - a leather cup that went under her chin and over her mouth where it fitted tightly over her upper lips. Over her mouth it had a two little holes, partly to help breathing and also, as she would soon discover, to enable her to to suck up water, or the fruit juices and special soups that would form a large part of her diet.

Osman now produced a hood and put it over the head of the frightened Amanda. It had a little wire mesh at the side to allow for breathing, but she could see nothing. She felt the hood being strapped round her neck and her heavy manacle chains being fastened to the buckle.

After what seemed hours, she felt her collar chain being unfastened. Holding her collar chain in one hand, Osman drove her forward with the whip in his other hand. At first she felt sand under her feet, and then wood. She seemed to being driven up a wooden ramp, like that of a cattle truck. She felt her collar chain being fastened behind her. She was now chained, standing with her back to the side of the truck.

Soon she heard the sounds of other women being driven up the ramp and chained just like her. She tried to call out to them, but thanks to her muzzle all that came out were little grunts, that were answered by other muffled grunts.

She heard the engine start, and then with a jolt the truck set off along a bumpy track.

She had been sold again!

PART V - BROKEN IN

27 - DISCIPLINE - A TERRIFYING START

The truck containing Amanda and some other purchases came to a halt alongside a long white painted building. Although the hooded Amanda could not see it, next to this building was an attractive air conditioned bungalow surrounded by flowers, and next to that a small air conditioned barracks. The contrast between the comfortable looking bungalow and barracks, and the bleak looking windowless farm-like building, with no sign of air conditioning, was marked.

The bungalow was for the whipmaster, Osman, and his wife. The little barracks was for his young negro assistants.

Beyond these buildings was just sand and scrub and beyond that the brilliant blue sea. Only a pile of dirty straw, on a concrete pad and surrounded on three sides by a white painted wall, showed that the farm building was in use. Behind the bungalow was a well laid out vegetable and fruit garden that, like the flower beds, seemed surprisingly fertile for this bleak landscape - until one realised the evident role of the pile of straw and manure!

The ramp at the back of the truck was lowered. Although light now streamed into the truck, the women were still in darkness, under their hoods. There was the menacing crack of a whip and the sound of excited voices, boys' voices. Amanda heard the deep voice of Osman laughing as the boys climbed into the truck. She tried to shrink back as she felt eager young hands on her breasts, on her belly and parting her hairless beauty lips, but she was stopped by the side of the truck pressing against her naked back and buttocks.

Then she heard Osman give an order and the unseen hands fell back except for one rather pudgy pair which went on examining her and then unfastened her collar chain from the ring in the side of the truck. She felt a sharp tap on her buttocks as if from a cane, and found herself being driven down the ramp - apparently by a small boy!

Still hooded and muzzled, Amanda was urged on by the cane through an end door of the windowless building, her heavy wrist chain clinking as she nervously held her hands out in front of her. She now felt cobble stones beneath her naked feet. There was an animal-like smell and she heard the clinking of more of chains and whimpers that seemed to be coming from all around her.

She felt the hands of the boy pushing her up a step and then turning her round. There was a noise behind her as her collar chain was again fastened to something. She was left alone, standing there nervously and unable to see.

Then suddenly there were small hands unfastening the strap of the hood round her neck and it was lifted off. She blinked in the unaccustomed light, and looked around her, and then gasped in horror, only her tight muzzle preventing her from crying out.

She was standing in small white washed open stall, in a large airy and well lit building. There were ventilation slits below the roof through which sunlight also streamed. Overhead, large fans slowly rotated.

The stall was deep enough to allow her to lie down, but only a few feet wide. In the back of the stall was a vertical bar with a sliding ring to which her collar chain had been fastened. To one side of the vertical bar was a small shelf and on it a simple metal comb, a lipstick and some eye make up. Above it a small mirror was fastened to the wall.

Down on the floor of the stall, along one wall, was a feeding trough, and along the other a water trough. Fresh straw had been pushed back to the sides and in one of the back corners was a small pile of it.

Standing next to her was a small black boy of perhaps ten, wearing a simple sarong. In his hand he was proudly holding a small whippy cane with a curved handle with which he pointed to a gutter which ran down the centre of the cobbled stall to an open gutter which ran down the side of the passageway.

Like the stall, the passageway was cobbled - with the open drain running down each side. Several other young black boys, also carrying canes, were striding importantly up and down the passageway.

But it was none of this that had made Amanda gasp in horror. It was the sight of other young women, naked like herself, standing in the stalls facing her across the passageway. Like her, they were muzzled and their wrists were joined by a heavy chain. Like her they had the sign of two palm trees tattooed onto their right forearms, followed by some Arabic numerals. Like her, their mounds and beauty lips had been completely depilated.

In front of each stall was a blackboard on which a number had been painted. Below it was a lot of Arabic written in chalk and various tick marks.

The boy pointed to the Arabic numbers painted on the blackboard outside her stall and then at her own forearm. She saw that they were identical. The boy then again pointed to the numbers and called out something in Arabic. He repeated it twice and pointed to her. He was teaching her her number!

Suddenly she heard the deep voice of Osman, shouting something in Arabic from the far end of the passageway and the women opposite began to comb their hair, put on lipstick, and make up their eyes.

They were all very attractive. Some looked Indian, some Chinese, some Siamese or Filipino - and some clearly were European.

There was another shouted command from Osman, and the frightening crack of his whip. The black boy gave Amanda a sharp tap with his cane and held up one finger. He pointed to the stall opposite, where a very pretty Chinese girl was now straddling the central gutter that ran down the centre of her stall.

There was another another crack of the whip. The black boy held up two fingers and again pointed to the Chinese girl who now bent her knees, put her chained hands up behind her neck, thrust her belly forward and looked straight ahead. Amanda saw that all the other girls had done the same, and that the other black boys were walking up and down the passageway, using their canes to make some of the women part their legs more, some bend their knees more and others hold themselves up straighter.

There was yet another crack of the whip and the black boy now held up three fingers.

Immediately the Chinese girl, still standing rigidly upright with her legs apart, started to pass water into the gutter of her stall, and all the other young women were doing likewise.

Then came another shouted word of command. The women opposite stepped forward right to the edge of their stalls - their collar chains taut behind them. They knelt down on all fours on the cobble stones, their knees and the palms of their hands on either side of the gutter, heads lowered so that muzzles were touching it. Their long hair was flung forward over the edge of their stalls. They made a perfect picture of abject submission.

The large figure of Osman now came slowly down the passageway, looking at the women on the opposite side. Again the black boy gave Amanda a sharp tap with his cane and pointed to what was going on.

Amanda saw that as Osman came up to each stall the boy overseer would call out her number and the girl would jump up and stand at attention, with her right forearm held out in front of her, showing off her tattooed number. Then, still holding out her right arm, she would bend her knees and part her beauty lips with the fingers of her left hand, displaying her womanly charms to the burly great Negro.

After Osman had passed each girl would smartly resume her former humble position on all fours.

The huge figure of Osman slowly passed down in front of her, looking at the girls on the opposite side of the passageway. Amanda eyed him with fear and respect as he passed.

Show Respect! Yes, that must be the purpose of this degrading position!

When Osman reached the end of the passageway, he turned back towards the stalls on Amanda's side. The little black boy left Amanda and stood in the passageway.

Again came a shouted order which Amanda recognised. She hesitated, as if pretending she did not know what she was supposed to do. But she did! And when the boy raised his cane warningly, she too started to comb her hair, put on lipstick and paint her eyes.

Then after some minutes came another familiar shouted order, and the crack of Osman's whip. For the benefit of Amanda, the black boy raised one finger. Oh no, thought Amanda, not that! But when the black boy again raised his cane, she found herself standing astride the shallow gutter of her stall.

The whip cracked again. The boy held up two fingers.

Very nervously Amanda bent her knees slightly and put her chained hands behind her head as she had seen the Chinese girl do. The negro boy was striding up and down the passageway looking at his several charges. When he came back to Amanda, he gave her an angry look and hit her hard across her buttocks with his cane, pointing to her knees. Biting her lips with shame, Amanda bent her knees more.

There was now a long pause. Amanda knew that she must get herself ready to perform the next time the whip cracked.

Suddenly she heard it. At first she was too shy and embarrassed to do anything, but then nature took over and she too performed into the shallow gutter between her widely spread feet.

It took several strokes of the little black boy's cane before Amanda could bring herself to assume the humiliating position on all fours kneeling in her stall, with her forehead touching the gutter, and her long air flung forward over the edge of the stall.

She could hear Osman slowly coming down the passageway. She heard the piping voices of the boys calling out the numbers of the women as Osman passed, and the rattle of chains as each woman in turn jumped up and assumed the humiliating position of Show Respect. She heard the deep resonant voice of Osman as he commented on each woman to her boy overseer.

Finally Osman reached her stall. The black boy put his foot on her neck to make her keep her head down into the gutter. Out of the corner of her eye she could just make out the black feet of Osman as he stood in front of her. She heard him say say something to the boy and boy reply. Both laughed.

Then suddenly she heard the boy call out something. She recognised her number and knew what she had to do, but she simply couldn't bring herself to do it.

Suddenly there was a line of fire across her naked buttocks as the little boy brought his cane down across them. She screamed behind her muzzle. But she immediately jumped up and stood at attention, her head raised and her eyes looking straight ahead above the huge Osman, as he stood below her in the passageway. She held out her right forearm across her body, showing off the tattooed numbers.

But she knew that this was not enough, but she just couldn't do the rest of it, she just couldn't...

The boy brought his cane down again across her buttocks. With a little yelp, Amanda put the fingers of her left hand down onto her beauty lips. Still not satisfied, the black boy again raised his cane. With a sob of shame and despair, Amanda parted her beauty lips and displayed her womanly charms.

28 - DRILLED AND DISCIPLINED

Osman passed on down the passageway and the blushing Amanda relaxed from the humiliating position of Show Respect and renewed the humble position of Submission, kneeling on all fours astride the shallow gutter, with her head lowered, her muzzle in the gutter, and her hair thrown forward over the edge of the stall's raised floor.

Then she heard the black boy who seemed to be her particular overseer step into her stall. His name, she had learnt, was Batu. He reached down and holding her hair with one hand raised her head. She felt him release her muzzle momentarily, but before she could cry out he thrust several large pills into her mouth and then quickly refastened the muzzle. She choked and the boy patted her back and stroked her throat to make her swallow the pills.

She saw that he was carrying a small flesh coloured plastic plug. It was several inches long and curiously shaped with a long softly pointed nose, like a bullet, and a cut-in narrower waist. At the bottom it opened out into a flat flange.

He pushed her head down again and went behind her. She gave a jump as she felt his hands on her buttocks, but remembering his vicious little cane she kept her position. She was horrified as she felt him slowly part the cheeks of her bottom. He put something greasy onto her rear orifice, and rubbed it in with his finger.

Then she gave a gasp as he pushed in the plastic plug. She felt it going deeper and deeper inside her, until it was stopped by the flange pressing against her bottom. She tried to push it out with her muscles, but near the flange it was narrower - shaped to be gripped by her sphincter muscles, making it impossible for her to eject it.

She had been plugged! Plugged and dosed! Plugged, presumably, so that she would not disgrace herself in her stall until Batu had time to instruct her in how to do it to his orders.

But she had little time to reflect more on the uncomfortable plug, for there came a sudden shout of what she would later learn meant 'Exercise!'

The woman all jumped up and stood standing in their stalls, their manacled hands raised with the heavy manacle chain behind their necks. Then the little black boys came down each line of stalls, each now carrying a long whip, like a boy's riding crop.

One by one they unlocked the women's collar chains from the sliding bar at the back of each stall and at a word of command each woman stepped forward into the passageway. It was a brief moment of freedom, but the young overseers made their charges keep their hands clasped behind their necks before fastening the end of their collar chains to the ring on the front of the collar of the woman behind.

When Amanda felt her chain being released, she rushed into the passageway and ran up to the end, seeking to escape from this awful place. But to her horror a steel gate barred the way out. Crying out, beneath her muzzle, with disappointment and frustration, she ineffectually tugged at the closed gate and hammered at it with her manacled hands.

She heard Osman laughing behind her. She turned and saw him standing half up the passageway, grinning, his feet apart and his whip raised. Slowly he beckoned her back. She gave the closed gate a final shake and then turned back towards Osman.

But Osman was pointing to the cobbled floor of the passageway. His meaning was unmistakeable. With a sob she fell onto all fours and started to crawl back to her stall, her collar chain dragging behind her. As she passed Osman, he brought his whip down across her back. She screamed and scuttled back to her stall like a whipped cur.

Moments later, she too, was standing on one side of the passageway, one of a line of a dozen silent women being chained up to form a coffle, with a similar number forming a chained coffle on the other side of the passageway.

She heard a creaking noise as the barred steel gate at the end of the passageway was opened. Then there was a sudden crack of a whip. Amanda saw that the women straightened up as if expecting another order. Another whip crack and the two lines of women broke into a high-stepping trot, raising their knees high in the air and keeping their hands clasped behind their necks.

Amanda felt a sudden jerk forward on her collar as the woman in front of her, a young Indian-looking girl who was kept in the stall next to hers, broke into a prancing run. Then her collar was jerked backwards as the woman behind her, who was also new to all this, was pulled forward. Both women were encouraged by Batu's whip to keep up a steady prancing pace as they ran down the passageway, past the now open gate and out into the warm evening sun.

Amanda saw that the two chained coffles of prancing naked women were now running onto a small concrete parade ground on which various white lines had been painted.

The two women leading the coffles, big strong-looking women, now separated. One, a coffee coloured Indian girl, led her coffle round the outside of the small parade ground in a clockwise direction. The other, a Scandinavian-looking European woman who was the leader of Amanda's coffle, led hers round the opposite way, so that the coffles kept passing each other.

Amanda saw that everyone was running in step and she tried to follow the step of the Indian girl in front of her. But she was also becoming increasingly conscious of the cleverly shaped plug and, moreover, she could feel her belly beginning to respond to the pills.

In the centre of the parade ground stood Osman, cracking his whip menacingly and calling out the pace.

"One, two! Left, right!"

At each corner of the parade ground stood one of the little black boys, also cracking his whip, shouting orders to individual women as they pranced past him, and applying his whip to the bottom of any woman he felt was not straining to raise her knees properly.

The boys were grinning and shouting to each other, obviously thoroughly enjoying the opportunity to use their whips.

Amanda recognised her own number being shouted out by one of the black boys, but did not understand what he was saying. Seconds later his whip fell across her buttocks, making her stumble with the pain.

"731! Knees up! Up! Up! Up!" she realised he must be shouting in Arabic.

Moments later she passed another little black boy, and his whip, this time, caught her across the shoulders. Again came the shouted order.

"731! Up! Up! Up!"

Desperately Amanda tried to raise her knees higher. Every time that she did so, she could feel the plug. She was now passing another black boy. She saw that he was looking at her, his whip raised. But this time he was pointing at her head and elbows.

"Head up! Elbows back!" he seemed to be shouting.

Terrified of the boy's raised whip, Amanda strained to obey. Soon she was out of breath with the effort and she could feel the sweat beginning to run down her body.

There was no respite for the straining women as they pranced round, each coffle keeping perfect time, all raising their knees to the same height whilst keeping their heads up, their elbows and shoulders back, and their eyes fixed on the head of the woman in front.

Suddenly the panting Amanda heard a blast from Osman's whistle. The women halted smartly and caught their breath. What a relief! Then a minute later there was another blast of the whistle, and raising their knees high, in military fashion, the well drilled women turned smartly into line. Only the new girls were slow in reacting to the whistle.

Amanda was terrified of getting the whip again, for not having turned properly.

"Please," she tried to call out from under her muzzle, "please don't beat me. I'll do it properly next time."

But one of the boys had noticed her awkwardness. Shouting with anger, he came over to her and raised his whip. He held up an admonishing finger and brought the whip down - this time across her belly.

Amanda screamed behind her muzzle, but she did not dare to break position. Never again, she swore, would she fail to turn in the smart military way that was evidently expected on this parade ground. Indeed driven by her fear of the whip, Amanda was learning fast!

Just off the parade ground stood a luxurious looking four wheel drive vehicle, its windows tinted to hide its occupant. The engine was running to keep the air conditioning going.

Sitting comfortably within, Sheik Turki watched his women being drilled. In particular he watched Amanda, gloating as he did so.

This was revenge indeed!

Her slim but shapely body was straining with the effort of keeping up the prancing step, and he saw her eye the boys' whips with fear. How frightened and mystified the once arrogant and condescending television interviewer must feel now! Now it was she who was humiliated - a mere naked, prancing, muzzled, plugged and manacled creature.

And she still had no idea of the fate that awaited her...

He turned to his driver and told him to drive back to the club house and his waiting helicopter.

The two coffles faced each other across the small parade ground, with the women in each one spaced, by their collar chains, exactly three feet apart.

Again the whistle blew. This time the women dropped to their knees, their manacled hands touching the ground. Amanda was slow in following them, and was rewarded with a smart crack of a whip across her buttocks. With a gasp of pain, she quickly assumed the same position as the others.

There was a long pause whilst the boys strolled up and down the coffles their whips at the ready, the women quite still and silent behind their muzzles, their eyes looking straight ahead as each one prayed that she had not done anything to attract the attention of these demanding little monsters.

Satisfied at last, Osman blew another blast on his whistle. The women quickly straightened out their legs behind them and took their weight on the palms of their manacled hands and on the tips of their toes, as they strained to keep their bodies quite straight, a few inches above the concrete ground.

Again the black boys walked up and down, giving a stroke of their whip to any woman whose body was not quite straight. This time it was the other Englishwoman who received the whip. She strained to try and obey, but it took several strokes before the black boy was satisfied.

Again Osman blew his whistle: six short blasts, followed by a longer one. Immediately the women bent their elbows and, keeping their bodies quite straight, performed a perfect press-up, lowering their bodies until their nipples just touched the concrete. Then Osman cracked his whip, and in unison the women slowly straightened their arms again, before repeating the exercise slowly, six times.

Poor Amanda got the whip when she allowed her exhausted body to collapse onto the concrete, and again when she failed to keep her body in a straight line. But by the end of the exercise, although she was panting with the exertion, she was doing it quite well.

There was a short pause and then the whistle blew eight times, again followed by a long blast as the signal for the women to perform again - this time eight times.

The exercise was repeated several times, and each time the number of short blasts varied. Amanda, like the other women, found herself counting the number of short blasts so as not to make a mistake and get the whip across her backside.

29 - MORE HUMILIATION FOR AMANDA

Half an hour later the women, sweating and exhausted from their exercises, stood chained up in the coffles outside the building. Two showers were running and Osman sat between them on a small stool. At a word of command the lead woman of the coffle containing Amanda stepped under the first shower.

Moments later Amanda found herself being dragged by her collar chain under the shower. Her manacled hands were still clasped behind her neck. But it was gloriously refreshing.

Seconds later she was dragged on to stand in front of Osman, who had a bar of soap in his hand. Still sitting on his stool, he ran his hands over her dripping wet shoulders, breasts, belly and thighs, feeling her muscles as he did so. Then, kicking her ankles apart, he ran his hands on down between her legs, feeling her in a knowing way as he did so.

Amanda longed to brush his probing hands away. But one warning glance from his stern eyes was sufficient to make sure she kept her hands gripped tightly together behind her neck.

Seconds later she was pulled under the second shower - to wash away the soap. Then the whole coffle was marched up the passageway and one by one the women were released and their collar chains secured again to the sliding bar at the back of their stalls.

The dose had now taken effect and, with the plug preventing her from relieving herself, Amanda felt very uncomfortable. She saw Batu come along the passageway with a wheelbarrow and a pitch fork. He stopped at her stall and with his whip pointed to the stall opposite her in which the pretty Chinese girl was chained.

Batu gave an order and then repeated it so that Amanda would recognise it. The Chinese girl had turned so that she was standing facing the corner of her stall where, as in Amanda's stall, there was a small pile of fresh straw. Her pretty little back was to the passageway.

The boy cracked his whip and turning to Amanda held up one finger. She was going to have to learn another sequence of orders.

She saw that the Chinese girl had bent down and placed a small pile of the straw behind her legs. The boy blew a second blast and held up two fingers to Amanda. The Chinese girl, still facing into the corner of her stall, now dropped onto all fours astride the small pile of straw.

"Oh no!" gasped Amanda behind her muzzle as, shocked, she realised what the Chinese girl was being made to demonstrate. Then Batu cracked his whip a second time and held up three fingers, and horrified Amanda saw the Chinese girl straining to perform.

Then, making sure that Amanda was paying attention, he made the Chinese girl repeat the whole drill again.

The boy turned back to Amanda and, raising his whip menacingly, twice put her through a practice run of the same drill. Then he reached down and removed the plug. This time, a greatly relieved but highly embarrassed, Amanda had to perform for real.

The boy cleaned Amanda with some fresh straw and then wrote something in Arabic on the board hanging in front of her stall. Then he picked up the pitchfork and deftly tossed the now dirty straw into the wheelbarrow, which he pushed down the passageway and out to the pile of dirty straw hidden behind its surrounding white walls. Meanwhile, a shocked Amanda still knelt on all fours facing the far corner of her stall.

A delicious smell of cooking began to spread over the lines of stalls, coming from the big feed boiler at the end of the passageway, and soon the black boys started to trundle a trolley up the passageway. It contained a large bowl of steaming hot, porridge-looking food: boiled oats and barley, with lumps of meat, nuts, rice, raisins and bran. As they passed each stall, one boy would unfasten the woman's muzzle and read out the feeding instructions written on the board. Another would then dollop one or more scoopfuls of the mixture into the woman's feeding trough. When they came to Amanda, they just gave her half a scoopful - she was to be slimmed down.

Amanda was thrilled to feel the muzzle being slipped off. She wanted to ask so many questions. But the boys put their fingers to their lips and raised their whips warningly.

She looked down into the trough. The food did not look exactly appetising. She put a finger down towards it to get a taste, but immediately the boys angrily pushed her back, and pointed to the stalls opposite. She saw that as each woman's trough received some of the feed, the woman would immediately stand at attention, facing the trough with their manacled hands clasped behind their necks. My God, she thought, there was even a routine for feeding!

Not until all the troughs had been filled was there a crack of the whip and the women fell to their knees in front of their troughs, their hands still clasped behind their necks, their heads up, their eyes fixed on the wall of the stall above the trough.

There was a long pause whilst the boys checked that each woman was kneeling in just the correct position. Then with the second blast of the whistle each woman lowered her head over the trough, her hands still clasped behind her neck and her mouth immediately over the food, but still not yet touching it.

Again there was a pause, whilst the officious little boys strolled up and down the passageway, angrily seizing the hair of some women to raise or lower their heads slightly. They were deliberately stopping the women thinking for themselves, and instead making them only obey their whips.

The whip cracked again and each woman lowered her head into the trough and quickly started to guzzle up the food. Amanda hesitated, and immediately felt her head being thrust down into the food and held there.

"Eat!" shouted Batu. It was one of the few Arabic words she had learned in Prince Rashid's harem. "Eat!"

She heard his whip being cracked behind her bent-over bottom and began to feed.

It was hardly a minute later when she heard another crack of the whip. Her head was lifted up and pulled back from the trough. She saw that the women were all kneeling up again, their hands still clasped behind their necks. Several were looking scared. The reason for this became clear as the black boys inspected each trough, and gave any woman who had not finished her allocated food two strokes of the whip across their naked backs before thrusting their heads back into the trough.

Amanda was trembling all over when her black boy keeper contemptuously looked into her own trough and saw the pile of uneaten porridge. She screamed with pain as she received the ritual two strokes. But when her head was thrust back into the trough, she started to eat in a frenzy, making sure that there was not the slightest sign of anything left in the now gleaming metal trough.

Then the muzzles were replaced and water was poured into the drinking trough. After her exertions on the parade ground, Amanda was desperately thirsty. But the little black boys enforced the same drill for drinking as they had for eating. It was unbelievably frustrating having to keep her mouth poised over the enticing cool water, waiting for the whistle.

It was now getting dark - and chilly. Batu and the other black boys came down the passageway. This time they fastened a ring in the centre of each woman's manacles to the ring at the front of her collar, preventing them from touching their bodies below their breasts. Then they threw a heavy jute cloak, like a stable rug, over each woman's shoulders and fastened it with a strap around the throat. It came down to the navel, leaving each woman's buttocks, belly and depilated intimacies exposed, and was open down the front. On the right breast was emblazoned the crest of a green circle and two bright red zig-zag lines.

Amanda found herself holding the edges closed over her breasts. She longed to be able to try and pull it down, but with her hands now fastened to her collar she could not reach down far enough. She must be an erotic sight, but she was thrilled not to be stark naked for once.

There were no windows in the building and the women could not see out. The only light came from the wide gap between the top of the side walls and the eaves of the sloping roof. Soon, with the suddenness of the short tropical twilight, the building was almost in darkness.

Osman pulled a big lever at the end of each line of stalls and Amanda suddenly felt herself being pulled down to the floor by her collar chain. The sliding bar to which it was attached at the back of her stall had been moved right down to the floor. She found herself lying on her back on the paving stones.

Across the passageway she could make out the other women on the floors of their stalls reaching out with their manacled hands for handfuls of straw and trying to tuck the straw under their backs to make a little bed to lie on. Amanda copied them, but remembering the humiliating use to which the straw had been put earlier, did not dare to use more than just a little of it, so as to have enough left next morning.

With her head kept chained to the back of the stall, and her wrists chained to her collar, Amanda now lay on her back, her legs towards the passageway.

She was horrified when Batu came to her stall, several straps in his hand. Silently, he parted her ankles and strapped each one to a ring bolt in the front corner of the stall. Angrily he smacked her face and pulled out the straw that Amanda had put under her buttocks and tossed it back into the corner, leaving the straw only under her back and shoulders.

Amanda had learned another lesson! She must not risk dirtying her straw except when ordered.

Then he checked the straps and then left her.

Amanda could now feel the bare sides of the gutter beneath her buttocks. The gutter itself, she realised, ran up between her outstretched legs and was immediately beneath her beauty lips. She blushed as she realised why Batu had chained her down like this, especially as she had drunk so much water earlier on.

30 - AMANDA IS PUT TO WORK

At dawn next morning, a sleepy Amanda was vaguely aware of her ankle straps being unfastened by Batu.

Then she was rudely awakened, as she lay asleep again on the meagre straw of her stall, by her collar chain jerking her upwards as Osman pulled the lever at the end of the passageway. With her manacled wrists still fastened to her collar, she stumbled awkwardly to her feet.

She recognised a shouted order. Oh no! She remembered having relieved herself once during the night. The liquid had splashed down into the little gutter between her legs. She remembered the noise of it running down to the edge of her stall, and then falling into the drain at the side of the passageway. It had seemed so awful. But, she realised, although the women were apparently allowed to perform in private at night, tied down over the little gutter, by day they must only do it to order, together - and this was even more humiliating.

But she was now ready to do so, she knew, as she stood straddling the little gutter.

"Two!" came the shouted order.

There was a cracking of whips from the boys in the passageway. She saw the women in the stalls opposite positioning themselves. Like Amanda they were still wearing their short little jute cloaks with the straps fastened round their throats, under which their wrist manacles were still fastened to their collars which, in turn, were still chained to the vertical bar at the back of their stalls.

Blushing, Amanda, like the other women, clasped her hands behind her neck, bent her knees, thrust out her belly and looked straight ahead. This was something she would never get used to, something which she could never learn to do voluntarily. Presumably the other women felt the same - hence the cracking of whips.

Again there was a long pause as Batu and the other boys proudly strutted up and down making sure that each woman was in exactly the right position.

"Three!"

Amanda could hardly bring herself to do it. But there was more cracking of whips. She relaxed and let the water fall into the gutter.

Soon there came the familiar noise of the feeding trolley being wheeled down the passageway. Once again Batu slipped off Amanda's muzzle. Once again, like the other women, she turned and stood silently at attention, facing her feeding trough, and waiting for the whip crack that was the signal for them to fall to their knees in front of their troughs.

When the whip cracked, she hesitated. Why should she be ordered about like a performing animal? She'd show these awful young black boys! But when Batu's whip cracked just behind her buttocks, she found herself hastily kneeling down, her hands dutifully clasped behind her neck and her eyes fixed on the wall above the trough. She shivered with fear as a boy drew his whip across her soft little bottom.

When the whip cracked again, she remembered that she had to lower her head over the trough without touching the food.

Then came the crack of the whip that was the order to feed. She started to swallow it all up in a desperate rush.

Then the boys came into each stall, replaced the muzzles and unfastened each woman's manacles from her collar. Amanda stretched out her arms with relief. She brushed some of the remains of her feed off her jute cloak. She saw that the women in the stalls opposite her were now combing their hair and making up their faces and eyes, and she followed suit.

Osman shouted another order. The other women had turned and were now standing facing the far corner of their stalls. Again the whip cracked, and Amanda, like the other women, bent down and put a tight little pile of fresh straw between her legs.

At the second crack she knelt down on all fours astride the straw, her head up, her eyes fixed on the wall, her buttocks left bare by the short cloak and thrust back towards the passageway. Desperately she tried to get ready ... Yes, she realised with relief, it would be alright!

The whip cracked yet again. There was more cracking of the boys' small whips and a trembling Amanda performed.

Still kneeling on all fours, she heard Batu enter her stall. Not daring to look round, she felt him clean her with fresh straw and then heard him lift up the soiled straw and put it aside, put a tick on her board, and then go onto the next stall.

Still Amanda did not dare move. Not until the offerings of each woman had been removed did the whistle blow again as the signal to stand up and face the passageway for the morning inspection.

Amanda, like the women facing her across the passageway, was now standing at the front of her stall, looking straight ahead, her collar chain drawn taut.

"Position of Submission!"

This time Amanda knelt down on all fours like the other women, her knees and the palms of her hands on either side of the little gutter, her head lowered so that her muzzle was touching it and her hair flung forward over the edge of her stall.

Unable to see anything except the gutter, she was trembling again as she heard Osman make his way slowly down towards her stall. She heard the noise of the wheelbarrow being trundled down the passageway after him.

"731! Show Respect!"

It was the shrill young voice of her black overseer, Batu.

Amanda jumped up and held her right arm across her body, displaying her tattooed number. Then, blushing again, she shyly parted her beauty lips with her left hand.

Osman was standing in front of her. Because the stalls were raised above the passageway, his head was level with her navel. She looked straight ahead above his head, whilst he discussed her in Arabic with Batu.

Batu was holding out the neat little pile of straw onto which she had just performed. Oh how awful! Was there no end to the humiliating control these people had over her body?

Finally Osman moved off to the next stall, and Amanda dropped back onto all fours to the Position of Submission.

The young black overseers now unfastened the collar chain of the dark skinned coffle leader of the stalls opposite and took off her short jute cloak, before leading her up the passageway.

Amanda saw that Osman had a list in his hand. He called out a number and the black boys quickly released another woman opposite and removed her cloak. Then, holding her by her collar chain, they brought her to stand behind the coffle leader. They fastened the coffle leader's collar chain to the ring on the front of the second woman's collar.

Meanwhile the number of a third woman had been called out and now she too was released, her cloak removed and her collar fastened to the chain of the second woman.

They certainly took great care to limit the number of women who were not properly chained at any one time. It reminded Amanda of stories about the way white galley slaves had been treated two hundred years ago in the Barbary States.

It did not take long before twelve women had been selected and chained together.

They were left standing in a line on the far side of the passageway and Amanda was surprised to see that several women had been left still chained in their stalls.

Then the Scandinavian-looking coffle leader from Amanda's side was released and brought along the passageway. Although her little overseer was holding her collar chain, she held up her head with pride, tossing her head arrogantly as she passed the other women. It seemed that being a coffle leader was a source of pride.

Amanda noticed that both coffle leaders had been allowed to grow a little carefully trimmed moustache on her mound in the shape of a lance-corporal's stripe. But her beauty lips and the rest of her mound were as hairless as those of the other women.

As she passed Amanda's stall, she turned and looked Amanda up and down, making Amanda give a little shiver of repulsion and fear. She saw the boy leading the woman laugh at the woman's evident interest in Amanda.

A dozen women were now selected from her side of the passageway and chained up one by one behind their coffle leader. The other new European woman was selected, but Amanda herself was not. Standing there chained in her stall, she did not know whether to be relieved or disappointed.

There was a sudden crack of a whip and the women in the two coffles started to prance on the spot, raising their knees high in the air, whilst the black boys walked up and down between the two lines, cracking their whips to make the women raise their knees even higher.

Then after several minutes there came the creaking noise of the iron barred gates at the end of the passageway being opened. Osman shouted an order and the two lines of women pranced down the passageway and out of the building in perfect step.

Moments later Amanda recognised the noise of the ramp of the cattle truck being raised and closed with a bang, and then the truck drove off.

Time passed slowly for Amanda and the half dozen women who had been left behind. They just had to stand in their stalls with nothing to do.

Amanda could feel the heavy weight of both her collar chain and the chain linking her wrist manacles. She longed to lie down to ease the strain of their weight - but this was forbidden. She found herself walking to and fro in her stall, like a caged animal, trying to change the weight of the chains from one set of muscles to another. Was this why the collar chains were so heavy? To help get the women muscled up?

Her thoughts were interrupted by Batu coming down the passageway, shouting in his boyish voice and cracking his whip. He seemed to be in charge in the absence of Osman. His whip might only be a small one, but how it could hurt!

"Position of Submission!"

Amanda saw that the few women who had been left behind were again abjectly kneeling on all fours in the front of their stalls, their muzzles touching the gutter, so that their collar chains were taut and their hair was flung forward over the edge of the stall. She did the same.

Not daring to look up, she heard Batu enter her stall. She gave a little tremble of fear as he went behind her to unfasten her collar chain. Then she heard him step down into the passageway.

Suddenly she felt a sharp tug on her collar. She started to stand up so that she could follow Batu out onto the corridor, but he shouted at her angrily and brought his whip down across her back so that she screamed under her muzzle.

Then, still tugging her collar chain, Batu pressed his foot hard down on her neck. Keeping her head down, she was led crawling along the passageway to where she saw that four other women were kneeling alongside each other in pairs, their heads down, one pair behind the other.

The collar chains of each woman had been fastened to the ring in the front of the collar of the woman kneeling alongside her. In this way each woman was secured to her partner's neck by two chains. The women in each pair were kneeling a little apart so that the two chains were almost taut.

Batu half led and half drove Amanda right up to them, until her lowered head was between the outstretched ankles of a white skinned girl. Another black boy took her collar chain from Batu and waited whilst he went back down the passage and brought up another crawling girl, who was made to kneel alongside Amanda. Then the other boy bent down and fastened Amanda's collar chain to this other girl's collar, and then fastened her collar chain to Amanda's collar.

There was a long silence as the muzzled women knelt there humbly, their foreheads touching the cobbled floor.

As she knelt behind the buttocks of the woman in front of her, Amanda wondered whether this degrading way of forming a coffle of crawling women was just a cruel whim. Were they just enjoying humiliating some of their charges whilst Osman was away with most of them? Or was it a deliberate piece of extra security, to make sure that they could not escape in the absence of Osman?

Then, out of the corner of her eye, Amanda saw Batu and the other black boy bringing up what looked like several thick planks. The planks seemed to be hinged at one end and to have holes cut out in the middle. The black boys did something with the planks to the two pairs of women in front of her, but she did not dare to raise her head to see properly.

Then she felt something wooden being fitted round her neck above her collar. She saw it was one of the planks, now held open at the hinge. The other hole in the plank was being fitted round the neck of the girl kneeling next to her. Then the two halves were swung together and bolted closed. She and the other girl were now yoked together by the neck, their heads some three feet apart, their collar chains still taut.

Fastened to the front of the yoke was a length of stout chain hanging from a ring in the centre of it. Batu bent down and fastened this to the ring in the yoke of the two women in front. The half dozen women were all now safely coffled together in pairs. Then, and not until then, was the barred gateway at the end of the passage opened.

Batu shouted an order and cracked his whip over the women's naked backs. Amanda felt her neck being jerked upwards as the other girl, a French or Italian looking young woman, jumped up. Like the other women, now yoked in pairs like herself, she was standing rigidly at attention, her head held up above the plank, and, half hidden below it, her arms straight down her sides, her hands on her thighs, her fingers stretched down and her manacle chains taut across her legs. Batu flicked his whip across Amanda's naked buttocks and hastily she assumed the same position of attention.

Batu shouted another order and cracked his whip. Then her wooden yoke was jerked forward as the first two pairs broke into the usual high prancing run. Amanda heard another shout from Batu and felt a painful little flick of his whip as he called out what was evidently the step. Hastily Amanda tried to fall into step with the other women, though it was awkward because the plank round her neck prevented her from seeing her own legs. But with the whip cracking terrifyingly behind her buttocks she just had to concentrate.

At least Amanda was spared having to prance along with her manacled hands clasped behind her neck, for the plank prevented the women from reaching up above their shoulders. Instead she was able to run with her hands naturally raised.

The line of prancing pairs, encouraged by the cracking of the boys' whips, ran down the passage, passed the barred gates, and into the bright sun light. However, instead of going onto the parade ground they were driven round to what seemed to be a well. On top of the well was an old fashioned water pump for pumping the water up into a tank on top of the building in which the women were housed. The pump was worked by a long bar that projected out on either side of the well.

At a shouted word of command from Batu, the line of prancing women halted smartly - in military fashion which Amanda, scared of Batu's whip, tried to copy. The heavy chain attached to the centre of the first pair's yoke was unfastened, and instead fastened to a ring some way along the bar. Then each of the women's manacles were fastened to other rings on either side of the first one.

Then two remaining pairs of women were made to prance round to the other side of the well. Batu's whip was raised, but this time Amanda not only managed to keep in step, but also to halt in perfect time with the others, raising her right foot high in the air and bringing it down smartly alongside her left one. Batu smiled to himself and lowered his whip. This woman was learning fast!

The chain linking them to the second pair of women was now unfastened, and the other women, still yoked together, were led off to be attached to the other end of the bar. There was now one pair on either side of the pump, each pair attached to a different end of the pumping bar.

Batu cracked his whip. Immediately one pair of yoked women strained to pull their end of the bar back towards them, whilst the other pair pushed their end hard away, taking a step forward as they did so. A moment later, encouraged by another terrifying crack of Batu's whip, their roles were reversed and the first pair were pushing their end of the bar away, and the second pair were pulling back, in a push-pull pumping action. There was a little tinkling noise as a cupful of water fell into the tank.

Amanda watched spellbound as, driven on the by the boys' whips, the women strained and strained as the water was slowly pumped up.

Her thoughts were interrupted by another black boy who picked up the chain hanging from her yoke and gave a sharp order. Obediently Amanda and her yoked colleague broke into a prancing run, as they were now led off towards a large upright stone wheel standing in a narrow circular cement channel full of oats and barley. It was held upright by a simple wooden axle which, in turn, was fastened to a pole in the middle of the circular channel. The axle protruded some way beyond the wheel and here it too was fitted with iron rings like those she had seen on the bar attached to the water pump.

The heavy chain attached to her yoke was attached to the axle. Then like the other women, their wrist manacles were fastened to other rings on either side of the one to which their yoke chain was attached.

There was a crack of a whip and the two yoked women lent forward to start pushing the axle, and so push the heavy wheel round and round the narrow channel containing the oats and barley. The whip cracked frighteningly behind them, but there was no question of running. It was all they could do to inch the heavy wheel forward over the corn in the channel. Amanda was soon sweating as driven on and on by the boy's whip, she and her muzzled companion silently strained to push the wheel round. Periodically the boy would pour fresh corn into the channel, to be crushed into porridge by the heavy wheel.

And all the time Amanda wondered why? There was electric power available. Why do it this way? Why, why why?

31 - AMANDA IS MADE TO PERFORM A NEW TRICK

Several hours later came the noise of the cattle truck returned. There was the noise of the ramp being dropped, shouting and the crack of whips. Then the showers at the end of the passageway being switched on and moments later the women of one of the coffles, naked and dripping wet from the shower, still chained one behind the other by the neck, half ran and half stumbled down the passageway.

At a word of command they halted and one by one were detached from the coffle, and chained up again in their stalls. They were allowed to drink from their water troughs and lie down on the cobbled floor.

As the new European woman passed her, Amanda was horrified not only by her state of exhaustion but also by the fresh marks of a whip across her back. Several of the others had been whipped too!

After the women of the second coffle had been put into their stalls, Osman came down the passageway, smiling and rubbing his hands as he looked at the women on Amanda's side of the passageway but looking angrily at the women on the other side. She saw the women on her side, those who had been taken out in the coffle, were now smirking with pleasure, whereas those on the other side, and those on both sides who had been left behind, were all looking angry and jealous.

The reason for this soon became evident, for Osman started to throw bits of chocolate into the stalls of the former, whilst ignoring the latter.

This chocolate was evidently a rare reward and the delighted women hastily picked up the pieces in their manacled hands and bowed their heads gratefully to Osman. Then the boy keepers came and momentarily loosened their muzzles. Quickly they popped the bits of chocolate into their mouths and then started to chew them slowly, behind their now refastened muzzles, as if wishing to draw out the unusual sensation of being allowed something sweet.

They now looked full of pride and much less exhausted. How easy it was for Osman to get the best out his women! He merely had to chuck them a few bits of chocolate!

Osman now clapped his hands. The women opposite came shyly to the front of their stalls. Oh no, thought Amanda, not another inspection! But she saw that this time the Indian-looking coffle leader opposite had been unfastened from her stall and was being led up the passageway by her little overseer.

Osman gestured to the women in the stalls opposite as if inviting her to choose. The coffle leader looked delighted. Above her muzzle, her eyes sparkled with anticipation. She hesitated for a moment and then pointed to the slender and very pretty Chinese girl in the stall opposite Amanda.

Amanda saw the Chinese girl give a little jump of fright and back away in her stall. But Batu jumped into her stall, unfastened her collar chain and with his whip drove the wretched girl forward to the edge of her stall and then made her turn so that she was sideways to the passageway. Standing behind her and gripping her collar chain in one hand, his whip raised in the other, he made her kneel and clasp her manacled hands behind her neck.

Amanda was astonished to see that he then reached forward and unfastened her muzzle. He jerked her collar chain and gave an order. She straightened up and raised her head, but Batu was not satisfied. He repeated the order. The Chinese girl shook her head and looked up at Batu imploringly

Again the same short order was repeated, this time accompanied by a stoke of the whip across the slender back. She gave a little cry, and then to Amanda's astonishment she thrust out her tongue.

The other young black overseer, holding the Indian coffle leader's chain, looked enquiringly at Osman, who nodded. Her small overseer then motioned her with his whip to step up into the Chinese girl's stall, so that she too was sideways on to the passageway. She was now standing facing the kneeling diminutive Chinese girl, her strong thighs level with the girl's face. Her hands, like those of the Chinese girl, were clasped behind her neck.

The Indian woman started to look gloatingly down at the Chinese girl, but instantly the other black boy used his whip to raise her chin so that she was looking straight ahead over the head of the Chinese girl. Then he made her bend her knees and part her legs. Reaching down with one had, and still holding the whip raised behind the coffle leader with the other, the black boy parted the Indian woman's prominent and hairless beauty lips.

The Chinese girl's thrust-out tongue was now only an inch away from the coffle leaders proffered beauty lips, which were now glistening with desire. But her young overseer, now gave her a sharp tap on her belly, making her frustratingly pull in her stomach, away from the Chinese girl's tongue. She was trembling with desire and arousal as she was made to stand still, looking straight ahead, her head raised, and her belly sucked in, knowing that a deliciously soft little tongue was almost touching her aroused beauty bud. What an illustration of Osman's discipline, Amanda thought - and of the power of the whip.

There was a long pause, whilst Osman and his grinning young assistants silently watched the two young women. Above her muzzle, Amanda's eyes were wide with amazement as she took in the astonishing and erotic scene.

Then on a sign from Osman, the other boy, still holding the Indian woman's beauty lips apart with one hand, tapped her buttocks with his whip. She moved her hips an inch towards the kneeling Chinese girl, who was looking at the approaching beauty lips as if hypnotised. She started to move her head back, but a sharp tap of the whip from Batu, still holding her collar chain, stopped her. Her tongue was now just touching the Indian woman's beauty bud.

Again there was a pause as the coffle leader desperately tried to control her instinctive desire to thrust forward against the soft little tongue and the Chinese girl tried not to pull back.

Then Osman clapped his hands.

The boys pulled both women back by their collar chains, whilst Osman shouted angrily at the now wretchedly frustrated Indian woman, smacked her face twice and pointed back at her stall. Clearly, Amanda realised as the now sobbing woman was led away, by being led to believe that she would be allowed satisfaction and then being deprived of it at the last moment, she was being cruelly and ruthlessly punished for some lack of effort by her, or by her coffle.

Moments later, indeed, the Scandinavian-looking coffle leader, a smug smile on her face, was led down the passageway. Amanda saw that below the neat chevron of hair on her mound, her moist beauty lips were glistening as she passed the other women on Amanda's side - all standing nervously at the front of their stalls as if offering themselves.

The woman did not hesitate. Unable to speak because of her muzzle, she pointed at Amanda.

Horrified at the implication of the woman's gesture, Amanda shrank back against the back wall of her stall - just as the Chinese girl had done. Grinning, just as he had when handling the Chinese girl, Batu jumped into Amanda's stall, unfastened her collar chain and drove her forward with his whip.

Batu removed her muzzle and shouted an order in his boyish voice. Amanda may not have understood the words, but their meaning, accompanied as they were by a sharp tap on her buttocks from young Batu's whip, was quite clear.

She reached out with her tongue. The tip was just touching the Scandinavian woman's own parted beauty lips. She could taste the woman's juices. Appalled, she started to turn away but a tap of the whip stopped her.

Now Amanda's natural masochism began to take over. Appalled at her own sensuality, she felt her own beauty lips begin to moisten in sympathy with those of the Scandinavian woman. Horrified, she began to want to lick. What a natural slut she was!

Then, even more aghast, she felt Batu reach down between her legs as if testing her state of arousal. Was there nothing these awful little black boys did not know about white women?

Meanwhile Ursula, the Scandinavian coffle leader, was being driven almost mad by being kept at the height of excitement with the tip of Amanda's hot little tongue tantalisingly bringing her to a high pitch of arousal. She could hardly restrain herself from bringing her manacled hands down from behind her own head and seizing Amanda by the hair and then pulling her head violently towards her beauty lips. But with her overseer standing behind her and tapping her buttocks warningly with his whip she did not dare to do so.

Only her muzzle stopped her from screaming out aloud in her prolonged frustration and growing arousal.

The two women were kept like that for what seemed hours, too terrified to move, as their arousal was cunningly brought on. Amanda could hear the increasingly heavy breathing of the Scandinavian woman from behind her muzzle. It was all too awful! Too humiliating!

"Wriggle tongue!" at last came the order as the watching Osman judged that Ursula was now ready. It was an order that Amanda recognised. The Princess had used it in Prince Rashid's harem. She started to arouse the proffered beauty lips.

The effect on the highly aroused Ursula was almost immediate. Her overseer had to hold her back by her collar chain as she almost doubled up and thrust against the penetrating tongue. Moments later a muffled scream came from behind the muzzle and her whole body shook with climatic ecstasy, leaving poor Amanda frustrated but overwhelmed with her masochistic feelings.

Osman clapped his hands. The performance was over.

PART VI - GALLEY SLAVE!

32 - AMANDA LEARNS THE TRUTH ABOUT HER FATE

"731!"

Amanda recognised her number, suddenly called out by Osman. She hated being called by a number. She was Miss Amanda Aston! At least in Prince Rashid's harem she had been called Sky Blue. That was humiliating enough, but being just a number was even worse.

"731!"

This time she jumped to attention!

Amanda's heart was in her mouth as Batu came into her stall and unfastened her collar chain from the sliding bar on the wall at the back of the stall and took off her short cloak. Then he led her down to where Osman was standing by a weighing machine. Astonished, she was made to step on it and Osman seemed to be carefully comparing the weight showed on the machine with that in his notebook.

Still not satisfied, he noted the result and said something to Batu who produced a tape measure and began to measure Amanda's breasts and hips and then her waist, calling out the figures in Arabic to Osman, who seemed to be doing some sort of calculation in his notebook.

Now Amanda was led back to the end of the coffle and chained up, sixth in line behind the Scandinavian coffle leader. Her long hair, and that of the other women, was now pulled back and fastened with an elastic band into a pony tail hanging down her back.

The selection of the two coffles continued and when a dozen naked women had been chained in each coffle, there was the sudden crack of a whip, the signal for them to start warming up their muscles by prancing on the spot, their hands as usual clasped behind their necks.

Amanda screamed behind her muzzle as Batu brought his little whip down across her buttocks, but she also now strained to raise her knees high enough. Batu stood alongside her using his whip to drive her on and on.

Soon she was beginning to sweat freely, and it was a relief to hear the iron gates at the end of the passageway swing open. Seconds later Amanda's collar was painfully jerked forward and her coffle pranced onto the parade ground, accompanied by the inevitable cracking of whips.

Amanda, like the other women, was concentrating not only on raising her knees up high, but also on keeping in perfect step with the women ahead of her, and on keeping perfectly spaced so as to avoid jerks on her collar.

She was expecting the two coffles to start running round the parade ground in opposite directions, but this time a large cattle truck with its ramp down was parked in the middle of the parade ground.

The two coffles were led up to the ramp. There was a shouted order and the crack of a whip, the signal for both coffles to start prancing on the spot at the foot of the ramp. There was another crack of the whip, and Amanda saw that the other coffle ran up into the cattle truck, like well trained circus animals. When they were all in, standing pressed tightly one behind the other, there was another crack of the whip and the women all raised their manacled wrists high above their heads and one of the boys passed a long light metal bar under their manacles and fastened it to the front of the truck and to a metal support hanging from the roof near the ramp.

Then it was the turn of Amanda's coffle. She could feel the breasts of the woman behind her pressing into her back as she was pressed into the woman in front of her. Then, when the whip cracked, she too had to raise her arms. She found herself standing almost on tiptoe as the bar was passed under her manacles.

The two coffles were facing forward in the truck as the ramp behind them was raised, plunging the truck into half-darkness. A little light and air came from slits in the side, but they were too high up to see out of. Amanda heard Osman and one of the boys climbing up into the cab, then they moved off.

After a bumpy drive of some ten minutes, the truck stopped and Osman and the boy climbed down. There was the sound of voices - many voices, laughing and talking in Arabic. She heard other trucks arriving and ramps being lowered, more shouts and the cracking of whips.

The women were kept shut up in their truck for perhaps ten minutes - ten desperately anxious minutes for Amanda. She longed to ask what was going on, but her muzzle kept her silent.

Suddenly the ramp of her truck was lowered with a crash. Sunlight flooded in. There was a clinking of chains as the two coffles of women shuffled nervously. Then the support hanging from the ceiling that held the bar over the first coffle was taken down. Gratefully they dropped their hands to behind their necks. There was shouted order and the crack of a whip and the women all started to move carefully backwards down the ramp.

Then it was the turn of Amanda's coffle.

As she stepped into the bright sunlight, she blinked in sheer terror.

Facing the coffles were several tough-looking armed Arab guards in camouflage uniforms carrying sub-machine guns which were aimed at them!

Her truck and a dozen others were parked on what seemed to be a quay, to which several dhow-like craft were moored stern on. Each truck was brilliantly painted with a different crest and so were the sterns of the vessels. Beyond the craft she could see the brilliant blue sea. glistening in the sun.

Several small vessels were under way, but before she could take them in properly her attention was caught by the sight of another two coffles of naked women. They were not muzzled, but their heads had been shaved! Dear God! Was it so that their hair would not interfere with whatever it was that women were used for in this terrible place? Was that why her own hair had been fastened back into a ponytail? To keep it out of her eyes? But at least it had not all been shaved off!

She saw that these others were chained by the neck like her own coffle, but were marching along the quay in a very strange way, keeping their legs straight and raising them high in the air, whilst a large Negro walked alongside them cracking a whip. They were goose-stepping!

She saw that several guards were keeping their sub-machine guns pointed at the other two coffles, as if ready to open fire at the slightest sign of revolt or mutiny. A slave revolt! Yes, she could see that with several coffles on the quay at any one time, this was the moment when the desperate women might make a mass break for freedom - even if they were still chained by the neck and wrists.

The two coffles of bald-headed women had now reached what seemed to be a special strip of sand marked out in white. At a word of command, they halted smartly and then, raising their manacled hands straight out in front of them, until they were level with their shoulders, squatted down on their parted ankles.

Dominating the scene was a raised terrace, shaded from the sun, on which a small crowd of men dressed in pristine white Arab robes were looking down, their faces half masked by sun glasses. Blushing at her nakedness, she saw that the men were looking at her companions and that one man was even pointing, it seemed, at her.

Her mysterious owner?

The other two coffles now rose up on the marked off stretch of sand and, goose-stepping again, marched off under the orders of their whipmaster. Immediately, Osman cracked his whip and gave an order. The two coffle leaders led the two coffles prancing past the watching Arabs up on their balcony to the same stretch of sand. It was slightly damp under foot. Osman gave an order and the two coffles began prancing on the spot on the sand. Another order and they halted and, keeping their hands clasped behind their necks, parted their legs.

Suddenly Amanda realised what she and other women were supposed to be preparing their bodies to do - and what the other two coffles had been doing when so curiously had squatted down. This must be a last chance to relieve themselves. But why? And to have to do it in perfect time, altogether and in front of the watching Arab men! How awful! But when Osman's whip cracked as the order to perform, perform she did!

Osman's two coffles now pranced off towards the edge of the quay, towards a vessel prominently marked on the stern with a large green circle and in it two bright red vertical zig-zag lines.

The coffles halted. Amanda saw that she was looking down into a strange but beautifully made, and highly varnished, lightly built vessel. It was long and thin with a raised deck aft which was covered with an awning and on which was a steering wheel, like the helm of a yacht. Forward of the raised poop deck, and down almost level with the water, were several rows of benches, with a raised catwalk running along amidships from the foot of the poop up to the pointed bows, where to her surprise she saw a native drum.

Amanda's coffle was made to climb up from the quay onto the raised poop, and then step down a companionway to the catwalk. Their leader marched up to the bows and then turned, and seeing that the end of the coffle had stepped down the companionway, marched back towards the poop again, passing Amanda.

Now the coffle was spread out along the catwalk, facing aft, the strong coffle leader nearest the poop with several other strong-looking European and Indian women immediately behind her and the more delicate Chinese, Siamese and Filipino women towards the bows. Amanda was half way down.

She looked up to the raised poop deck and saw that one of the armed guards was now standing there, his sub-machine gun at the ready. Another guard was pointing his gun at the other coffle still standing on the quay side.

Osman appeared on the poop and gave an order. Taking their time from the coffle leader, the women in turn sat down on the benches on the starboard side of the craft. Being very light, it listed slightly under their weight.

Whilst the guard kept the women covered with his gun, Osman and his boy stepped down onto the rowing deck and lifted up oars from below the catwalk. They thrust each one through the small port in the side of the vessel by each woman's left side. As they did so there was a rattle of the women's manacles which Amanda could not, at first, understand.

Then when it was her turn to be given an oar, she saw that each had been fitted with a locking metal clasp. Deftly Osman closed the clasp with a click over her manacles. She was now chained to her oar - as well still being chained by the neck to the women sitting on the benches immediately in front of and behind her.

Chained to an oar!

The expression reverberated round her feverish brain. Like the galley slaves of yore! But they had been men, not women. And anyway this was the twentieth century, almost the twenty-first.

Nevertheless, this must be a sport! The galley was built for speed - it must be a racing galley!

This then was why she had been brought here. To be a galley slave for the amusement of some rich Arab, Osman's Master!

Everything fitted into place: the emphasis on everything being done as a team, working together, eating together, relieving themselves together; the emphasis on doing everything to the whip; on blind and instant collective obedience rather than each woman thinking for herself; and being kept cowed - and muzzled.

This also explained the emphasis on fitness, on prancing, on exercising, on the careful individual feeding, on the examination of wastes, and on the prevention of any self abuse.

Now she began to understand the emphasis on security to keep the women controlled and docile, the manacles, the collar chains, the barred gate at the end of the passageway, the whips of the young black overseers, the armed guards, the importance of the coffle leaders who were also the key stroke oars of the galley, and the spare women left behind, ready to be step into the place of a sick or unfit woman.

All this, and so much else, was now beginning to make sense.

Desperately she rattled her manacles as if seeking to be free. But they were firmly attached to the oar and the oar was strong and had been firmly pushed through the little port in the side of the vessel. Quite apart from her collar chains, which were now nearly taut, and which, she realised, would help ensure that the women all rowed in perfect time together, there was no way that she could get away from her oar, or pull her oar inboard again.

She was secured to her oar as firmly as the male galley slaves of olden times that she had read about. But they had pulled huge war galleys or galleys used for trade, she was going to be used just for sport!

Whilst these thoughts had been racing through Amanda's brain, the other coffle had come onboard and had been chained to oars on the other side of the catwalk: the port side. The armed guards now left. Osman, the galley's whipmaster, was walking up and down the catwalk, a short black whip in his hand. His boy assistant sat in the bows holding the drum expectantly. Up on the poop stood the Arab coxswain who took charge of the vessel on practice runs, in the absence of the Master.

There was silence in the craft as the muzzled women sat silently at their oars, each with her eyes nervously fixed on the back of the woman chained ahead of her.

Suddenly there was a roll on the drum. It was bad enough having to do everything to the crack of a whip in the building and to the whistle on the parade ground, but now, it seemed, she would have to learn a new set of routines to the beat of the drum.

Amanda would learn that this particular drum beat signified that the Master was on the island and was about to come onboard. Immediately the women straightened up, their manacled forearms straight and holding the looms of their oars out in front of them, with the blades horizontal and clear of the water in a perfect line. They also parted their legs and thrust their bellies out up towards the poop in a humiliating sign of respect.

Osman brought his whip down across the back of a woman who had been slow to assume the required position. She gave a little moan from under her muzzle and, like a whipped cur, quickly assumed the correct position. Osman grunted angrily. He insisted on instant and unthinking obedience.

Amanda had been terrified when she heard the whip cracking across the woman's back. Now Osman was coming towards her! Desperately, looking at the other women, she tried to copy them. She looked pleadingly at Osman as if to say that she was trying to do the right thing, she really was!

Osman smiled as he looked down at her. Yes, this buxom but slight European woman had the makings of a good docile and yet strong galley slave. Clearly she was terrified of the whip. Already she was holding her oar correctly, and had thrust out her belly in the proper way for showing respect to the Master. But he motioned with his whip to part her legs properly so as to complete the sign of respect by also proffering her beauty lips. He saw Amanda blush as she obeyed. Then he pointed to the back of the woman in front of her, to remind her to keep her eyes down and not to look up at the poop until she was ordered.

There was another roll of the drums, and although Amanda did not dare raise her eyes, she was aware of a short, plump, bearded figure in a white robe, taking his seat in a chair up on the poop. His cold and expressionless eyes and face were hidden behind large sun glasses and she did not recognise him.

Osman bowed to the Master and then straightened up and looked down at Amanda's hairless beauty lips. He smiled as he saw the telltale signs of her womanly masochistic instincts taking over in the presence of her Master. He had seen it so often before: the more strictly the women were controlled and humiliated in the name of their Master, the more they came to respect and worship him!

Indeed, despite herself, Amanda could feel her body becoming aroused at the thought of being naked and chained in front of the cruel and powerful man who now owned her, body and soul, to whom she was now having to thrust up her exposed and parted beauty lips as a sign of respect.

Sheik Turki stirred on the comfortable chair on the small poop deck. His face was hidden behind his sun glasses, as he looked down onto the rowing deck with pleasure - the pleasure of ownership. He looked suave and relaxed in his spotless robes. But he also looked the epitome of cruelty, as with a dominating air he tapped a short cutting whip against the palm of his hand.

He surveyed the naked women cringing at their oars below him with a contemptuous and yet possessive smile. The contrast between his own elegance and their animal-like nakedness was particularly gratifying.

Two dozen naked, collared and muzzled women were sitting expectantly at their rowing benches, chained to their oars and to each other, their heads up with eyes looking straight ahead, their breasts quivering, and their arms held straight out in front of them. Each was gripping the oar to which she was chained, holding it so that the blades were in the horizontal saluting position just above the water. None had dared to raise their eyes to him. Each was thrusting forward her belly, and below that had parted her legs wide to display hairless beauty lips.

Yes, he thought, Osman was an excellent disciplinarian as well as an efficient whipmaster, keeping the women at a peak of fitness. It had been with pride that he pointed out to his fellow members the way all the women of both coffles had simultaneously performed to Osman's order onto the sandy strip, before going onboard the galley.

He looked up and down the rows of silent women. Each had been personally purchased by him. Each knew she only existed to pull his oars, to provide him with the excitement of driving his racing galley faster and yet faster, to win him races, and to win him prizes and bets. Yes, they were fine looking lot. Every single one of them was a beauty - and all relatively buxom for their different races. Certainly being made to row did wonders for the firmness of their upthrust breasts.

Their hair was well groomed and gleamed - a tribute to Osman's care in the stalls in which they were kept. Some of his fellow members preferred to keep the heads of their galley slaves shaved, but he liked to see long hair hanging down a galley slave's back - just as he also liked them to be kept muzzled.

He felt his manhood stir strongly under his robes. It was a pity that he had to return so quickly to his palace and only had time to take the galley out for a couple of hours. But he would return in a week's time, and meanwhile the women of his harem could well satisfy the physical arousal that the sight of his straining, sweating, galley slaves always provoked.

They were available any time he wished to use them, of course.

And there half way up the starboard side was the blond figure of Amanda! She was in his complete power at last!

Slowly and ponderously Sheik Turki stood up and gripped the rail of the poop. There was another roll on the drums. Osman tapped Amanda on the shoulder and pointed up at her Master. She saw that the other women were now all openly looking up at him. She did the same.

She heard little moans coming from the muzzled women all around her, as if they were excitedly greeting their Master, and Amanda found herself joining in. Osman turned and smiled contently at the women, his obedient little creatures! The Master would be pleased.

Slowly Sheik Turki removed his sun glasses. The moans increased in intensity.

Amanda gasped!

There were the unmistakable features of the man she had last seen when she had interviewed him on television!

More and more was now falling into place!

Sheik Turki gave a cruel laugh as he saw the horror on Amanda's face. He felt his manhood stirring again. Well, she could keep until his return. Meanwhile she wouldn't be going anywhere!

33 - THE MONTAH ISLAND SPORTING CLUB

The ancient sport of racing galleys pulled by teams of female galley slaves had recently been revived in secret by some twenty Arab Princes and Sheiks. They were all immensely rich, bored by their life in Arabia, and looking for a stimulating way to use their wealth.

The isolated island of Montah, previously uninhabited, had been chosen as the base for the new sport. Not only was it well away from the normal shipping routes, but it was within easy helicopter or speed boat range of several of the oil rich sheikdoms and of a little known airstrip where those coming from further away could readily leave their private planes and aircrews.

Thus the exclusive Montah Sporting Club had been established. In addition to the accommodation for the women there were luxurious villas for members and guests situated in the clubhouse complex near the quay to which their galleys were moored.

To ensure secrecy and fairness, the galleys were built on the island to a standard design.

The traditional design of a rather high sided galley, with an awning covering the rowing benches, when required, had been retained to prevent any casual observer from seeing that the rowers were women.

The rules of the Montah Sporting Club were almost as complicated as those governing certain well known yacht races in the West. But whereas the latter referred to inanimate sailing craft and their various sail measurements, the racing rules of the Montah Sporting Club referred to the bodies and measurements live women.

The basic rule, of course, was that the twelve oars on each side a galley were be pulled only by women and that to ensure that this rule was strictly observed the women were to be naked. Each member was responsible for the training and security of his team of women, but to ensure secrecy all women were to be registered by the club on arrival in the island, their registration numbers prominently marked on their forearms. Once registered no woman could ever leave the island without the express permission of the club, who would want to know what steps would be taken to ensure that she could never speak about her experiences.

Races were held twice a week during the racing season that ran from

October to December and again from March to June. Races were not held during the height of the hot summer, since so many of the wealthy members went to Europe at this time to avoid the heat, nor during the worst of the winter weather. There was also, of course, a break during Ramadan.

However, even during these off periods, the teams of galley slaves had to be regularly exercised and kept fit, new techniques tried out and new slaves acquired and broken in to the oar. So there was always something going on - which, quite apart from the excitements of the actual races, partly accounted for the popularity of this absorbing sport. But perhaps it was more the feeling of power that came from owning and controlling two dozen young women.

The light galleys were fast and manoeuvrable. Handling both the craft and the women called for a high degree of skill and ruthless cruelty, as did feeding and exercising them to keep the women racing fit.

Owners normally steered their own galleys around the zig-zag courses. Rounding the marker buoys, steering between the buoy and another vessel, and training the crews to spin round by holding water with the oars on one side and pulling hard with the oars on the other, called for skill, perfect timing and a well trained crew.

But success in the races also depended on the owner knowing the stamina of his crew: when to conserve their energies, and when to order his whipmaster to flog them into a desperate effort to overtake a rival or to maintain a lead. If the owner was away then his galley could be steered by his Arab coxswain who was in charge of the maintenance of the galley.

For centuries in the Middle East, uneducated but cunning black eunuch Sudanese slaves had been used to supervise and control the women in the harems of rich Beys and Pashas. It had been found that whereas the predominantly white Balkan or Circassian slave girls were able to get their own way with delicate white eunuchs, they were terrified of the hugely fat and grotesque black ones. These black eunuchs had therefore been able to maintain a high level of discipline and obedience in the harems, and could be largely left to run their busy masters' harems for them - attributes that were now needed here by the owners of teams of female galley slaves.

Beys and Pashas did not discuss their women with other Turks or Arabs. Instead, the owners of harems of nubile young women found it easier to discuss them with an experienced black overseer. They would enjoy discussing their women's progress in the harem, their level of training and obedience, and the state of their bodies. They found it less inhibiting discussing with an uneducated black man the acquisition of new women, and the disposal of women whom they no longer found attractive. Indeed, the close relationship between a rich owner and his chief black eunuch had been in many ways similar to that of a rich Western man and his stud groom, in charge of a large stable of high spirited carriage horses, hunters and hacks.

What was more natural, therefore, when rich Arab Sheiks had replaced rich Turkish Pashas, than to employ negroes as whipmasters for their female galley slaves? But the role was very different from that of a harem supervisor. They combined the roles of an old fashioned overseer of slave labourers with that of a modern athletic coach. They were not eunuchs.

However, to prevent whipmasters being tempted to treat women of their own race with special kindness, and partly to make the acquisition of suitable women more interesting, the use of black women on the rowing benches was banned.

Similarly to make it all more interesting, and to prevent an owner merely filling his rowing benches with the biggest women he could find, there was a strictly enforced but variable upper weight limit for the twenty four galley slaves used in a particular race. Thus owners were encouraged to also train slim women to the oar.

It was recognised that whereas it was relatively easy to acquire Indian, Ceylonese or Filipino women as galley slaves, it would be far more difficult and expensive to acquire the erotically more satisfying white women. However, the use of white women would be penalised because they were usually heavier than their Eastern sisters. Therefore, to reward owners who acquired white women, their official weight was reduced.

It was also recognised that there was a need to reward the acquisition of women with more opulent womanly charms, or else an owner who merely used dull, but strong, flat chested women with a boyish figures would have an unfair advantage. Thus the weight of a woman could also be reduced by a formula that compared the measurements of a woman's breast, waist and hip measurements. This had the effect of making it well worthwhile using an erotically more satisfying buxom woman, and owners were always talking to each other and to their whipmasters about the bosom-to-waist ratio of a particularly valuable galley slave, or of the average ratio for all their galley slaves. The greater the ratio, the more flexibility an owner would have in selecting a crew for a particular race, whilst remaining within the overall weight limit.

The effect of these rules was that the occasional buxom European girl, provided she was fit and strong, could be an invaluable asset to any team, of which an owner would boast to other owners.

Indeed, whereas rich Arabs did not discuss, or show of to other men, the inmates of their harems, they felt quite differently about their galley slaves - and would proudly invite each other to come and inspect them both in practice rows and in their stables. Such visits would often result in exchanges - which would, of course, be registered with the club.

Different owners and different whipmasters often had their differing views on the stamina of different races and on age. Some, for instance, swore that Chinese and European women were excellent for longer races, as were older women, but that Indian women and girls were better for short ones. Others insisted on the reverse!

They also held differing views on the best way to house, feed and exercise their galley slaves. Some, like Sheik Turki, liked to keep them in individual stalls, fed individually, with their wastes individually inspected and recorded. Moreover they could then be prevented from wasting their energies in self or mutual abuse.

Others swore that this was an unnecessarily complicated and expensive system. Instead, they maintained large cages with communal feeding and drinking troughs and another water filled trough, which the women could straddle, for their wastes.

The twice weekly races varied, not only in the permitted overall weight of the rowers, but also in their length. Some were over 30 miles in length, with many laps over the same course. Such races, of course, tested not only stamina, but also the owner's skill in varying the striking rate so that the women did not become totally exhausted before the end of the race.

Other races might be only five miles long, and here the women could be kept at full stretch for longer periods. The aim in both cases was to exhaust the crew totally just as they passed the finishing line. But many a losing owner would feel that he would have done better if only he had had the whip applied harder earlier in the race!

Once a month there was a special 24 hour race, with the women being kept rowing all through the night. These races were greatly feared by the women, though most whipmasters deliberately kept their women ignorant about when the next race would be and what sort of race it would be. Indeed, it was partly to help keep them ignorant, that Sheik Turki kept his women muzzled.

Because of the need for secrecy, great care was taken to prevent the galley slaves from escaping or staging a revolt. The basic rule was the galley slaves must be kept chained to each other whenever they were outside their slave pens, as the buildings in which they were housed were called. Whenever the women of several galley owners were present in one place, such as on the quay before races and or practices, armed guards were to be present with orders to shoot at the slightest sign of trouble.

The women were also to have a metal collar, marked with the crest of the club, riveted round their necks and their wrists were to be kept manacled.

This latter was also to assist in ensuring that they were properly chained to their oars. To ensure fairness, these collars and manacle chains were to be of a standard weight. They did, of course, form part of the weight of each woman when the crews were officially weighed before each race on the special weighbridge on the quay.

To further ensure secrecy owners were not allowed to bring women from their harems to the island, unless they were destined to stay there as galley slaves. It was therefore appreciated that owners staying the night at their luxurious villas would want to have galley slaves brought to them for their overnight enjoyment. Indeed the galley slaves also formed for many owners the functions of a second, highly disciplined, harem.

So, these villas had to be within the security perimeter of the clubhouse and to be provided with secure cages or pens in which galley slaves could be held until they were called to their Master's bed.

Once a week a sale of surplus and new galley slaves was held and there was a considerable turnover of women as owners and whipmasters adjusted the mix of their crews. A trained galley slave might be bought for a high price by another owner seeking to improve the stamina of his own crew or to reduce their overall weight - especially if she had a good bosom-to-waist measurement ratio.

34 - ROW, GIRL, ROW!

Sheik Turki looked past the lines of chained galley slaves to the young boy crouching in the bows by the drum. He called out an order, and gripped the wheel of the galley. There was a long and distinctive roll on the drums and an air of excitement ran through the galley slaves.

Osman went down the catwalk, whip in hand, correcting the position of individual women. He put a cushion under Amanda's still soft bottom to stop it blistering until it had been hardened properly, and also slipped a pair of gloves onto her hands. Then he made her turn her oar so that the blade was vertical again, reach right forward until the loom of her oar was almost pressing against the back of the girl in front of her, straighten her back, and press her feet against her foot bar.

The boy gave a sudden bang on the drum and immediately twenty four oars stuck the water. Amanda felt a sudden jerk on her collar chain from behind her as twenty four arched backs swayed back in perfect time, twenty four female buttocks were lifted off the benches, twenty four pairs of arms were pulled back to each woman's shoulders so that the looms of the oars touched their breasts just below their nipples, and twenty four bellies were now pointing up at the sky.

Then Amanda was jerked forward by her collar chain as the women immediately swayed forward again, their hands slightly lowered to raise their oars out of the water, and their arms out straight again as they reached forward, ready for the next stroke.

There was another beat on the drum and the whole process was repeated, this time to the accompaniment of the crack of Osman's whip across the naked back of a young Chinese girl.

The drum beat again and again.

The crack of the whip against naked flesh had terrified Amanda and had made her strain to reach out forward at the end of each stroke. Perhaps if she did that, then Osman would not notice if she did not pull the heavy oar back very hard!

Crack! Amanda screamed under her muzzle as the whip caught her under her arms and across her breasts. The pain was awful. But for the next few strokes she strained as never before to pull the oar right back.

She soon learnt to avoid the awful jerks on her collar by keeping in perfect time with the swaying back of the woman in front of her and with those of the two coffle leaders seated on stroke's benches from where they gave the time to the entire crew.

The drum beats alternatively increased in tempo or slowed, as the galley slid away from the quay and as Sheik Turki exercised his women.

He liked to work at a steady slow stroke for a few minutes, then put on a sudden spurt at high speed with the stroke increasing rapidly as the galley surged ahead.

He knew from experience with horses that such changes in pace were the best way of attaining fitness. It also realistically practised what the women would have to do in a race as the various galley owners jockeyed for position.

Soon Amanda was dripping with sweat. Four times Osman's whip came down across her back when, feeling exhausted, she tried once again to go through the motions of rowing in time with the other women without really putting her back into it. Putting her back into it! Was this where that expression came from? But anyway Osman was far too experienced a whipmaster for her to get away with it!

Four times he had silently come up behind her. Four times his whip had slashed across her back with the knotted tip flicking round under her arms to catch her breasts as well. Four times, driven by fear and pain, she had forced herself to really pull her oar for several minutes, until exhaustion, and the hope that this time Osman would not notice her, had persuaded her to slacken off again - only to be driven on again by the whip.

Amanda was astonished to see two smartly dressed women appear on the poop from the little cabin below. One, a hard-faced German looking woman in her early fifties, was dressed in a cool well-cut cotton dress with high heels and a wide hat to keep off the sun. The other, a Chinese woman from Singapore, Mrs Lee, was dressed in a simple long cheongsam Chinese dress, slit at the side to show off her slim legs.

Amanda could hear the other women gasping with humiliation under their muzzles. It was bad enough to be seen naked and chained to an oar by their cruel owner and his terrifying whipmaster, but to be seen as galley slaves by two elegantly dressed women was somehow far worse.

The two women were courteously welcomed by the Sheik, who handed over the wheel to his Arab coxswain and invited them to sit down on the comfortable chairs on the cool poop deck under a striped awning. The little black boy temporarily abandoned his drum and ran down the catwalk and up to the poop deck where he offered the women iced drinks as, fascinated, they looked down at the straining women below.

The German, Frau Smitt, was a society woman, well known in both England and Germany. For some years she had built up a lucrative business supplying discreet young women companions to visiting wealthy Arabs. For this she received a substantial fee and a percentage of the large 'salary' paid to the attractive 'private secretaries'.

More recently she had found her services being requested by wealthy European women who wanted a pretty young woman, in whom their husbands were showing an embarrassing interest, removed from the scene - completely removed to somewhere where their husbands would never find them. She had found that several of her former visiting Arab clients had been only to happy to receive a beautiful young European woman for their harems!

However, Frau Smitt was always worried lest a girl might escape back to Europe and expose her. But now, as she looked down on the two lines of chained and manacled women, and saw the registration numbers tattooed onto their forearms, she felt she had found the ideal outlet - the chance of escape was minimal.

Mrs Lee specialised in the Far East in getting rid of young women, often European ones, who had become an embarrassment to their wealthy Chinese lovers. Sometimes such women had overplayed their cards by becoming too demanding or possessive. Sometimes their millionaire friend had simply tired of them.

Looking down on the straining naked women, she too smiled as she too thought of how she could reassure her clients that the women who had annoyed them would be used in future to strain at an oar, driven on by the cruel whip of a negro.

The Sheik now had his women practised at 'racing starts' - a dozen very quick short strokes of the oar intended to get the galley moving as fast as possible, followed by another dozen gradually lengthening strokes. As the Sheik and his guests watched, the galley slaves had to pay close attention to the drum and to the stroke oars, the coffle leaders, or else there would be disaster as oars became entangled - followed by terrible retribution as the offenders knelt on their benches, still gripping their oars, and presented their buttocks for Osman's whip.

Amanda felt like a naughty puppy when she too had to kneel up and offer her buttocks to the whip. It was bad enough having to do so in front of Osman, the drum boy and her fellow galley slaves, but to do it in front of the Sheik himself and his sophisticated women guests was too much. It was made even worse when Osman, before applying his whip, pulled her head up by her hair and pointing to the Sheik, made it clear that she was to look at him throughout her punishment.

She saw the Sheik pointing her out to his guests.

"Yes, she's an Englishwoman," she heard him call out in his strongly accented English. "She had the effrontery to criticise me in public - on television! - and now she's paying for it. But I think she has the makings of an excellent galley slave!"

The two women laughed, and then laughed again as Osman brought his whip down across Amanda's bottom. But being formally beaten in front of her Master had a strange effect on her. With the first stroke she felt herself becoming moist. By the time Osman had applied the regulation four strokes she was dripping wet. How utterly shame-making it was! But as she screamed with pain under her muzzle, she also resolved not to make any more mistakes when they next had to practice 'racing starts'.

The Sheik now took the helm again, and for the next half hour showed off his galley slaves to his guests, putting them through different speeds from the gentle 'Paddle' or Slow Ahead, to the dreaded Full Ahead, when every woman was driven by Osman's whip into putting her back into pulling her oar as if her very life depended on it.

"Up two!" he would order and the drum beat would increase slightly.

"Up four!" he would cry and the stroke would appreciably increase, as would the sweat running down between each woman's breasts.

"Down six!" and the gasping women would give little sighs of relief under their muzzles - but for how long?

Then he made them practice suddenly holding water with the Port or Starboard oars as if rounding a buoy at high speed, with the oars on the other side still keeping up a high rate of stroke. Amanda's arm and shoulder muscles were repeatedly almost at breaking point as she strained to hold her oar in the water.

At last the Sheik was satisfied. The drum gave a long roll similar to the one that earlier had greeted his arrival onboard. Once again, as a sign of respect, the women had to hold their oars still above the calm sea with their arms outstretched, their heads up, their bellies raised and their legs parted.

Then the Sheik escorted his guests down onto the catwalk.

"I need good well breasted women," Amanda heard him say as they came down towards her. They stopped at the white woman in front of her. Osman gave a word of command and the woman, awkwardly because of her manacled wrists being chained to her oar, knelt up on her bench.

"This one has been in training for a year now. Look at her thigh muscles and see how firm her breasts are! And not an ounce of fat on her anywhere."

They moved towards Amanda. Terrified, she heard Osman tell her to display herself. No! She couldn't do it! The whip cracked. She forced herself to assume the kneeling position. Osman thrust her head down. Her buttocks were now raised and he gave her a sharp tap with his whip to make her part them. Horrified she realised that not only was she on display but she was again becoming wet!

"Just in case you feel that using a woman as a galley slave is unnecessarily cruel," Amanda heard the Sheik say behind her, "just look how this new girl is enjoying being trained!"

Amanda blushed with shame, but blushed even more when she felt hands feeling her from behind.

"Yes, she's soaking!" she heard the German woman exclaim. "What a little slut!"

She heard the Sheik laugh. "You'd be surprised how nearly all the women react like this to the whip. They just can't help it. Despite themselves, they really love being my galley slaves - even if they hate me at the same time! They long to serve and please their Master, but they're terrified as well."

"I'm not surprised," the German woman laughed, looking at Osman's whip.

It was then that something occurred to her. Sometimes when she was asked to get rid of an attractive young woman, the situation was more complicated in that in order to get her lover away from his wife, the girl had deliberately allowed herself to become pregnant. Often she kept this fact hidden until it as too late for anything to be done about it. It was of course the oldest ruse in the world and a very effective one. A young woman in this state was much more difficult to dispose of - even to white slave dealers in the Middle East. But here?

She turned to the Sheik. "Would you be interested in taking a woman in an Interesting Condition?"

The Sheik's eyes suddenly gleamed as the implication of the question struck home.

"Another Secret Weapon!" he laughed.

"Secret Weapon?" queried Frau Smitt. "What do you mean?"

"It's too long to explain now, but certainly if I send you a telegram saying 'Secret Weapons now acceptable', please go ahead and send me details of any such young woman."

35 - THE SHEIK APPLIES A LITTLE PSYCHOLOGY

Two hours later Amanda tottered back into her stall and allowed herself to be chained up again by the neck. She was physically exhausted. She was also emotionally exhausted by the realisation that she was now the helpless galley slave of Sheik Turki - and overcome with shame at the memory of how her body had reacted to being whipped in front of her awful new Master.

Listlessly she watched as one by one the remaining women were unfastened from the coffle and chained up in their stalls.

Then suddenly something caught her eye in her own stall. A large photograph of Sheik Turki had been fixed to the back wall! Whenever she was tethered facing the wall, as she so often was, she would have to look at the cruel, sneering expression of her dreaded owner.

Then, as she was looking at the picture, Osman came and silently placed two other even larger photographs, one on each wall of her stall. She saw that the first one showed Sheik Turki, wearing his long Arab robes, standing proudly with his raised foot on the neck of a frightened-looking naked white woman and looking straight at the camera. Meanwhile another younger looking white girl was kneeling and kissing his other foot in a gesture of utter obeisance. In his raised hand was the same short cutting whip that she had seen him carrying onboard the galley. It was a most striking photograph, symbolising the Sheik's utter domination of his women. She could not help identifying with the women in the photograph and as she did so she could not help feeling a little tremble of excitement.

Ashamed, she turned to the other photograph. This time the Sheik was sitting on a sofa, his legs open. The same two white women were kneeling naked on the floor their tongues outstretched towards the edge of his robe. His hand was raised over them and in it he again held the same short cutting whip.

Having securely fastened both photographs, Osman left Amanda trying not to look at the scenes of female subjugation. But no matter how she might turn her head, the cold eyes of Sheik Turki seemed to be on her, as if ordering her too to kneel at his feet. Her thoughts were dominated by the idea and by thoughts of the erect manhood hidden under the long robes, and of his raised whip.

36 - THE SHEIK'S TOUR OF INSPECTION

Amanda had now been subjected to the life of a galley slave for a week. Sheik Turki had not reappeared in person, but the terrifying photograph hanging in her stall ensured he was never absent from her thoughts. Every day she been exercised at her oar. Her hands and buttocks had become hardened, thanks to Osman's daily applications of alcohol, and he had removed her gloves and the mat. She was becoming a good galley slave, pulling well up to her weight - especially when the official reduction given for her large breasts was taken into account.

She had also been frequently exercised at the water wheel and the corn crusher. These not only helped develop her muscles but also her sense of dumb obedience - so essential for a galley slave in a racing galley.

But it should not be imagined that she was becoming an ugly muscular giant. On the contrary, the importance of keeping her weight down and her breasts well developed ensured that Osman kept her slim and attractive.

Except for little slices of meat, she had been largely fed on the special high protein porridge. The exact composition was Osman's closely guarded secret - and one that his rival whipmasters would have been only too anxious to know.

Amanda had learnt how to keep her stall spotless whilst performing her natural functions to order, for checking by Batu and recording on the blackboard at the front of her stall

A new development had been that as well as the embarrassing daily intimate inspections of her body by Osman himself, his young black assistants would now amuse themselves by starting to arouse her sexually whilst she stood stiffly at attention, chained up in her stall. Batu would order 'Inspection!' and she would raise her manacled hands and clasp them behind her neck, whilst moving her legs apart, bending her knees, and thrusting forward with her belly.

In this humiliating position, she had to look straight ahead whilst one of the boys would play with her beauty bud, and Batu would watch her, his whip raised, ready to punish her for the slightest movement - even of her eyes.

They never let her climax, but the effect, coupled with the erotic photographs of Sheik Turki hanging in her stall, had the inevitable effect of keeping her secret thoughts turn more and more towards to her powerful and ruthless Master. Previously she had always regarded him with repulsion, now he seemed her only chance of sexual relief.

Twice, not daring to actually touch herself, she had been caught by one of the boys secretly rubbing herself on a little ball of straw in her stall. Twice she had had to stand at attention whilst Osman was fetched - and angrily ordered her to be whipped.

One day the women were woken before dawn and taken down to the galley for an exceptionally early exercise. Then when they returned to their stalls they were all exceptionally carefully brushed and groomed by the young black boys. Electric trimmers were run over their mounds and down between their legs. They were made to make up their eyes and faces, and their beauty lips were outlined with black kohl. Then each woman had to scrub the floor of her stall with a nail brush until it was spotless.

Amanda heard the noise of a helicopter. Minutes later Osman called the women to attention and walked slowly down the spotless passageway past the lines of beautiful young women. Each stood at attention at the front of her stall, her collar chain to the wall at the back of her stall taut behind her, and her blackboard carefully showing her physical state and record.

There was the noise of a car outside, followed by the unlocking of the barred gate at the end of the passageway. Amanda longed to look and see what was going on, but with Batu quietly patrolling his section of the passageway she did not dare to move her eyes away from the stall in front of her across the passageway.

There were voices, and then the boy responsible for the section at the end of the passageway gave his women the order for 'Inspection'.

Amanda shivered with fear as she realised that Sheik Turki was slowly making his way down the passageway, pointing to each woman's body with his short cutting whip as he discussed her in Arabic with Osman and with the woman's own boy overseer.

Each woman stood stock still as her body was felt and as the Sheik barked out his instructions to Osman who was carefully noting them down. It was all desperately humiliating for an intelligent and educated woman - as Sheik Turki clearly intended it to be. He was impressed by the degree of discipline that Osman and his boy assistants exerted over the women in their charge. It was clear that the women were suitably scared of the young black boys even though they were only half their size. He grunted in approval.

Amanda was called to attention, and out of the corner of her eye she saw Batu go up to the Sheik, salute smartly and report his women ready for inspection. Moments later, the Sheik arrived in front of her stall. She longed to cringe back against the far wall, but she knew she must remain right at the front and keep her collar chain taut.

Osman began a brief description of her progress, inviting the Sheik to feel the muscles of her arms, shoulders and thighs, and to read the strange Arabic notations on her blackboard.

The sheik touched first one of Amanda's nipples and then the other with the tip of his whip. She felt her nipples harden and found it hard not to look at him. Still talking to Osman, he lifted her breasts with his whip, evidently pleased with their increased firmness.

Then Batu said something to the Sheik, and reaching forward to part her beauty lips for the Sheiks's inspection. Amanda gave a little jump backwards, but Batu's whip caught her across her buttocks. Then, still parting her beauty lips with one hand, he used his whip in his other hand to make her thrust her hips right forward towards the Sheik, standing in the lowered passageway. Her head now raised again, and her eyes looking straight ahead above the Sheik's head, Amanda could have died of shame as she felt the tip of her Master's whip between her parted lips.

Now the Sheik gave an order, and Batu ran up with a little stool which he placed in the passageway in front of Amanda. Then Batu sat down and began to play with her, demonstrating to the Sheik, as she stood trembling all over, but still stock still, both her level of fear induced discipline and her sensuality. Soon Osman was pointing out the changing colour of her cheeks and breasts, as her breath became shorter and shorter.

Never in all her life had Amanda been more ashamed as, despite her efforts at self control, she felt herself being brought to a climax in front of her Master by the horrible little boy. Was this why he had so often played with her? So that he could give the Sheik a demonstration of her sensuality - and of his control over her?

Apparently satisfied with the demonstration, the Sheik gave some more orders in Arabic and turned to the woman in the next stall, then the next section, and Batu ordered his women to relax from the position of Inspection. Gratefully she lowered her arms, closed her legs and straighten her knees.

A little later, still standing nervously at attention, Amanda heard her Master slowly coming back down the passageway. The stables resounded with youthful shouted orders, as each boy ordered his women back into the position of Inspection as the Sheik passed. Just as a sentry presents arms as an officer passes, so each section had to show their servile respect for their all-powerful owner by presenting their intimacies for his gaze as he strode by.

37 - TAKEN BY HER MASTER

That afternoon, Amanda saw Batu pushing a trolley containing several large bottles down the passageway to her stall.

He made her kneel down on all fours at the edge of her stall and face the wall, thrusting her buttocks up towards the trolley and keeping her head down on the floor. Then he fastened the chain linking her wrists to the ring at the back of her collar. She realised that this was so that she could not interfere with whatever he was going to do to her and moaned in fear.

Suddenly, she felt Batu tapping the inside of her thighs with his dog whip to make her part her legs. She felt him pull her buttocks further apart and then touch her with something that was greasy and firm. She gave a little shudder as she felt whatever it was being inserted into her.

Then he tied a strap over her buttocks and round her waist. As he fastened the strap, she felt it being pushed a little more into her. It was now firmly attached to her, and although she tried to use her muscles to expel it, to her dismay she found that the straps were holding it firmly in place.

Then to her surprise she was made to stand up again and face the passageway and the tall trolley. Batu used a second strap to fasten the first one to a ring on the trolley. She was now tightly strapped to the trolley as well as held to the ring at the back of her stall by her neck collar. She could hardly move.

Horrified, she saw a long rubber tube coming up from between her legs. Even more horrified, she saw that the tube led up to a large open bottle in a metal holder high up on the trolley level with the top of her head.

The bottle contained a thick green liquid. It seemed to be fizzy and slightly bubbling, like a freshly opened soda water bottle. As she watched Batu poured a small bottle of soda water into the large bottle, making the liquid fizz even more and bringing it exactly level with one of the numbered graduations engraved on the side. He stirred it with a wooden spoon until it looked like a sort of green sparkling wine.

Then he added a large handful of what seemed to be soap powder and stirred again. Soon there were large soap bubbles on the surface of the liquid, with little bubbles making their way up to them.

As she gazed at the bottle she saw that there was a tap where the tube joined it. Batu put down the wooden spoon and went off, leaving a petrified

Amanda gazing in horror at the bubbling bottle to which she was attached by the tube.

Osman came and inspected the bottle, nodding in approval. Then he checked the strap round her waist that held the nozzle of the tube up inside her. Then he patted Batu on the head and stood back.

Batu now felt Amanda's belly. She nearly died of shame. But worse was to follow for with his other hand he slightly turned the tap leading out from the bottle. Seconds later, Amanda gasped behind her muzzle as she felt the liquid squirt under pressure deep up inside her.

Above her muzzle her eyes started from her head. Batu nodded at Osman as now with both hands he felt her belly begin to swell and as he heard the bubbling liquid begin its cleansing task. Then he reached up and turned off the tap. It relieved the pressure but the horrible liquid still bubbled away inside her.

Osman came up and also felt her belly, nodded with approval and put a red mark on one of the graduations some way below the already lower level of the liquid. Then, with an experienced hand, he opened the tap just a shade, and led Batu off to work on another of the women in his charge.

Now Amanda could feel the liquid trickling into her, still under pressure. Her eyes were fixed on the bottle and on the red mark, down to which the top of the green liquid was very, very, slowly dropping. Already her belly felt huge and uncomfortable. She simply could not absorb any more! She tried to cry out, but her muzzle muffled her cries.

Desperately she tried to expel the nozzle, but the strap held it tightly in place. She tried to edge away from the trolley but the strap linking her belly strap held her tightly in place. Standing there, on display at the front of her stall, she was helpless to prevent the liquid from continuing to enter her drop by drop.

Suddenly there was a commotion at the end of the passageway. Amanda heard the distinctive rattle of the barred gate being unlocked and opened. Then striding down the passageway came Sheik Turki!

He stopped in front of her stall. Once again Amanda felt that she could die of shame at being seen like this by him.

Osman came running up. The Sheik barked several questions at him in Arabic. As he answered, Osman was pointing to the red mark on the bottle and feeling Amanda's swelling belly.

The Sheik slowly walked round Amanda, his eyes taking in the strap that held the the nozzle inside her, her terrified eyes and, of course, her swollen belly - something which seemed to fascinate him. Revenge! Then turning on his heels he strode away down the passageway and out of the building.

Five minutes later the top of the liquid had dropped to the red mark. Batu came and turned off the tap. But there was no relief yet for Amanda. For another ten minutes she was left standing there whilst the liquid completed it task.

Only then was she unstrapped from the trolley, the nozzle removed and under the watchful gaze of Batu was she allowed to empty herself onto the straw in the corner.

Later that evening Batu came back to Amanda's stall, washed her all over, and powdered her body. Then he began to paint her eye-lids. He dropped something into her eyes that made them seem huge and soft. He put her into short white gloves and long white stockings, an abbreviated white suspender belt and white high heel shoes.

He wrapped a very short white frilly skirt round her waist. It stuck out like a ballerina's tutu, leaving her shorn and now powdered beauty lips on display.

A big white satin bow was tied around each of her upper arms and round her neck. A little white bridal hat and veil completed her outfit. Her breasts were still bare and she was still muzzled.

Amanda looked at herself in the mirror in her stall. She gasped at the sight of the beautiful and erotically dressed girl who stared back at her with huge eyes, a girl dressed to pander to the lusts of a man, and once again felt a mixture of pride and shame - and mounting excitement!

Now Osman arrived, and having looked her up and down with evident approval he unfastened her collar chain from ring on the rear wall of her stall, and led her down the passageway.

Amanda noticed how the other women turned in their stalls and looked jealously at the beautiful and exciting creature into which Amanda had been transformed. She tossed her head proudly, though she also blushed at her scanty clothing, which somehow seemed more revealing than when she was naked.

The barred gateway at the end of the passageway was unlocked and she was taken out to the otherwise empty cattle truck. Her collar chain was fastened to a ring in the side of the truck and her hands fastened behind her neck. The ramp was raised and she was left in darkness.

The truck moved off down the bumpy road. Then it stopped and the ramp was lowered. Osman came in to the back of the truck and unfastened her collar chain. Then, holding her chain in one hand and his inevitable dog whip in the other, he led down her down the ramp.

Amanda looked around in the darkness. She was back on the quay. The high stern of the galley loomed up above her.

Osman led her up the gangplank that led to the poop of the galley, and then down to the rowing deck. But instead of being led to her rowing bench, they went to the door of the small cabin under the poop.

Light was coming from under the door and through a curtained small porthole. She heard the sound of someone moving about inside the cabin. Osman fastened her collar chain up to a hook above the door that was out of her reach. He gestured with his whip for her to kneel down on all fours. Then he knocked on the door and went in, leaving Amanda kneeling outside, in the warm evening air, like a dog chained up by its lead outside its owner's front door.

She heard the Sheik's strong voice, speaking in Arabic. Her Master! Suddenly Osman came out. The door remained open, lighting up the erotically dressed and kneeling figure of Amanda. She saw that Osman was now carrying a beautifully decorated and distinctive short whip. She trembled as she recognised the Sheik's own cutting whip.

Osman gestured with the whip for her to raise her buttocks. Then he put his foot on her neck and pressed her head down onto the deck, tapping her underneath on her belly with his whip to make her push her buttocks up, then used the whip to lift up her absurd little white skirt and bare her bottom.

Osman coughed, as if seeking permission to proceed. Nothing happened. Amanda tried to scream, but only a little gurgle came out from behind her muzzle - a gurgle that was greeted by a sardonic laugh from behind the door.

Again Osman coughed. She heard the noise of pages being turned. The Sheik was reading a book! Reading whilst she was being kept waiting for a beating - a beating which was purely for the Sheik's amusement.

Amanda heard the Sheik say something in Arabic. Osman raised the whip. Then he brought it down slowly and methodically, across Amanda's buttocks. A muffled scream came from her. The pain was awful, but so too was the humiliation and, she realised, the excitement of knowing that the Sheik would have heard the crack of his own whip across her skin.

There was a long pause and the sound of more pages being turned. Then the curtain across the porthole was drawn back. Another page was turned. Would the Sheik now be able to look up from his book and see his insignificant new galley slave being beaten for his amusement as well as listen to it? My God! She felt utterly dominated. To her shame, however, she felt herself becoming more aroused at the thought. She remembered the Sheik callously telling his guests how his women galley slaves could not help themselves from becoming aroused when they got the whip. It was true!

Then she heard the Sheik snap his fingers as he read. She felt the tap of the whip signalling her to raise her buttocks high in the air again. As she strained nervously to do so, she felt Osman's boot pressing hard down on her neck. The whip came down again. Again there was the noise of a muffled scream.

Osman kept his boot on her neck, as she tried to reach back behind her with her manacled hands to ease the pain in her buttocks.

She realised that the casual snap of the Sheik's fingers was the signal for the administration for each stoke. She found herself desperately listening for the next click of his fingers.

Suddenly she heard a double snap. Terrified, she raised her bottom for the whip. Nervously, she clenched her buttocks. But nothing happened. What now? She felt Osman raise his boot from her neck. Then, holding her by her hair, he lifted her up.

Osman gestured to her to raise her short little skirt with her manacled hands. Ashamed, she did so and then, with his whip, he tapped her forearms making her strain to keep her elbows right back. Then he tapped her buttocks, until she also straining to thrust out her belly under her raised skirt. He looked her up and down. He was still not satisfied! She felt him tap her under the chin making her lift it and so thrust her head right back until she was looking up at the stars.

She knew that Osman, and hence presumably the Sheik, had no more compunction about beating a girl across the belly, than he had of beating her across her buttocks. And, she realised, her soft little belly was now perfectly positioned for the whip. She bit her lips nervously.

Osman coughed again as if signalling to the Sheik that the girl was now ready. Amanda glimpsed a shadow behind the porthole. There was a long pause. Osman tapped her elbows, and then her buttocks and her chin, keeping her straining to hold position.

Suddenly she heard the snap of fingers from behind the door. With a splattering noise the whip came down across her beautifully presented belly. A line of fire seemed to cross her and she doubled up with the pain.

Osman let her writhe in pain, and then pulled her up again by the hair and used the whip to reposition her. Once again she stood there, her belly thrust out, straining to hold position, her ears cocked for the dreaded snap of the cruel Sheik's fingers.

At last the stroke came - was it imagination or was it less hard? Did Osman feel that he had achieved his aim of making her realise that she was nothing more than an obedient slave?

Osman pointed to the deck with the whip. Obediently Amanda fell to her knees. Osman unhooked her collar chain. Then he thrust the Sheik's cutting whip into her mouth and picked up his own dog whip. He gave a sharp pull on her collar chain, just as an impatient dog owner might give a sharp pull on a lead.

The Sheik was lying back on a comfortable sofa, dressed in a long caftan. Osman handed him Amanda's chain and bowing deeply left the cabin. For the first time, Amanda was alone with Sheik Turki.

"Ah! My latest new bride," came the harshly accented voice. "And quite a pretty one too." Then he laughed and gave the chain an angry tug. "Give me my whip!"

With a sob of despair, Amanda crawled up to him. Like a well trained dog, she dropped the whip into his hand.

"Now, up onto the couch on all fours! Move! And stop snivelling or I'll call in Osman to give you another four strokes."

Furious at being ordered about like this, but too terrified to disobey, Amanda climbed up onto the big sofa, still kneeling on all fours. Holding her collar chain in one hand, and his whip in the other, the Sheik pulled her up alongside him, keeping her on all fours. Then he put down his whip.

"Keep your eyes on my whip, 731," he ordered. "The slightest sign of disobedience or any lack of respect and you'll feel it again. So just remember and keep your eyes on it."

As if hypnotised by his words, Amanda's eyes were fixed fearfully on the whip, as he reached forward and began to rub her nipples between his fingers. Excitement flowed through her body like electric shocks. She began to moan under her muzzle. Sheik Turki smiled and then moved his hand down between her legs and slowly began to stroke her.

Amanda found herself opening her legs to his touch, as if silently asking for more. He put down the collar chain. She was now too hooked on the pleasure he was giving her to try and run away. With one hand now rubbing first one nipple and then the other, he began to use the fingers of the other hand to feel round and round her beauty lips. The moaning increased. How sensible Osman was to keep his galley slaves muzzled.

Now he began to tickle her beauty bud. He could feel her trembling all over. Slowly and tantalisingly he began to feel up between the now well moist lips. He smiled again. First terrify a woman, then have her beaten and then play with her. It never failed!

Indeed, Amanda felt herself responding more and more deeply. The Sheik might be repulsive and cruel, but she was his! His to do with as he liked. She was just his slave. It was all too animal-like, but she just could not help it.

The Sheik saw that her eyes were becoming glazed, and her breathing heavy. Little gurgling noises of pleasure came from behind her muzzle. Her whole face, her neck and her breasts became flushed. It was time she was made to show her sluttishness!

He removed his fingers and keeping both hands quite still, with one he now merely cupped a hanging breast and with the other her intimacies. He heard a little moan of disappointment from behind the muzzle.

Then he felt her start to press both her breast and her intimacies down against his hands as she desperately sought to renew the earlier excitements. Soon she felt herself melting again, melting into the cups of his hands.

Suddenly he removed his hands. She moaned again in disappointment and tried to rub her beauty bud against his strong hand. But this time he picked up his whip and made her raise her hips and keep quite still.

Then, unbelievably, she saw him reach for a book, open it and start to read, leaving her aroused, shamed, frustrated and muzzled. How she hated him!

Idly he reached up with one hand, turned the page and stroked her breast. She sighed with pleasure. He rolled a nipple between finger and thumb. She moaned in ecstasy. She gave her breasts a little shake as if inviting him to hold them. She wriggled her hips as if inviting him to feel her again.

But he took his hand away to hold his book! What should she do, she wondered, as she knelt panting by his side on all fours? She looked at him as he read his book and ignored her. What a repulsive creature he was! How could she have been turned on by such an evil and horrible creature? She must have been mad! Anyway, he would not arouse her again!

Two minutes later, the Sheik casually reached down between her legs ... another two minutes and, despite her resolve, she was fully aroused again and panting with desire. Then again he took his hand away and concentrated on his book, leaving her feeling both dismayed and degraded.

From time to time he would absent-mindedly play with her body as he read. She began to plunge wildly, but he held her tightly by her collar chain, keeping her firmly kneeling on all fours by his side. Sometimes he would allow her to rub herself desperately against his palm and then take his hand away again to turn over a page, leaving her wondering if he would deign to bring his hand back again.

Slowly he brought her again and again towards a climax, paying no more attention to her than he would when casually fondling a favourite dog.

Amanda felt that she was being driven mad. Driven mad by desire for a man she hated and despised. How he must be enjoying his revenge!

Suddenly she plunged wildly as he touched her beauty bud with an idle finger. Overcome with desire and shame, she half climaxed. Now she needed to feel his touch more than ever. But again he took his hand away, leaving her appalled at her own behaviour.

Soon his hand returned, arousing her to yet greater heights. Slowly and intermittently he aroused her again and again. She felt utterly dependent on him, on his touch. Finally, feeling that she had now sufficiently demonstrated her sluttishness, he did allow her to climax - on all fours in front of him.

"You disgusting little creature," he called out as he gave her several gentle taps with his whip to bring on her climax. "Aren't you ashamed of yourself?"

But there was no respite, for he soon had her panting with desire again. This brute of a man was playing on her body, against her will, as if it was a musical instrument! She became exhausted. She collapsed onto the couch, but he quickly pulled her up by her collar back onto her knees again, back to his terrible fingers and their casual stroking, tickling and probing.

She wanted more. She wanted to feel him inside her. Yes, she wanted this awful man inside her. Oh how ashamed she felt!

Suddenly he put down his book. He came behind her. She was wet and ready for him. Half heartedly obeying some primaeval instinct, she tried to wriggle away, but he gripped her by the neck, and held her down.

Then slowly he penetrated her, enjoying the feeling of tightness and of her attempted resistance, enjoying both the physical pain and the mental anguish he was inflicting on her. Ah, revenge is indeed sweet but will be sweeter yet!

Amanda dropped her head in shame, but he gripped her hair and pulled her head back so that her back was nicely arched - all the better to take his manhood.

He kept her still in that position for several moments and then he thrust forward in an ecstasy of power over a beautiful white woman reduced to the status of a mere galley slave, knowing that she, in turn, would be experiencing a deep feeling of utter humiliation and excitement. Was this not what her own lust had made her secretly long for?

Slowly he forced his way up inside her. Never had she felt so stretched. He was so big. The pain was exquisite!

Then slowly he withdrew, leaving her feeling used and rejected.

Now she felt him apply a little grease. But in the wrong place! Immediately he pressed his manhood against her. No! No! She had not realised the significance of the preparations in her stall. Now suddenly she did! She tried to wriggle away but again he held her still by her hair, tighter than ever, making her arch her back even more so as to make her accommodate his thrusting manhood even better.

Suddenly he was inside her, deep inside her. No! No! But she still tightly held, and the more she wriggled and writhed, the more pleasure, physical and especially mental, she was giving to him. Exhausted, she began to relax. But that was the signal be was waiting for, and now he thrust violently in and out of her weakening body, taking her and dominating her in a way that she had never felt before.

Now she felt him grow bigger and firmer, and she felt a jet of something warm deep inside her, inundating her. She felt so helpless. So ashamed. So degraded. So much his slave. A slave who had been used to arouse and satisfy her Master, after previously being made to perform so humiliatingly on all fours. A slave who would now be ashamed to look her Master in the face.

Contentedly he clapped his hands for Osman to come in and take her away.

His revenge was coming on nicely!

38 - FINAL TRAINING AND THEN THE CREWS ARE PARADED.

A few weeks after the Sheik had enjoyed Amanda the Spring racing season began.

Twice a year, in the winter and summer off-seasons, the galley owners had the absorbing task of bringing their female galley slaves up to strength: the sheer fascination, skill and expense of selecting and acquiring suitable young women and of watching their whipmasters overcome their initial reluctance to obey.

Then, as the spring and autumn racing seasons approached, there was the art of whipping the women into a winning team. And in the actual racing seasons there was, of course, the racing itself.

Sheik Turki started attending more practice sessions. Impressed by the stamina and level of training reached by his own women, and confident of his own skill as a coxswain and helmsman, he had already placed large bets on their future performance.

Chained to her oar, Amanda could not bear to meet her Master's eye as he stood imperiously on the raised poop deck gripping the rail as he looked down on the straining women below, or as he spun the steering wheel, barking his orders to the boy at the drum and to the women at the stroke oars.

She no longer despised him as she had done when she interviewed him back in London. Now she feared him. She hated him certainly, but she also respected him. She dreaded him and yet she longed for him.

She watched breathlessly as he chose other women to be sent down to the galley, or to his villa, for his evening pleasure. Was she being deliberately ignored? Was she relieved or secretly jealous of the other women?

Although Amanda did not know it, the first race was to be four laps of a two mile zig-zag course intended to test the stamina and state of training of the various crews, and the expertise of their Owners and whipmasters.

The course would also test the skill of the Owners and their whipmasters in controlling both their galleys and rowers as they rounded the various buoys whilst surrounded by other galleys, each pushing and shoving to steal a lead.

Overtaking galleys did not have the right of way and must therefore keep clear of galleys being overtaken, and if an overtaking galley struck a galley it was overtaking, or if their oars touched, then the former would be disqualified. However in the muddle and melée that often took place as several galleys rounded a mark, it was not always very clear just which vessel was the overtaking one and which the overtaken. A craft whose rowers were tiring, and whose lead was being challenged by another galley with a fresher crew, might quite legitimately steer a zig-zag course to try and block the other galley, or to force him to touch oars inadvertently.

Such tactics made the the races more exciting, especially since, as the women were chained to their oars, the chaos and physical damage to them could be considerable. Not only could the oars be smashed or broken off, but the unfortunate women could well be injured.

If this happened then, by the Rowing Club rules, the Owner of the galley that had had the right of way could pick replacement women from the crew of the offending galley. This might result in the offending alley being out of action for the rest of the racing season whilst replacements were acquired and trained. However the performance of the galley that had been struck might also be affected as the new members of the crew settled down and learnt the ways of their new whipmaster.

This rule was intended to deter dangerous manoeuvres. However, not only were the galleys competing against each other during a particular race, but they were also desperate, as in the British Football League, to earn points towards each racing season Championship. So great were the sums involved in the betting, and so large was the Championship prize money, that it was not unknown for a leading Owner to bribe another Owner, who was out of the running for the Championship, to ram the galley of his closest rival in an attempt to disable as many of the crew as possible.

Another effect of this rule was that an Owner of an inferior crew might deliberately seek to be struck by a galley higher up the League table, so as to be able to replace his injured women with better trained ones. It was therefore important for the Owner of a successful galley to keep a sharp lookout for unscrupulous Owners seeking to collide with his galley, irrespective of who had the right of way.

As with a successful football team, it was also important to have reserve rowers, kept trained like the rest, ready to step into the place of any injured women.

Just as in horse-racing the runners are paraded around the paddock by their trainers before cantering off to the start, so on Montah Island the crew of each galley was paraded by its whipmaster on the rowing club lawn before being run off to their galley.

Not only did this enable the Club Members and their guests to judge the strengths and weaknesses of each crew before placing their bets, but also to get an idea of its state of discipline. A crew that, for instance, pranced eagerly onto the lawn in perfect time, their bodies all gleaming and showing no surplus fat, might be expected to outperform a crew that had to be whipped onto the lawn and in which the bodies of the individual women showed various states of fitness.

Each crew was watched carefully as it was paraded in front of the shaded terrace on which the Members and their guests enjoyed cooling refreshments before embarking in their own galleys, or in the boats provided for spectators and judges. The watching men would be looking for an impression of stamina in the crew as a whole, and also seeing if a crew gave the impression of moving and thinking as one.

Just as in horse racing there is often a prize for the best turned out horse in the paddock, so here there was a prize for the best parade.

Sheik Turki's women's wrists were chained with the Club's standard weight manacles that prevented individual crews getting an advantage over the others. They were also tattooed on the right forearm with the club insignia of two palm trees followed by their registered number in Arabic numerals. But they differed from the others by the well cut chevron of hair, like a Lance-Corporal's stripe, on the mound of the otherwise hairless mounds of the two coffle leaders, the stroke oars.

They also, of course, differed by being muzzled and by having the Sheik's own design of standard weight flexible stainless steel collars riveted round their necks rather than the more normal simple black iron ring or brass studded dog collars. The Sheik preferred his type as it enabled his name to be prominently engraved on the collar, as well as the insignia of the club. This, he felt, drove home to the women that they all belonged to him and formed part of his team.

Sheik Turki also liked to see his crew wearing a distinctive gold edged, short red cloak on their way to their galley before a race.

There was therefore no mistaking Sheik Turki's crew as, chained by the neck into two coffles and raising their knees up high, they pranced towards the club house, their red cloaks streaming behind them

Each Owner, of course, had his own ideas about how best to mark his women and give them a sense of identity. Amanda was shocked to see that the women lined up next to them all had a distinctive brown and white chequered pattern, a foot wide, tattooed right round their waist and over their bellies. The brown women in the team had white squares tattooed onto their bodies, and the white women brown squares. Each square was about two inches across. The effect of this pattern was most distinctive and bizarre looking.

In another crew, a distinctive partial circle of short hair had been allowed to grow on their otherwise hairless mounds. The two ends of the circle led down to half along the shorn beauty lips where there hung a brass infibulation ring.

Another crew also had yellow plastic collars round their necks, like those worn by cows in a modern cattle feeding system, so that their feed could be individually preset and automatically controlled.

Amanda recognised the crew that had had their heads kept completely shaved. Was this so that there would be no hair to get into their eyes during strenuous sessions at the oars? Or was it just a cruel way of making the women all feel part of one team?

One team had a bell hanging from their collars. The bells rang with their every movement. Would the bell of one woman, tinkling a split second later than the rest, bring down the wrath of her whipmaster?

Some of the teams had been branded on the shoulder or breast with an insignia, presumably that of their Owners. One had their Owner's insignia tattooed in bright green and scarlet on their naked bellies. At least, thought Amanda, Sheik Turki, cruel though he was, hadn't yet introduced that idea!

In some crews the women seemed to have had their hairless beauty lips sewn up. How awful! Was this so that they could not waste their energies by playing with themselves? Had they also had their beauty buds removed, to make sure? Then she saw that in one team the entire beauty lips seemed to have disappeared altogether. There was a long scar were the beauty lips should have been. My God! Amanda remembered reading about total circumcision being quite common in parts of the world - the removal of not only the beauty bud but also the sensitive lips which were then made to heal over to form a solid scar except for a small orifice low down. At least Sheik Turki did not do that.

Indeed the more she looked around her, the more Amanda felt that her Master, whom she had previously regarded as the most appalling swine, was not perhaps so bad as a Master after all.

Suddenly there was the crack of a whip, and the team of shaven headed women started to goose-step round the lawn, in perfect military formation, their straight legs raised high in the air. Every twenty paces they halted, performed a smart military about-turn, and then goose stepped ten paces back in the direction they had come from, before turning about again, and marching forward again another twenty paces.

Amanda realised that this was all more than a mere desire by the Owner to show off how well disciplined his women were. Thigh and stomach muscles all played an important part in pulling an oar, and just as the prancing step of Sheik Turki's crew provided an excellent way of exercising these muscles, so too did this team's goose-stepping.

A few minutes later it was the turn of a nose ringed crew. Their Owner must have been struck, on a visit to England, with the very fast march of the British Light Infantry, and on his return had introduced it as the normal marching pace for his galley slaves. The sight of two dozen naked women, marching smartly at the exaggerated Quick Step of 140 paces to the minute, their breasts swinging in time, was indeed an impressive sight.

At last, Osman gave a warning crack with his whip. Amanda and the other women straightened up and clasped their hands behind their necks, waiting for the next crack of the whip. At last it came and Amanda found herself prancing onto the lawn in perfect step with the other women, her breasts swinging wildly under her cloak, and the chains that linked her collar to that of the women in front and behind her bar taut.

As she followed her coffle leader round the lawn, she had a glimpse of the white robed men sitting nonchalantly on the shaded clubhouse terrace. The immaculate dress of these all-powerful individuals made her more conscious than ever of her nudity and helplessness, especially when she saw there in the middle was sitting Sheik Turki, smiling as he received numerous congratulations on the appearance of his team.

Obeying a crack of Osman's whip, they halted. Several of Osman's young black boy assistants ran onto the lawn and quickly removed the red cloaks. Again Sheik Turki's young women pranced round the lawn, this time their breasts on display. Many experienced Owners swore that they could tell the state of fitness of a team of galley slaves by the pertness of their breasts, and would place their bets accordingly. They would explain that nothing made a woman's breasts more firm, with the nipples pointing up, than rowing.

Finally, obedient to another crack of Osman's whip, they all pranced off the lawn and towards the jetty where their galley was lying.

39 - AMANDA'S FIRST RACE

Amanda and the other women were now marched to their galley. They embarked, as usual under the guns of the guards, and were chained to their oars.

The Club Inspector came on board and with Osman went down the central catwalk of the galley. He checked the number tattooed on each girl's forearm with a list that Osman had handed him and with his own handicap book that listed each girl's true weight and her official handicap weight.

Then, using his calculator, he added up the total handicap weights. Satisfied that the total was within the maximum allowed in this particular race, he stamped Osman's paper, handed it back to him, and went off to repeat the process in the next galley.

This was the galley in which all the girls had their heads shaved. A few minutes later there was a furious scene there as the Inspector discovered that the crew was just overweight. The embarrassed whipmaster had to unchain a large muscular girl, and replace her with a delicate Thai girl who he had brought down to the quay in his cattle truck as a reserve.

The naked women in Sheik Turki's galley sat waiting, silent under their muzzles, their manacled hands gripping their oars. With each of the galleys festooned with its Owner's personal racing pendants, the scene was one of beauty and exhilaration.

Amanda tried to peer through the small port in the side of the galley, through which her oar was passed. She glimpsed a group of white robed Owners approached from the direction of the club house, laughing amongst themselves as they strode along the jetty to their respective galleys.

Osman's whip cracked and hastily she turned her head. She knew very well that the galley slaves had to keep their eyes in the boat at all times, looking only at the back of the girl in front and at the stroke oars.

As she sat there, wondering what was gong to happen, she remembered the last time Sheik Turki had taken the galley out on a practice row. Hardly had they started out when two diminutive figures, dressed in immaculate white Arab robes and headdresses, had appeared from the cabin under the poop. The Sheik's young nephews!

For them this was an exciting day out. They were laughing and giggling as as they climbed up to join their uncle on the poop deck, and then watched, open mouthed, as the naked, muzzled, galley slaves, were put through their paces.

Amanda felt embarrassed at being shown off in this way to young Arab boys, and even more so when she saw one of them point to her and then, laughing, whisper something to his brother.

Their uncle said something to them and they scampered down onto the central catwalk and then, as the women continued to row in perfect unison to the beat of the drum, started to run up and down, looking at the numbers tattooed on each woman's forearm.

Suddenly there was a sheik of excitement as one of the boys found what they must have been looking for - the number on Amanda. Both boys clustered round her. She saw Osman looking at her, his whip ready. Then one boy put a pudgy hand on one of her naked breasts. He said something to his brother and soon there were two little hands kneading and squeezing her breasts as she swayed to and fro in time with the drum. It was a horrible and humiliating feeling but, with her hands chained to her oar and Osman watching her, there was nothing she could do.

Then they ran back up to the poop to join their uncle. One of them pointed to the steering wheel and, with a smile, the Sheik let him take over. The boy gripped the spokes of the wheel and proudly began to turn the galley first one way and then the other. Then, imitating the his uncle's voice, he called for greater speed and laughed as the drum beat increased and Osman cracked his whip menacingly.

Amanda was even more humiliated when the other boy pointed at the proud figure of Osman strutting up and down the catwalk his whip raised. The Sheik nodded indulgently and called out to Osman. The little boy ran eagerly down to the catwalk and Osman handed over his whip.

The boy practised cracking it several times and then, brought it down across the back of a straining young woman. Laughing with delight he began to run up and down the cat walk, his whip raised in imitation of Osman. He paused at Amanda and then, with a cruel little smile, brought the whip down across her back, making her scream with a mixture of pain and shame.

Finally the Sheik called the boy back to the poop and took over the helm again so that he could get down to the serious work of exercising his crew. But the memory of the shame of being made to perform as a galley slave by these two horrible rich young Arab boys was still in her mind as she now waited ... and waited.

Suddenly there was the roll of the drum that signalled that their Master was about to come onboard. Hurriedly Amanda straightened up, and with her manacled arms straight out in front of her, turned her oar so that loom was horizontal and in a perfect line with the other oars just above the water. Then she parted her legs and thrust her belly up towards the raised poop. Would she ever get used to this humiliating gesture of respect?

There was another roll of the drum, and out of the corner of her eye she saw the Sheik stride up the gangway onto the poop. As usual, and to her utter shame, she felt her displayed beauty lips responding to his presence and her own helpless nakedness.

The Arab coxswain and the negro drum boy now cast off, and the women slowly paddled the galley out to the start of the race, off the club house. There was a long pause whilst each galley moored itself by the stern to its starting buoy.

Suddenly there was the roar of the starting gun, fired from the club house lawn. The coxswain, standing on the poop deck deftly slipped the starting rope. Sheik Turki shouted an order and spun the steering wheel. The black boy began the quick drum beat of the racing start that the women had so often practised and Osman's whip cracked.

Twenty four female backs swayed back in the first of the initial short strokes and then forty eight naked nipples jerked as the women quickly reached forward again for the next stroke. The light galley shot forward, as did twenty other galleys, all racing for the first marking buoy half a mile ahead.

The dozen quick strokes were completed, and the women were lengthening their stroke as the drumbeat eased. The galley was moving fast.

"Full Ahead!" screamed the Sheik in Arabic as he lined the galley's bow up with the distant marking buoy. It was an order that the women had all learnt to recognise and obey.

Osman walked slowly back along the central catwalk, towards the poop, looking for any signs of slackness. Amanda sensed that he was coming down towards her, and strained hard at her oar. The fact that he was behind her spurred her to even greater efforts for she could not see when his whip might suddenly slash down across her naked back. No wonder the women were made to row naked - naked for the whip, she thought.

Suddenly she saw the whip slash down across the back of the girl seated opposite her as she reached forward. Osman had judged his stroke cleverly and the knotted tip of the whip whistled round under the unfortunate woman's armpits to catch her breast where it curved down just under the nipple - the most sensitive spot. Amanda saw the woman judder and strained even harder at the next stroke, as Osman stood behind her his whip raised.

But Amanda had made the mistake of slightly turning her head towards the other woman, instead of keeping her eyes on the woman ahead and on the stroke oars. As she pushed her oar back to the starting position for the next stroke, she too felt the whip crack across her soft back, the tip catching her, too, on the soft under-breast. The pain was excruciating, but her muzzle muffled her cry.

The Sheik kept them at Full Ahead for a whole minute. He was now in the leading group of galleys. He must conserve energies.

"Half Ahead! Twenty six strokes!" he ordered. The drum beat eased perceptively and the women slowed down to the less exhausting stroke.

Soon the galley was approaching the rounding mark. Another galley was challenging them from behind.

"Up four strokes!" ordered the Sheik grimly and the galley began to surge ahead of its rival as the striking rate increased to thirty.

"Hold water starboard two strokes!" shouted the Sheik and spun the wheel. Obediently Amanda and the women on her side of the galley strained to hold the loom of their oars in the water, as they had so often been made to practice. The galley spun found the mark ahead of the other galley which began to slow down.

"Give way together!"

Amanda and the women on her side resumed the stroke and the galley steadied on the new course for the next marker buoy.

The Sheik looked back with a smile. But he did not want to exhaust his women too quickly.

"Down six strokes."

The relieved women slowed down again to an easier stroke, but Osman still continued to patrol up and down, looking for any woman who might be using the excuse of a slower stroke to ease off too much.

And so the race continued with the stroke being altered up and down at frequent intervals, but with only the very occasional Full Ahead.

Amanda suddenly heard a terrible crash of breaking oars from astern of the galley. Daring to raise her eyes slightly she saw that a galley astern of them had slowed down just in front of another galley which had run into it.

Amanda, of course, had no idea of the significance of the collision, nor of its cunningly planned result, but from the noise of the crash and the shouting she realised that it was serious. Indeed it did not need much imagination to realise the awful effect the collision might have had on the wretched women chained to the smashed oars as they had been wrenched out of their manacled hands.

After half an hour the leading galleys began to drop back, their women exhausted by the over-fast stroke that their misguided owners had insisted on. Now the furious owners were screaming at their whipmasters to get more effort from them, but it was in vain. The whips cracked and weals appeared across the backs and breasts of the naked women, but the galleys slipped further and further back.

Sheik Turki's tactics of conserving his women's energies were now paying off handsomely. Soon there was only one more buoy to round and then a straight one mile to the finishing line off the club house. He looked down at his team. They were still rowing steadily in time with little sign of distress other than the sweat which ran down over their breasts and bellies. Osman was keeping an eye out for any woman who was pretending to be more exhausted than she really was. He knew the stamina of each of the women he had so painstakingly trained.

"Full Ahead!" ordered Sheik Turki in a cruel and decisive voice when there was still half a mile to go, and two galleys ahead.

Amanda could not believe it as the drum beat increased. She had no way of knowing that the finishing line was near, but she did know that she was nearing exhaustion.

The whip cracked across her back, making her forget everything except pulling her oar. She could hear other women being whipped also as Osman strode up and down, driving them on. He now had a shorter whip in his hand, a whip which he called his Finishing Whip, with a short thick leather tip. As he stood behind Amanda, he waited until she was leaning right back, her legs parted and her oar held back to her breasts. Then he brought the short whip expertly down over her shoulder and over her oar. The flat leather tip caught her lower belly between her open legs. The pain was terrible but it made her realise that, tired as she was, she simply must keep up with the new fast stroke and put her back into it. Such was the power of the whip!

The galley surged ahead, passing one of the other galleys still ahead. A quarter of a mile to go! Dare the Sheik risk keeping the women at Full Ahead? Or would they suddenly collapse under the strain before reaching the finishing line? He looked down at his women. He ignored their pleading eyes and desperate faces. He saw that they were still pulling in time and that, thanks to Osman's Finishing Whip, only a few were showing signs of real distress.

He gestured to Osman to redouble the whip. The galley resounded to the thwack of leather hitting flesh.

Fifty yards from the finishing line , Sheik Turki caught up with the only galley ahead of him and won by a nose!

Suddenly the drum beat ceased. Amanda collapsed over her oar like a dead woman, gasping for air. All around her the others sprawled on their rowing benches, every muscle aching, hearts pounding, sweat pouring down onto the wooden benches.

Osman came round and forced a slice of bitter lemon into each woman's mouth, reviving them slightly. But how Amanda and the other women found the energy to paddle the galley slowly back to the quayside was something she would never know. For Osman and his terrible whip were no longer on the rowing deck. No! He was now up on the poop deck with the Sheik and the Coxswain, a bottle of Champagne in his hand, as he gestured obscenely to the whipmasters of the galleys they had just passed.

Through half closed eyes Amanda saw the delighted Sheik congratulate Osman and present him with a miniature gold bar.

PART VII - AMANDA'S SPECIAL CONDITION

40 - THE MONTAH RACING CLUB INTRODUCES SOME INTERESTING NEW RULES

That evening, after the prize giving in the club house, there was a full meeting of the members of the Montah Racing Club.

An elderly grey bearded Sheik rose to his feet. His eyes gleamed and his voice was vibrant.

"My Sons and Brothers," he began, "let us not forget that we are all here because of one simple thing: we, like our fathers, our grandfathers and for generations before them, enjoy the supreme thrill of acquiring young women. Our ancestors relied upon slave markets, wars, or raids on rival tribes. We acquire ours, thanks to the new wealth provided by our black gold, oil, from all over the world."

He paused. His listeners were nodding.

"We, like our ancestors, all enjoy the thrill of running our hands over the tremulous young bodies of a slave girl, of having her crawl naked to our feet, of having her look up at us with fearful eyes, of having her sitting like a little girl on our knees, and of watching her being thrashed by our black servants, and of feeling her trembling body under us as, terrified by the threat of the whip, she desperately tries to please us.

"But our ancestors also enjoyed something else: the feeling of power that comes from having a pretty young slave girl put into a special condition. I do not necessarily mean that they themselves were the father. A man might sometimes have enjoyed getting his revenge on a hated rival tribal leader, whose wives, concubines and daughters he had captured, by making the women carry his own child. But more usually he enjoyed the cruel revenge of having them mated with a black slave to produce mulatto slaves for his service. The same fate awaited captured Christian women. My forebears enjoyed the feeling of complete power over a young slave woman that came, first, from an enforced mating, and then from making the woman carry a child that like its mother was destined for slavery. They enjoyed watching the slave girl ineffectively tearing at the chain mesh pouch locked tightly around her loins as she desperately tried to get rid of what her Master had ordered she was to deliver to him - and which, thanks to her maternal instinct she would eventually find herself proud to deliver. Meanwhile he would enjoy feeling the reluctant and frightened slave's slowly swelling bellies and breasts, and he later enjoyed drinking her milk, or having it made into yoghurt for the delight of himself and his guests."

Again he paused. He had the attention of all his listeners.

"But my brothers," he continued, "here we are depriving ourselves of the most basic ways of exerting our power over our galley slaves, and of the natural enjoyment that springs from it, by making no provision for the natural fate of a slave girl: enforced maternity.

"Let us also remember what the holy Prophet, may he be blessed for ever, taught us: that Allah has put women into the world for two reasons. The first was for the greater enjoyment of men, the second was to propagate the human race, by which he meant not only breeding sons from our wives and concubines, but also the traditional and fascinating art of breeding more slaves from our slave women. We should be following his teaching here!"

There was a roar of agreement as the elderly Sheik sat down, and a buzz of conversation as the men turned to each other, agreeing with every word that he had said.

One owner particularly caught the attention of his fellow members when he described how it had now been disclosed that the Russian communists had discovered that there was a link between maternity and the improved strength and stamina of young female athletes, due to to male hormones entering the blood stream. This had been the secret of the often astonishing success of the Eastern Bloc countries in the world Olympics.

But, he continued, all this was directly relevant to their own female galley slaves. It would be just another way of getting better stamina and fitness from them, like enforcing regular exercise and controlled feeding. All the more reason, he demanded amidst general applause, for the club rules to be amended to encourage owners to use this form of fitness training, and to stop owners using it from being penalised.

Other members also argued that the rules should be amended to reward owners who went to the extra expense and trouble of acquiring beautiful, but naturally heavier, white European women for their galleys and so enriching the whole sport. European women, particularly women from Northern Europe, naturally made better galley slaves, because of their build and physique, than small, delicate girls India or the Far East but, being heavier, they were penalised by the present handicap rules.

Although the present rules, based entirely on the difference between breast and waist measurements, gave some advantage to the owners of European women, it was not enough.

Amending the rules, they added, was now urgent, because the chaos that had ensued after the break-up of the Soviet Empire had made it easier to acquire suitable white women from Eastern Europe. This was an opportunity not to be missed and a mixture of women of different weights and physique from different parts of Europe would make building up a suitable team all the more interesting - but the present weight rules mitigated unfairly against having many white women in a team.

The easiest way of changing this gradually, without upsetting the present predominance of Far Eastern women in most owners' teams, or changing the overall weight limits for a team, would be simply to give a greater handicap to galley slaves who were in a special condition. Most young white women were naturally heavier and stronger than Far Eastern ones, but, if they were mated, then their official handicap weight should be reduced to that of a smaller boned Eastern girl.

Sheik Turki, the respected winner of that day's race, now rose to his feet. The murmur of conversation died down.

"My brothers," he said, "I also agree with every word that has been said. Why indeed should breeding not form an essential part of our operation - specially as it will strengthen the bodies of our galley slaves for their very arduous work? Why indeed should we not alter the handicap rules to encourage this?"

There were murmurs of agreement, and turning to the grey bearded Sheik, he went on.

"Our Brother here reminded us of what the Prophet, may he rest in peace for ever, taught us: that women were put into the world for the enjoyment of men. We all know the joy of looking down from the poop deck as our captive young women are forced by our black whipmaster's whip to strain at their oars, or of inspecting them chained up in their slave pens."

Again he turned to the elderly Sheik.

"But our Brother also reminded us of the traditional fate of slave girls in the days of our fathers and grandfathers and before them. He also reminded us of the exciting feeling of power that can come from deciding and controlling the mating of our young slave girls. Others of you have emphasised the need to allow for a growing number of heavier and stronger European white women in our teams. But there is a further important matter related to both these points."

He paused for effect.

"That is, that these European women are Christians. For centuries, ever since the Crusades, we Arabs, and the Turks as well, have enjoyed humiliating Christian women. We revenged ourselves on such women for all the humiliations that the Christians have heaped on us True Believers."

Murmurs of agreement went round the room. These were strong words, but clearly Sheik Turki had a receptive audience as he continued.

"Think of how for years these uncircumcised and godless Westerners have humiliated us. Now it is our turn to humiliate their arrogant and shameless women. Let us acquire more of these haughty and supercilious Christian bitches, and bring them here to be trained against their will as galley slaves - and let us breed from them without spoiling the racing!"

Sheik Turki's speech was greeted with shouts of approval, and the President of the Montah Sporting Club, an impressive elderly man wearing a black gold edged over-cloak, rose to speak. Immediately there was silence. He had the tall stature, prominent hook nose and small pointed beard that so often were the distinguishing marks of a member of an Arabian ruling family.

"My brother owners, we are all agreed then on the desirability of altering the rules to encourage breeding among our women? ... Then let us see how this might be done. I propose that the club Medical Officer be authorised to issue Certificates of Special Condition - which is the expression that, for security reasons, I feel we should use amongst ourselves ... That the existing authorised handicap weight for a woman for whom such a certificate has been issued should be immediately reduced by a quarter - or a half for twins. This will also allow for the fact that a woman in the special condition might well not be able to pull an oar up to her now increasing weight. Is that agreed?"

The murmurs of approval.

"I also propose" the President continued, "that if she is still in the same condition after six months, then the Medical Officer can issue a Certificate of Advanced Condition, reducing her official weight by another quarter. If, however, she is then no longer in a special condition, she will lose her handicap. This will discourage owners from having a girl put into the special condition merely to get the increased handicap and then simply having her aborted. It will encourage owners to make sure that women they have had put into a special condition are made, perhaps reluctantly, to carry their progeny through to the advanced condition and then to delivery - and to go on using her in his galley right up to the last moment - something which will make our races all the more interesting and unpredictable.

Many heads were now nodding in agreement as the President continued.

"I believe that pulling an oar will prove to be an excellent prenatal exercise, and that moderate use of the whip can do no harm!"

This was greeted with cruel laughter.

"So," the President went on, "this fifty percent handicap allowance will continue until the galley slave delivers her progeny. It will make it more attractive to include more heavier European women in your teams. But we should also agree further new rules to make the ownership of a team of galley slaves yet more interesting! We need large quantities of milk here in our club house, not only for use as a refreshing and invigorating drink, but also for the production of our traditional yoghurts and whey. And we all know, as our ancestors also knew, that there is nothing to compare with the milk of a young, and preferably white, slave girl."

There were many nods as he continued.

"So to further encourage owners to use larger breasted white women and to keep them in milk, a Milking Certificate will be awarded reducing the official weight of a woman producing a certain level of milk, and an Extra Milking Certificate if a really high level of milk is being produced. Her milk production will be officially checked and recorded by our Inspectors once a month and handicap allowances altered if necessary. These Milking and Extra Milking Certificates will be valid until a year after progeny has been delivered."

"And then?" asked one of the members.

"Then, of course, an owner will then be able to continue a high level of handicap by simply having her put into the special condition again, and getting a new certificate!"

The elderly President paused to let the implications of his words sink into the minds of his listeners. Then stroking his beard in a knowing way, he paused and took a sip of orange juice.

"Now, I come to the difficult question of mating. I think that many members will simply have their whipmasters cover a selected girl. This will also be a suitable way of rewarding a whipmaster. What we do not want is to have big strong male studs roaming this island, causing security problems, challenging the authority of our whipmasters or making them jealous. That would be a disaster. We must also be careful not to allow the new rules to upset our present very satisfactory arrangements here. So I must ask owners to be very discreet in implementing them. They might also like to consider the modern techniques of artificial insemination. I am told that whipmasters could quickly be trained in its use... I think that concludes our meeting. Thank you."

41 - AMANDA IS PREPARED

Sheik Turki had been quietly lobbying for the introduction of the new rule for some time and had made certain preparations.

It so happened that on a recent visit to Europe his eye had been caught by a handsome young refugee Romanian boy. He had persuaded the youth to enter his service and had taken him back to Arabia.

The Sheik liked to have a couple of intelligent and good looking white European page boys in attendance on him. It was a good way of showing off his wealth. He had them trained to act not only as his personal valets but also in pleasing him sexually, for he enjoyed both women and boys. In particular he enjoyed taking both from behind. But he had also found that there was little to choose between their tongues provided both had first been made sufficiently scared of the cane.

The young page boys were particularly useful when travelling for, unlike a young woman, they did not need the constant supervision of a black eunuch. There was, however, one little problem with a white page boy. In order to ensure his complete loyalty, and to prevent him from being distracted by the sight of many beautiful and half naked women, he had to be castrated. As the operation was often carried out after puberty, Sheik Turki insisted on infibulation with a large brass ring, the ends of which were brazed together to prevent removal, to stop any accidental erection.

The Romanian youth had no idea of the fate that awaited him when he so eagerly entered the Sheik's apparently well paid service. On arrival in Arabia he was sent to a nursing home to have what he was told was merely a minor operation on his nose. However in this case the operation was delayed 'for tests' whilst in fact a good stock of the boy's semen was built up.

Then the potency of the semen was checked by having two young black girls in the Sheik's service artificially inseminated. To the delight of the Sheik the young women conceived, later producing two little mulattos who were being raised on his estate as future workers.

Having ensured that he now had sufficient semen to fertilise numerous women, he gave orders for the boy to be castrated and infibulated.

However all this was to some extent merely a blind - something he could boast about when talking to rival galley owners, to throw them off the scent of what he was really planing to do. Indeed, Sheik Turki also had other plans, which he called his Secret Weapons and which he felt would be decisive in his battle to win and retain the galley racing championship.

Supposing that a galley slave was only carrying an exceptionally small child? So small that they would hardly notice it? Then, of course, their true weight would be only slightly increased and their rowing stamina would only slightly affected. Yet they would still receive the full handicap!

But how might this be achieved? By mating his white galley slaves with a dwarf? Perhaps. But would he breed true? Would the progeny really be smaller and lighter?

It was on a trip to Africa that he had stumbled on the first of his Secret Weapons: he had acquired two virile but very small pigmies! He wanted two partly so that they could keep each other company, for none else spoke their incomprehensible language, and partly as a precaution in case one of them proved not to be potent when crossed with a white woman.

He also had other two other Secret Weapons. Firstly, Frau Smitt. If she could regularly produce one or two young women already expecting a happy event, then they would be certified as being in the special condition to be given a much reduced official weight.

And he had read that doctors could now bring on a woman's milk well in advance of her giving birth. This also offered very interesting handicap possibilities! He had accordingly sent emissaries to obtain the new drugs.

Yes, one way or another, he would steal a march on his rivals, by taking advantage of the new handicap rules. Indeed, he would soon have a team straining at his oars that included more of the stronger and heavier type of white female galley slaves - many more than his rival owners could have without exceeding the maximum permitted weight. The true overall weight of his team would, of course, be greater than theirs but its official racing weight would be no more!

And as for Amanda, the scene had been set. Soon, as soon as Osman reported that her body was ready for mating, it would be time for action!

Ten days later, as Amanda lay chained in her stall dozing in the heat of the afternoon, Batu suddenly cracked his whip. Hastily the women all scrambled to their feet and stood at attention at the front of their stalls, their collar chains taut behind them, and their right forearms held out across their bodies displaying their tattooed registration numbers, eyes on the wall on the other side of the passageway.

She could not help realising that Osman was wheeling a trolley towards her. On the trolley was a large, strange looking trunk. He stopped at an empty stall almost opposite her, stood the trunk on its end, and unlocked it.

In the trunk was the naked body of a young woman!

She was unconscious and strapped in a sitting position. She was white! Amanda remembered reading about Arabs kidnapping people in Europe, drugging them and then flying them back to the Middle East in just such a trunk.

There was something strange about the girl, Amanda thought. Her breasts seemed strangely firm and her belly ... yes, it was slightly swollen!

There was a sudden second crack of a whip, much nearer, and Amanda screamed in pain behind her muzzle. Batu was standing by her side, his whip raised ready for another stroke as he shook his finger admonishingly and pointed at the wall opposite. Terrified, Amanda hastily raised her head again and looked straight ahead.

She did not dare to look down as the unconscious young woman was lifted out of the trunk, and a regulation muzzle fastened over her mouth, a regulation collar riveted round her neck, and manacles riveted round her wrists. Then she was lain down on the floor of her stall, chained to the wall at the back.

Then an Arab came down the passageway. Amanda knew his face - the Arab who had tattooed her registration number onto her forearm before she was sold. Sure enough, he tattooed the club's crest and registration number on this girl's right forearm.

Then an Arab in a white coat with a stethoscope round his neck came to the stall. He bent over the unconscious girl and examined her carefully before parting her legs and feeling carefully inside her.

Meanwhile, a trolley carrying some electronic equipment, and a monitor rather like a television screen, had been wheeled down the passageway. The doctor switched it on and began to run something over the unconscious girl's swollen belly. A series of bright images were shown on the screen and then, evidently satisfied, the doctor switched off the screen and wrote out what seemed to be some sort of certificate which he handed to Osman. Then he and his strange instrument left.

Amanda still did not dare to look down, but she could not help noticing, again out of the corner of her eye, that Osman had now produced a strange looking rather stiff triangular pouch made of silver filigree chain-mail. Astonished, she saw him place it over the girl's intimacies and turn her unconscious body over to lock it tightly into place. It was held in position on the front by two slender silver chains that were attached to each upper corner and joined by a tiny padlock in the small of her back. The pouch was also held down tightly over her beauty lips by a third chain, attached to the bottom of the chain mail pouch, which came up between her buttocks and was joined to the other two chains by the padlock.

Now Osman gave the girl an injection which roused her from her deep sleep. Slowly she sat up. Amanda saw that she was a very pretty young woman, rather Slav or Polish looking. Amanda watched sympathetically as the muzzled girl stared around her in sheer disbelief, gazing in horror at Amanda's naked, muzzled, manacled, collared, chained and tattooed body standing rigidly at attention just across the passageway.

Then she looked down in disbelief at her own manacled wrists, at the number tattooed on her forearms and at the crest tattooed on her belly. Horrified, she reached up and felt the silencing muzzle and the tight stainless steel collar.

Even more horrified, she reached down and felt the tight chain mail that denied access to her intimacies by even a little finger. Desperately she tried to reach under the tight sides of the tautly fastened chain mail pouch.

Amanda watched sympathetically as the girl silently looked around her, and then at her own body. In vain the girl tore angrily at her chain mail belt, and than at her muzzle, clearly longing to be able to cry out in horror or to ask a wild flow of questions - just as Amanda herself had longed to do on her arrival in the pens of Sheik Turki's galley slaves.

During the succeeding days, Amanda continued to watch sympathetically as the Polish looking girl was introduced to the harsh life and discipline of a galley slave, as she learned to obey the crack of a whip and the blasts on a whistle. Soon her muscles began to harden and her breasts often showed the marks of Osman's whip as she pranced back to her stall after exercise.

Amanda longed to whisper words of encouragement to the girl at night, or when Osman and the boy overseers were not looking. She also longed to ask her for news of the outside world. But, of course, both of them were kept tightly muzzled - even when their muzzles were removed at feeding time, Batu seemed to take extra precautions to make sure that neither of them uttered a word.

Unable to question the girl, Amanda was nevertheless now convinced that there was something different about the girl. Her naked belly did seem unusually large for a galley slave - and her breasts seemed strangely swollen.

She was pregnant! She must be! She couldn't be!

Unaware of the intricacies of the racing handicap system, unable to talk to anyone, Amanda decided that she was just letting her imagination run riot.

The girl was just naturally a little plump, that must be it.

Amanda was already used to her monthly cycle being closely monitored, and even delayed or brought on early to ensure her optimum performance on a race day. Batu seemed to enjoy degrading her when he inspected her for tell-tale signs.

Now Batu started to take and record her temperature twice a day. She never knew when it was going to be done. She just had to wait for a distinctive double crack of the boy's whip, as he strolled down the passageway towards her stall. Then abandoning anything she might be doing, feeding, grooming herself, or even relieving herself into the central gutter of her stall, she had to kneel very quickly on all fours facing the back of her her stall. Woe betide her if she was not properly in position, with her forehead to the floor of her stall, and her backside raised and proffered to the boy's well greased thermometer, by the time he reached her stall.

She did not know what was happening when, having calculated that this was just the right moment in her monthly cycle, Osman came to her stall and supervised her being specially well washed and groomed by the young Batu. He watched as the young black boy made her kneel on all fours, facing the wall at the back of the stall and again raise her buttocks - this time to be douched.

Then having performed to the satisfaction of her young keeper, there was the crack of a whip and the shouted order for her to turn round and stand at attention. She made a perfect picture of young disciplined womanhood as she stood at the edge of the stall, overlooking the sharp step down to the passageway, with her hands clasped behind her neck, her head raised and her eyes fixed straight ahead.

"Legs apart! Knees bent!" came the order from the young boy, now standing down in the passageway, his head level with her belly.

As usual, Amanda could not help blushing as she obeyed the orders. How she longed to hide her intimacies with her hand, but she did not dare to unclasp her hands, nor indeed did she dare look down.

"Thrust belly forward!"

Shamefacedly she obeyed, wondering what was going to happen. She felt something sticky being applied over her mound and down over her beauty lips. She was, she realised. going to be depilated again. Thank Heavens, she thought, very little hair had grown back since she had last been done. As the mixture set, Batu and Osman stood back. She did not dare to move, for out of the corner of her eyes she could see their whips. She also thought she saw something else - a strange looking bottle and a little applicator brush.

Then suddenly, as she stood there, not daring to move and keeping her head up and her eyes fixed straight ahead, whilst the burning depilatory mixture hardened, she was aware of voices coming down the passageway and stopping in front of her. She could have died of shame as she recognised the voices as those of Sheik Turki and his two little nephews. To be seen like this!

She longed to back away, to hide in the corner of her stall. But Batu raised his whip and she knew she must keep quite still as the mixture set. But how awful! And to make it worse her very feeling of humiliation, coupled with the presence of her all powerful Master, made her body betray her. She could feel herself becoming aroused.

"731!" came the order. She had long since learnt to recognise the Arab words for her registration number. Taking care to keep her body still, so as not to disturb the slowly hardening depilatory paste, she lowered her right arm from behind her neck and held it out to display her number to her Master.

Batu now stepped forward and, with a sudden gesture, ripped off the now solidified mixture. Amanda jumped with the pain and screamed out aloud behind her muzzle.

Then Osman himself stepped forward and drew his hand over her perfectly smooth mound and along her beauty lips. He turned to the Sheik.

"Your Highness, the galley slave is quite smooth," he reported.

Down in the passageway, the Sheik stepped forward. His beard was level with Amanda's hairless mound. Amanda gave a little shiver of anticipation, and, at a gesture from Batu, thrust her aroused intimacies forward towards her Master. Still not daring to look down, she felt his hand running over her mound and down her beauty lips. Then she gave a little start as she felt him touch her beauty bud itself, and began to stroke it gently. She heard herself moaning from behind her muzzle. Oh how she loved his touch, even if she hated him.

She heard the Sheik say something and then the two boys reached up and she felt their podgy little hands stroking her as well. It as if the Sheik was teaching them about women slaves, about how helpless they were, how when threatened with the whip they could not help responding to their Master's touch, how by playing carefully with a young woman's nipples and beauty bud they can arouse her despite herself, and how they can check the state of her arousal by parting her now moist beauty lips lower down.

Oh the shame of it - a shame made worse by the realisation that the Sheik was enjoying humiliating the woman who had dared to make him look a fool on television.

At last the lesson was over. Satisfied with the boys' progress, the Sheik dropped his hands and stepped back. Reluctantly, the fascinated little boys followed suit.

Osman now opened the strange looking bottle. There was a sudden pungent smell. He dipped the brush into the bottle and began to paint the liquid along Amanda's bare beauty lips. It felt oily and she longed to look down to see what it was.

Then she saw Osman gesture to Batu. She felt her lips being parted again, and held like that for the Sheik and the two boys to see. But worse was to follow, for suddenly she felt the oil covered brush inside her, deep inside her. It was being swivelled about so that the oil was well spread. She was now well lubricated for a deep penetration, but unknown to her she also now smelt just like a pigmy woman, prepared for mating.

The Sheik and his two young nephews went off down the passageway, pausing as the Sheik pointed out to the boys the key features of some of his other women, now all standing at attention, chained and muzzled in their stalls, their hands clasped behind their raised heads as they kept their eyes rigidly fixed ahead.

Whenever he stopped in front of a stall, the woman would quickly part her legs, bend her knees and thrust her belly out towards her Master, as he stood standing slightly below her in the passageway.

To make the forthcoming scene even more piquant, Osman now fastened a short wasp waisted corset round Amanda's slender body. It was boned and covered in pink satin and black lace. Over her full breasts were two thin lace cups that could be pulled down. At the bottom of the corset hung a fringe of short black silk tassels that hid her body lips tantalisingly.

Amanda was thrilled to be wearing such a garment after being kept naked for so long. Looking in the mirror in her stall, however, she could not help being a little shocked by the erotic picture that stared back at her.

Osman also stood back and looked at her. With her long carefully brushed honey coloured hair hanging prettily down her back, her eyes made up and sparkling with arousal, and the tight corset showing off her slim waist, voluptuous bosom, and good child bearing hips, she was ready to meet her new little lovers.

42 - WELL AND TRULY MATED

Amanda was driven prancing down the passageway by Batu - gripping her collar chain in one hand, whilst tapping her buttocks under the fringe of the corset with his dog whip, he forced her to run slowly in front of him. She made a fine sight as she raised her knees high into the air, still muzzled, but dressed in her pink and black fringed corset, with her hands clasped behind her neck.

She was driven into the darkness beyond the screen that had been put up at the end of the passageway, and held there by her collar chain, lit up by two blindingly bright spotlights. She was so surprised at what she saw that she almost forgot to go on prancing on the spot. There in front of her, lit up by other bright spotlights, was a high cage with straw on the floor.

Straining to keep on raising her knees sufficiently high in the air to satisfy Batu, she saw something beyond the lit up cage - a table laden with drinks and cakes. Her mouth watered. How long was it since she had been allowed to drink anything but tepid water or eat anything sweet?

Then beyond the table she made out three comfortable chairs. And standing at attention in front of the chairs, muzzled and naked, were three pretty Far Eastern girls, their backs to the cage. As she watched, taps on her buttocks from Batu's whip making her going on prancing, she suddenly saw Osman crack his whip.

The three girls immediately dropped to their knees in a gesture of humble obeisance. Sheik Turki and his two horrible little nephews came and sat down on the chairs. She saw the boys excitedly reach forward and start to play with the naked breasts of the girls kneeling at their feet.

Then the boys started to laugh, pointing across to herself and to the way her fringed corset fluttered tantalising up and down over her bald mound and hairless beauty lips, as she strained at her prancing. The Sheik was also looking intently at the erotic sight and, as he did so, Amanda saw him reach down and thrust the head and shoulders of the delicate young creature at his feet under his long white robe. Soon she saw the girl's head going up and down under the robe.

Finally the Sheik nodded and Osman opened a gate into the cage and thrust Amanda into it. He led her up to what looked like a gallows to one side of the cage. Hanging from a beam that projected out from the gallows was a noose running over a pulley. Amanda screamed in terror behind her muzzle as Osman brought the noose over towards her.

But it was not round her neck that the noose was fastened but to the manacle joining her raised arms. Osman pulled the noose tight and fastened the end of the rope to a catch on the side of the gallows. Then, with a little bow to the Sheik, he left the cage, carefully locking the gate behind him.

Amanda was alone now, lit up by the spotlights and held standing up on her toes, helpless, under the gallows. Suddenly she heard dogs barking from beyond the metal door. My God! Oh no! She screamed behind her muzzle as she saw the Sheik nod to Osman. But it was not a dog that came bounding into the cage, but two small black naked figures - not boys but miniature men, fully developed, their muscles gleaming in the bright spot lights, and their surprisingly large manhoods hanging between their legs.

The little men uttered whoops of excitement and rushed up to where Amanda was standing on tiptoe, hanging by her manacles from the gallows-like wooden post. They were only half Amanda's size. They gazed at her chained-up figure in amazement and awe, as if they had never seen a white woman before at close quarters - and certainly not one just wearing a satin and black lace corset.

Indeed it seemed they had never even seen a corset. But the erotic sight, coupled with a pungent scent that had been painted onto Amanda's intimacies, was clearly having its effect as their long manhoods slowly came into erection.

One of the pygmies ran his hand wonderingly over the skimpy cover that half hid her breasts, and then jerked it down, baring one entirely. Amanda tried to back away, but almost hanging by her arms as she was, she was quite unable to do so. The second pigmy seized a prominent nipple. He began to suck excitedly as, with his free hand, he bared her other breast.

Then, disappointed at not finding Amanda in milk, unlike so many of their own pigmy females, they angrily abandoned her breasts. The first pigmy then smacked Amanda's face.

They now stood back and one pointed to the fringe on the bottom of Amanda's corset. The second pygmy lifted it up, grinning happily as he disclosed her smooth and hairless body lips, onto which had been painted the scent he associated with his own females when they wanted a male. He knelt down and began to apply his tongue, happily licking up the painted-on liquid.

The first pigmy watched, laughing as Amanda's reddening cheeks and neck disclosed her arousal, an arousal which, thanks to the expert and persistent licking, she found she was quite unable to subdue. It was even worse when the first pigmy began to suck her breasts again.

Suddenly they both stood back, chattering again to each other in their strange-sounding tongue. They were looking at the straw bales that seemed to make a rough bed and to the manacles hanging above it from the bars that formed the roof of the cage, then one of them unfastened Amanda's manacles from the noose above her head. Together they marched her across to the bales of straw. She tried to wriggle out of their grasp, but in vain. They were surprisingly strong for such little men.

They threw her onto her back across the bales, and fastened her wrist manacles to the wooden post. Then they pulled her body forward and raised her legs. Holding them wide apart they fastened her ankles to the manacles hanging down from the roof of the cage, so that her buttocks were partly raised off the straw.

Amanda lay helpless on her back. She could not use her hands nor kick out with her feet. She was wide open. All she could do was wriggle - which excited them even more.

They stood on either side of Amanda's writhing body, their manhoods in their hands.. She watched in silent horror as they rubbed their now erect manhoods against her equally erect nipples - a traditional form of pygmy foreplay.

Then they came round and stood between her outstretched legs as she lay on the line of straw bales, and started to rub their manhoods between her raised and proffered body lips. Lying helpless on her back, her legs held high above her, Amanda could not stop herself becoming increasingly aroused.

Then suddenly one of the pygmies thrust his manhood up inside Amanda. She tried to resist him, but her body had been well oiled to receive him and she felt him penetrate deeply. She tried to scream but her muzzle muffled her cries. Desperately she began to wriggle, but the more she did so, the more excited he became. Suddenly she felt him explode inside her.

Moments later, she was even more horrified when his place was taken by the other pygmy, and his seed also was implanted deep inside her.

Well pleased with their enjoyment, the two naked pygmies left the cage. The metal door dropped behind them.

Amanda was horrified to see Osman come into the cage carrying a stiff rubber paddle mounted on a short handle.

"Now you boys," the Sheik was saying, "our ancestors learned that when breeding from a reluctant slave woman, conception is helped if she is given a good thrashing after the seed had been implanted, so as to get the blood racing! And a good thrashing is what Osman is going to give her. But note how he uses this paddle now, rather than his dog whip or a cane, so as to spread the pain better."

The boys watched fascinated as Osman slowly went up to the prone Amanda. He reached up with a hand to hold her raised ankles steady, and then with the other brought the rubber paddle hard down across her proffered buttocks and upper thighs.

Amanda screamed with the pain, but her muzzle made it sound like a little moan. Six times Osman brought the paddle down, until he was satisfied that the increasing reddening of her buttocks showed that indeed the blood was racing round!

Then Amanda saw her terrifying Master and his nephews rise from their seats. The Sheik congratulated Osman on what looked like a satisfactory conception and a spectacle that had been a useful lesson for his nephews and above all had well served to satisfy his desire for revenge.

Amanda lay back exhausted. But soon, she knew, Batu would come and douche her. The horrible seed would be washed out.

She was therefore astonished that when Batu came into her cage he was not carrying the rubber douche but something made of filigree silver. He held it up with a grin and handed it to Osman. It was a triangular chain mail pouch, just like the one she had seen being locked onto the girl who had arrived in the trunk - a belt that, she realised, would prevent the insertion of any douche, or for that matter, anything else.

Deftly they lifted her up and locked the chain mail belt around her loins. Then they left her, left her lying there stretched out and helpless, her legs raised high in the air. She gave a little moan from behind her muzzle, but they paid no attention and, turning off the bright lights that lit up the cage, left her in the darkness. She could feel the pigmies oily seed slipping deeper and deeper inside her.

An hour later, the lights were suddenly switched on again. Sheik Turki and his nephews had returned! There was a cruel expression on the Sheik's face as he watched Batu go into the cage and unfasten Amanda's wrist manacles from the post behind her head. Eagerly she tried to sit up, but with her ankles still manacled above her, she could only raise her head.

Quickly she put her hand down to the chain mail belt. She heard the Sheik and his young nephews laugh as she tried in vain to pull it off. Then they laughed again as she tried to put her fingers underneath it, only to find that the edges of the pouch had been stiffened with a flexible bar that kept each edge tightly pressed against her skin. There was no way in!

Again she was left in the darkness, still alternatively trying in vain to pull off the awful belt or to get her fingers underneath it.

And all the time she could feel the pigmy seed still slipping up inside her.

43 - SHEIK TURKI ENTERTAINS

Sheik Turki raised his head and looked round the room. A dozen white robed guests were sitting cross-legged on the priceless carpet, around a huge silver dish. They were discussing Arab politics as they helped themselves with one hand, in Arab style, to delicious morsels of well spiced cooked lamb.

Several more months had passed. Thanks to being able to take advantage of the new handicap rules, he had done well in the spring racing season and had won a lot of prize money. He had also won a lot of money in bets with his fellow galley owners, for none of them had quite realised how much stronger many of the white women he had introduced into his team really were, bearing in mind that their official all-up weight was no more than that of their teams.

Then, for Sheik Turki's female galley slaves, had come the relief of the three months hot-weather gap in the racing calendar. Their wealthy owner had sought refuge from the heat in his air conditioned harem or in Europe. He had left his galley slaves to swelter it out, chained up in their pens, or, under the eagle eye of their whipmaster, chained to their oars in the darkness of a pre-dawn practice training session in the galley before the heat of the day - for he had told Osman not to let his women's bodies get slack, but to keep them fit and ready to resume racing again in the autumn.

It was going to be a tricky winter racing season for Osman, for Amanda and several of the first women to be impregnated with the pygmy seed would soon be due to deliver their little progeny.

Indeed the Polish-looking woman and another young woman sent to the Sheik by Frau Smitt already in the required Special Condition, had already done so. Under the eye of their experienced whipmaster, they had delivered their progeny in a special stall, their muzzles tightened to ensure that they did not disturb the other women.

Thanks to all the hard exercise they had been subjected to the deliveries had been quick and simple - seated on Osman's special birthing chair with their manacled wrists chained above their heads.

Indeed, delivery in a seated position in a special cut-away chair, into a straw filled basket below the chair, was an old local and Turkish tradition for slave girls. Apart from its efficiency, it was also ideal for preventing the still muzzled and manacled young woman, now of course also blindfolded, from having any contact with her progeny before it was taken away.

"What the eye does not see, the hand does not touch, and the nose does not smell," Osman would say as he ordered the infants to be removed, "the heart will not grieve for."

Except for their still regularly milked large breasts, the women's well muscled bodies were now slim again, and with their extra milking handicaps they remained valuable members of the crew, trained, fit, and disciplined.

But care was still having to be taken with Amanda and the other Advanced Condition women. On the one hand Osman and the Sheik wanted to make full use of their official handicaps to help win races. On the other hand, they preferred not to have a woman deliver in the middle of a race. However, the club had ordered that a special prize should be given to the first galley that completed a race in which one of its crew had given birth without missing a stroke. And the Sheik had been half tempted to try and win it.

Accordingly, Osman had taken the precaution of having one of the rowing benches on each side of the galley cut away and fitted with a basket underneath - just in case.

Osman had moved Amanda and the other women now well into their Advanced Condition into adjoining stalls. Here he could keep a close eye on them as they lay chained down on their backs, their hands chained back behind their heads, and their ankles chained on either side of the little central gutter, pointing towards the front of their stalls.

A few were girls who had arrived mysteriously from Europe already in the desired condition, but most, like Amanda, came from the existing team who had been selected to be inseminated from his stock of pygmy seed. Even without moving from the passageway he could see the varying swell of each young woman's belly, and could check that the silver filigree belts were still in place, tightly locked over their body lips.

The women were, of course, kept muzzled to prevent them from accentuating their worries by talking to each other.

It was a position from which they were released only to be chained up in their coffles, either to be marched out onto the parade ground for a spell of drill and exercise, or marched out to the waiting cattle truck, chained with their manacled wrists fastened to rings high up on the walls of the truck, and taken down to the galley.

Now the Sheik was back, ready for the start of the next series of races. To celebrate this he was giving a dinner in his new sumptuous villa near the club house.

To decorate the dining room, and to show off his power and his wealth, he had ordered Osman to have one of his Advanced Condition women chained standing up in front of each of the marble columns that decorated the four raised alcoves in the corners of the room. Two of the women had been procured already in an interesting condition some months previously. Like Amanda, the other young woman had been put to the pygmies.

The centre ring of each woman's wrist manacles had been dropped over a hook high up on the wall above her head, so that they were standing up on their toes, breasts raised.

For once the chain-mail belts had been removed. Then, each of the four women had been spread-eagled on her back on the floor of her stall.

Amanda was terrified as she felt Osman first wash her beauty lips and then paint them a brilliant scarlet. Next he rubbed a strange liquid along them. It felt ice cold. Then with a special punch he had painlessly pierced the now temporarily anaesthetised lips four times - making two little holes on each side.

Through the two front holes, which guarded her beauty bud, he threaded a pretty black ribbon which he tied in a large bow. But through the two back holes, which guarded the entrance into her body, he threaded the hasp of a strong padlock which closed with a firm click, before repeating the entire process on the other three young women.

Looking down contentedly on the four wriggling and hugely embarrassed young women, Osman had wondered whether in future this simple treatment might suffice to replace the rather more cumbersome chain-mail belts. It seemed just as effective and was much prettier to look at!

To preserve a semblance of modesty the four chained women were dressed in long dark blue velvet cloaks, edged with gold, that covered their bodies from their necks to their ankles. But the front of the cloaks were open and were gently thrust aside by the women's contrastingly white swollen bellies.

To give an appearance of equal swelling, the bellies of Amanda and the other girl who had been fertilised by the pygmies had been thrust forward by a cushion discreetly fastened to their columns, level with the small of their backs.

To maintain the Islamic proprieties, Osman had put each of the women into a black chador that covered their heads, hiding their hair. He also had them heavily veiled with a leather mask over their muzzles, so that their features were completely hidden. Even the little slits over the eyes were masked with a tiny strip of black gauze, through which they could only just see. The same masks were used when Sheik Turki invited male guests to come out on the galley to see his fine team of galley slaves.

The Sheik smiled cruelly as he reflected that one of the masks hid the features of Amanda. He looked across to the corner in which she was standing stock still, her swollen belly prominent, her beribboned and padlocked beauty lips well displayed, a perfect picture of subjugated and well disciplined womanhood.

A feeling of power surged through him. Power and revenge were a satisfying combination!

But even more satisfying was the thought that one of the immaculately dressed men sitting cross legged on the carpet was none other than his arch enemy Prince Rashid!

The busy Prince had come to the island for a brief visit as the guest of a fellow member, who, not realising the enmity between the two men, had brought him to Sheik Turki's feast!

When the meal was nearly over, Sheik Turki gestured to one of the negro servants standing back against the wall. Immediately each guest was handed a little chastened silver cup. Then a door was flung open. The Sheik`s guests looked up.

Batu and three other small keepers entered the room. They were carrying little dog whips. They were followed by Osman carrying his dreaded short whip. They all bowed to the guests.

Then each boy went to one of the chained women, and drew back the dark blue velvet cloak to disclose the firm breasts that were the typical of galley slaves. Each nipple had been painted scarlet to match the painted body lips.

But, the guests noticed, the breasts were heavily veined - the sure sign of being in milk. Mystified, they glanced down to the swollen bellies that showed that their progeny had indeed not yet been delivered.

Then the boys slowly unfastened the women's big black satin bows, leaving the long ribbons hanging down their thighs from their beauty lips, and disclosing the padlocks that guarded their special condition.

There was a gasp of admiration from the guests at the way these beautiful white women were being so exquisitely humiliated and humbled.

Osman went to where Amanda was standing, stretched up on her toes, and blushing with embarrassment behind her mask. He reached up and unhooked her manacled wrists from the hook high up on the wall. He gave an order and Amanda quickly clasped her hands behind her neck. Batu snapped a short chain onto the ring at the back of her collar and, tapping her swollen belly with his dog whip, drove her forward towards the seated guests.

Osman repeated the process with the other three women. Soon there was a line of four women standing at attention, their heads raised, their hands clasped behind their necks. Each woman's collar chain was held in one hand by her boy keeper, standing behind her, whilst with the other he held back her cloak to display her white swollen body and her full breasts.

Suddenly the room filled with the strains of Arab music. There was a pause and then Osman cracked his whip and immediately all four women began to sway in time to the music, and to rotate their swollen bellies and padlocked beauty lips in a parody Arab belly dancing, with the boys using their little dog whips to make sure that each woman kept up the tiring movements.

The guests murmured their appreciation of the erotic sight. Then at last the music died away. There was a pause as the women again stood at attention. Then Osman again cracked his whip, and obediently the four women fell to their knees, still clasping their hands behind their necks.

Each boy now stepped forward and unfastened the strap of his woman's cloak from her neck. Then he drew the cloak off her, leaving her kneeling up on her ankles, stark naked except for her mask and chador, head humbly bowed.

It was a pretty scene, and one that showed off how well disciplined the women were. There was a buzz of appreciation from the guests.

Then Osman cracked his whip yet again, and the women dropped onto all fours like dogs, their heads raised, their collar chains still held by their boy keepers.

Again there was a pause to allow the guests time to appreciate the erotic scene. Then there was another crack of the whip and the women, pulling on their collar chains like eager little dogs pulling on their leads, crawled forward a little towards where the men were sitting.

Then came the final, well rehearsed, crack of the whip, and the women crawled forward again so that each was kneeling between two men.

The man on her right was - amazement overcame her - it was her very own Prince Rashid!

Sheik Turki gestured expansively to his guests.

"Help yourselves, my friends, to a little refreshing sustenance. These women, all from my team of galley slaves, have been giving delicious milk for several months now!"

There were murmurs of appreciation and astonishment from the guests as they each reached up and began to squeeze a heavy and trembling breast. Soon jets of milk were squirting into their small silver cups.

Amanda, like the others, remained kneeling silently on all fours between two men, her head again raised as she looked straight ahead. She was trembling all over with excitement as each of her breasts were milked by the men seated on either side of her. Oh, the relief of being milked! Oh, the unbelievable sheer thrill of her former Master's touch on her right breast as he deftly pulled, stroked her breast to bring on the milk and then gently pulled and released her nipple. She gave a little appreciative moan.

Prince Rashid had been fascinated by the breast that was offered to him. There was something about the nipple that was familiar. He remembered how Amanda's nipples had been artificially elongated before he bought her from the slave dealer. This nipple also seemed a little unusually long. He looked down at the raised head of the woman. Might this really be his long lost Amanda?

He could not make out any of her features under the chador and mask. Anyway, he thought, it seemed most unlikely that Amanda could have ended up here as one of Sheik Turki's galley slaves. But then he remembered that she had also insulted the Sheik on her television show, and how the Sheik's chief black eunuch had unsuccessfully tried to outbid him at the auction. Well!

Yes, this was Amanda! He was sure of it. A rage against Turki rose in him, but he did not show it.

44 - SHEIK TURKI ENJOYS A LITTLE LIGHT DISTRACTION

The dinner was over - Amanda and the other three women now stood at attention in a line in front of Sheik Turki's huge bed.

Amanda was the right hand girl. How many times had she been lined up like this? How many times had the Sheik taken his revenge on her body? She had lost count.

She should be dreading what as going to happen, but as always, to her shame, she could not help feeling increasingly excited. Was it the long wait and the anticipation? Was it the feeling of helplessness and the strict discipline? Or was it simply the primeval reaction of a helpless woman who knew that she was going to taken by a cruel and powerful Master?

As usual the women's hands were clasped behind their backs. They held their shoulders back and their bellies thrust forward. Their eyes were fixed straight ahead. They were wearing their blue velvet cloaks and their ugly chadors and leather masks. Under their masks they were still muzzled.

Amanda could feel the way her beauty lips were being held compressed tightly together by the padlock and by the black satin bow, which Batu had re-tied.

Batu was walking up and down in front of them, his whippy cane in his hand whip. He paused in front of Amanda. She held her breath. What had she done wrong, she wondered anxiously, as she peered nervously through her mask at the boy's whip.

In his hand he held a bag of delicious chocolate creams, into which he would periodically dip. The smell and sight of the chocolates was overpowering for the women. How they longed for such a chocolate. How long was it since they had been allowed anything sweet? Their feeds had been increased since they came into the Advanced Condition, but nothing sweet was permitted - they still had to remain fit to pull an oar and Osman was determined to minimise the extra weight that their condition might cause.

And yet each girl knew that the reason why the boy was showing off the chocolates was to remind them that the prize would be given to the woman who gave most pleasure to the Sheik and who would be rewarded by receiving his offering deep up inside her. Naturally, in view their Advanced Condition, she would have to receive it like a boy, for the Sheik did not want to risk disturbing her precious progeny in his lust.

Batu smiled to himself, the women were reacting to the chocolates like little girls: helpless little galley slaves, displaying their swollen bellies, and too terrified of his cane to dare to move an inch as they waited to give their Master pleasure.

He smiled again as he put his hand down to feel the moisture between each woman's beauty lips. Each was glistening prettily around her infibulating padlock. The anticipation and excitement, coupled with the threat of the cane, never failed to arouse them, even against their will. What sluts these white women were!

Batu looked at his watch. It was time to get the women ready for Sheik Turki.

"731!" he called out.

Amanda straightened up. How she still hated being called by a number - and by a number that was humiliatingly and conspicuously tattooed on her forearm and engraved on her collar.

"731!" Batu repeated impatiently, his cane raised.

Amanda stepped forward to the end of the extra wide bed and knelt on it. She felt her ankles being fastened to the foot of the bed - Sheik Turki did want to run the risk of being kicked by his women!

Then she was pushed forward over a padded bar that had been specially put across the bed. It came just below her breasts, and above her stomach. Then Batu fastened the manacles that linked her wrists to the top of the bed.

Soon all four women were secured kneeling on all fours on the huge bed. with their heads down and their buttocks raised.

Amanda trembled as she heard Batu come the line of women, pulling back their velvet cloaks from their now proffered little bottoms. But that was not all. He now held a pot of grease in his hand. She trembled even more as she felt him carefully insert a little grease up inside her.

"Oh no, not there!" she tried to scream behind her muzzle. However, she did not dare to look round.

For several minutes the women knelt there in enforced silence, each a prisoner of her own fearful thoughts. The only noise was of Batu walking up and down behind them, whip in hand as usual, making them occasionally practice wriggling their bottoms to attract their Master.

Suddenly Amanda heard the door being flung open. The Master had arrived! Batu's whip cracked. Obediently, like her equally well trained companions, she started to wriggle her buttocks to and fro. Her beauty lips, she knew, would be well displayed as she strained to attract the attention of her Master in the only way now left to her. She felt utterly humiliated, like a female animal displaying itself before the male, but she was too scared of Batu's cane not to go on wriggling.

But was it really merely fear of the cane that make do so, or it was it also her feeling of helpless excitement and servitude?

It was no means the first time that she had been made to offer herself like this to her Master, together with other women galley slaves. It was all very humiliating, but what made it even worse was the thought that the woman who finally received her Master's offering, even though it would as if she were a boy, would rewarded by a little all those delicious chocolate creams!

The very thought made her mouth water, and she realised that her longing for something sweet, so long denied her, would make her do almost anything to earn the bag of chocolate creams. How she desperately longed longed for them. She was willing to debase herself to earn them!

So it was not merely fear of Batu's whip that was making her wriggle her buttocks. Putting her encounter with her much loved and feared former Master out of her mind, she was now concentrating on attracting the attention of her hated and equally feared present Master. Deprived of the use of her eyes and her pretty face, her voice, and even her arms, she fell back to the only weapon left to her: her well rounded little bottom and what lay beneath it.

Sheik Turki slipped out of his silk dressing gown and handed it to Batu. He looked along the line of anonymous little white wriggling posteriors. What a line of excellent child-bearing hips!

He looked approvingly at the way between the cheeks of each little posterior hung an infibulating padlock. The erotic sight and the feeling of power made his manhood surge - a feeling even more enhanced by the thought that the right hand women was Amanda. Oh, the feeling of revenge that he had enjoyed when parading her before the unsuspecting Prince Rashid, naked, masked and muzzled!

And now he would be taking further revenge!

He moved up behind the right-hand woman. They had all been secured on the low bed so that he could drive down into them from a standing position. He reached down and untied the satin bow that guarded the woman's beauty bud - something that was greeted by a muffled moan. She thrust her buttocks back more towards him. How well these galley slaves were trained, he thought, as he felt the little silver rings threaded through the lips on either side of the now prominent little bud.

He reached down and pulled off Amanda's chador, disclosing her long blonde hair. It was a sight that further aroused him. He could feel a new surge from his manhood. Then he flung her cloak back, up towards her shoulders, delighting in the contrast between her hips and a waist, then further back, over her head and shoulders, leaving the girl in darkness whilst he enjoyed the sight of her long white back. With her head now hidden under the velvet cloak he was dealing with a mere body.

It was a thought that again made an exciting feeling of power surge through him. It was a feeling further accentuated by the sight of the girl arching her back well down to receive him - just as he always insisted.

He drove down into her. She gave an exciting buck, as if trying to throw him off, and screamed under her muzzle. But he held her and now started to drive in and out. He could feel her giving way to him. Suddenly he realised that he was approaching the point of no return. The mental excitement and feeling of power was getting too strong. Quickly he withdrew from her before he lost control.

Amanda moaned with a strange mixture of disappointment and relief. It was, the Sheik knew from numerous previous experiences, typical of what could happen when you took a woman in the same way as you might take a boy. She would be appalled and humiliated, yet she could secretly learn to like it.

Moments later Amanda heard the woman next to her being mounted. She was overcome with jealousy and frustration. For a moment she forgot to keep her eyes looking straight ahead, through the tiny half covered slits in her mask, and turned to look angrily at her neighbour. Instantly Batu's cane caught her across her naked shoulders. She did not dare to look round again.

Sheik Turki went on down the line, trying out each of them in turn. Then he stood back. There was no hurry!

But Amanda simply could not now help herself. She could feel her buttocks and beauty lips wriggling to try and catch her Master's attention. Oh, what a slut she was! And behaving in this way within hours of seeing the man she had so loved, Prince Rashid! But the fact was that, after Sheik Turki had so aroused her by playing with her beauty bud, she just could no longer control her desires.

Moments later Sheik Turki was again riding a bucking little anonymous white creature. And the more she bucked to throw him off, the tighter he held her and the deeper he thrust down into her, until the inevitable final explosion came ...

Ten minutes later the women, now chained together by the neck, were being driven by Batu up the ramp of the cattle truck to be taken back to

Sheik Turki's slave pens. There was nothing very unusual in this - what was unusual was that proudly clutched in Amanda's manacled hand was a little bag of chocolate creams - and, equally proudly, she could still feel, deep up inside her, her Master's oily seed.

45 - ESCAPE!

After she had given birth, the Sheik continued to summon the still muzzled Amanda to his couch, together with others of his galley slaves. However, he felt that he now needed some new humiliation to inflict on Amanda to satisfy his desire for revenge.

Suddenly he thought of just the thing: his young nephews. They were now approaching the age when, traditionally in rich Arab households, it had been the custom to provide a boy with his first slave girl - usually a white girl whom he could use both for his pleasure and to beat, depending on his whim.

Now that it was the winter off-season, the Sheik would be going abroad for a few weeks. But meanwhile, whilst he was away, his nephews could visit the island and be given Amanda to play with!

So it was that Amanda found herself at the Sheik's villa one evening dressed in her long blue velvet cloak. But instead of the Sheik waiting to torment her, she was horrified to find the two nephews.

Eagerly they took her over from Batu - and borrowed his cane, whilst he returned to his comfortable bed near the pens.

Thrilled with having a real woman at their mercy, the boys removed her cloak and, fastening her wrist manacles to the ring at the back of her collar, began to play with her slim again body.

Soon, a game of Doctors and Patient was under way with Amanda as the patient. The only redeeming feature of this humiliating game was that they removed her muzzle so as to be able to give her some 'medicine'. But if Amanda thought that this would lead to a general conversation she was very disappointed, for the young boys' English scarcely went beyond: 'We boys. You just a girl!'

It was at this stage when a strange looking Arab servant brought in a tray of delicious cakes. Delighted, the boys started to eat them, flinging a couple onto the ground for Amanda, still with her hands chained behind her neck, to eat up like a dog, whilst they stood over her, Batu's cane raised.

Suddenly Amanda saw them seem to totter. They went and sat down on a couch ignoring her. Within seconds they were asleep.

Then Amanda, too, began to feel unbelievably drowsy. She lay down, and within seconds was lying unconscious on the floor.

Moments later the strange-looking servant entered the room again. He looked around and smiled as he saw the deeply sleeping boys.

Then he beckoned in another strong-looking Arab who was carrying a sack. They picked up the sleeping Amanda and put her into the sack. Then they slipped out of the house and, carrying the sack, made their way in darkness down to a nearby jetty where a boat was moored. Quietly they slipped its moorings and rowed gently out to sea. Not until they were well clear of the land did they start the outboard motor.

Half an hour later they flashed a signal. There was an answering light from ahead. It had all gone off very well!

It was light when Amanda slowly recovered consciousness. She was lying in the small cabin of a motorised dhow. She was dressed in the long all-enveloping black dress of an Arab woman. Astonished, she found that her wrists were free. She put her hand up to her neck - so had her collar. And there was no sign of her muzzle. She pulled back the wide sleeve of her right arm to look at the number tattooed on it - it was hidden with a large strip of sticking plaster.

Still half drowsy, she staggered to the door. It was locked. Through a little porthole she saw land. Had she been rescued - or abducted again?

Her mind in a confused torment, she fell asleep again.

She was awoken by the rattle of a key in the door. She realised that the dhow was no longer under way.

In came a large smiling Arab. She sat up in the small bed and began to question him, eagerly asking him where she was and what had happened to her. But he merely put his fingers to his mouth and shook his head. Clearly he did not understand English.

He gestured to her to cover her face properly and then beckoned her to follow him onto the deck.

Peering through the slit in the veil in the bright sunlight, she saw that they were moored to what seemed to be an abandoned jetty. On the jetty a taxi was waiting. A taxi!

The Arab led her up a gangway to the taxi and opened the door for her to go in. Scarcely had she sat down than she heard the motors of the dhow being started up. The taxi drove off down the jetty and onto a track that lead across the desert. Looking back, Amanda saw that the dhow had cast off and was heading back to sea.

Soon they came to a town and were driving through a newly built area with large hotels and office blocks. But behind them was just the sand of the desert. They stopped at a small building. A Union Jack hung limply from a short flagpole that stuck out into the dusty street. Over the door was a metal crest - with her heart in her mouth, she recognised the Lion and the Unicorn. This must be the British Consulate!

The driver got out and rang the bell. An Arab servant came to the door. The driver spoke to him, pointing at Amanda sitting in the back of the taxi. The servant nodded. The driver opened the door and gestured to Amanda to get out. She followed the servant into the house.

She was safe!

"Now let me get it straight," said the consul. He was an elderly man near to retirement who did not want any trouble. "You were brought here by a taxi, whose driver says he knows nothing except he was told to go to a remote jetty, pick up a woman being landed from an unknown dhow, and bring you here. And you say you have been kept a prisoner - and also put into a harem?"

"Yes, yes," cried Amanda, "by Prince..."

"No, please!" interrupted the worried looking man. "It's best if I don't know. You must understand the primary role of this Consulate is to protect our highly sensitive and very important business interests here. Any scandal effecting members of the ruling class anywhere in Arabia could have repercussions that could seriously affect our oil supplies and our trade. It could allow in our rivals. You are an intelligent woman, you must understand that."

Amanda opened her mouth in astonishment.

"Yes, I see," she murmured. "Well I don't want to make trouble. I just want to get back to London."

"Then the sooner we get you out of here the better. You have no money and no passport? Very well I can issue a temporary travel document and get you some clothes. Then we can probably get you back on the flight later this morning. But only if you sign the Official Secrets Act."

"What!" exclaimed Amanda.

"You must agree not to disclose to anyone just what happened to you. You are not the first Englishwoman to escape from a rich Arab's harem, and in nearly all cases it has been successfully hushed up - and in the interests of the unfortunate woman herself."

"What do you mean?" cried Amanda.

"You must understand that the arm of these wealthy and powerful men is very long, and certainly reaches back to England. They would be supported by the various extreme fundamentalist terrorists who also have their agents in Europe. They are also bitterly opposed to anything that smacks of feminism, women's rights, lesbianism, liberalism, or merely equal opportunities for women. They are also fervent opponents of journalists and writers, especially if they are female and hated Western women, writing critically about the Middle East!"

He paused to let his words sink in.

"So let me make it quite clear, if you start opening your mouth when you get back about what happened to you out here, or even if rumours start circulating, then your very life would be in serious danger. Sooner or later they would silence you."

"My God!" gasped Amanda. "You can't be serious!"

"My dear," he replied. "We are dealing with immensely rich and ruthless men, who are determined to maintain their lifestyles whilst avoiding any scandal. They also have an attitude towards women that is ... well, quite different from that of our own - as you must know only too well. It is, moreover, an attitude that they feel is sanctioned by their religion. A woman, who enters their harems or service, does so for life. They boast that their women only go out of the house when they get married and when they die! Here even a wife cannot travel abroad without her husband's written authority. For it to be known that one of their women, particularly a white woman, had escaped abroad would be a slur on their honour."

"My God!" murmured Amanda.

"My dear," he continued, "you said I can't be serious. Let me assure you I am deadly serious. Unless you want to be found with your throat cut, I must advise you, that when you get back to London, you should start a new life, using a different name, with a different career and a new address - and above all do not say a word to anyone about what happened to you out here."

PART VIII: ENVOI

47 - A CHANCE MEETING?

It was several months later, back in London, that Amanda suddenly saw Prince Rashid across the room at a crowded diplomatic cocktail party to which she had unexpectedly been asked.

Yes, there across the room, was the tall, handsome figure of Prince Rashid himself!

She could feel her heart pounding with the sudden excitement. Had he seen her? Was he deliberately ignoring her?

A feeling of jealousy surged through her as she watched him flirting with some girl. She felt like going up to her and telling her some home truths about the way the Prince liked to treat women. Equally she wanted to slip away unseen.

Suddenly she saw that he was coming over towards her. Her heart jumped.

"Miss Amanda Aston? It's a long time since we last met. But how well you look! And, may I say, how beautiful."

His voice! His attractive accent! His smooth manner as he bent over and kissed her hand! And yet, she reminded herself, this was the man who had so cruelly tricked her into entering his harem. This was the swine of a man who had thought nothing of having her beaten for his amusement, nor of giving her to his second wife as a maid servant. And yet ... and yet this was also the strong and powerful man with whom she had fallen in love and who in humbly serving she had satisfied some primaeval need.

She stood there, staring, unable to say a word.

He thrust a card into her hand.

"Don't say a word now," he said with a commanding air. "But come round to this address tomorrow at five o'clock. You'll also be interested to meet an old friend."

With that he smiled, nodded his head graciously and turned to go back to the pretty young girl he was with. Damn that girl! Damn that Prince! Who did he think he was, ordering her to appear at five the next day as if she were his servant. Well, she certainly would do no such thing!

She turned angrily to leave.

When she got home she found she had put his card into her bag. Perhaps she might go there after all...

Amanda pressed the bell of the smart Mayfair flat. All day she had been telling herself not to go, but here she was, and it was spot on five o'clock. She was deliberately not wearing a pretty dress, but instead a smart business suit.

An Arab servant opened the door.

"Miss Aston?"

She nodded. Silently he led her across the expensively decorated hall and opened a door into what looked like a sumptuous drawing room. Would she collapse into the arms of Prince Rashid and thank him for apparently rescuing her?

The Arab ushered her through the door, and then closed it. Amanda looked round the room. It was empty! She turned back to the door. It was now locked!

Then another door slowly opened. This would be the Prince! Her heart was beating fast.

But into the room came a tall young woman, with a boyish figure, huge eyes outlined with black kohl, and dressed in a beautifully cut silk cocktail dress.

Princess Leisha held out her arms.

"Darling!" she cried in her fluent, and attractively accented English. "Darling Sky Blue!"

Speechless with astonishment, Amanda drew back for a moment. Then with a sudden sob of happiness she fell into the Arab Princess's arms.

"Oh, Your Highness!" she cried. "Oh Mistress!"

"Well, Sky Blue!" laughed the Princess. "I hear you've been having all sorts of little excitements."

"Little excitements!" Amanda cried. "You've no idea what was done to me!"

"Oh, but I have!" laughed the Princess. "But it won't make any difference. You're going to be in my personal service again - as well as being a concubine."

"But..." stammered Amanda, thinking of the number tattooed on her forearm. "The Prince may not like..."

"His Highness to you!" corrected the Princess. "And if you're worried about your tattoo, he's decided to leave it. You're going to be a living trophy, a permanent reminder to him of the way he got his own back on Sheik Turki. So you see, it's all arranged. Getting you secretly out of England will

220

be child's play compared with getting you secretly away from the island. You'll be leaving with us to go back to Shamur to-morrow."

"What! But I haven't agreed, and anyway I shall need a passport and visas, and time to arrange things and..."

"Here is your new Shamur passport," laughed the Princess, "showing that you are a servant in my employment - and as such you don't need a visa. And as for your personal affairs, everything has been taken care of - even the rest of the rent on your flat has been paid."

"Oh!" gasped Amanda. "But I haven't got any clothes for travelling."

"You will travel with my other servants, veiled, covered in a long black robe and sitting in the back of His Highness's private plane."

"But I shall need hot weather clothes over there..."

"I think not," said the Princess sharply, as she rang a bell.

Instantly in came a negro servant. It was Faithful, the Princess's young personal black eunuch. He was carrying one of her old harem costumes - the harem dress of the Prince's concubines: cut-away transparent trousers, a bolero, turned-up slippers and a little tasselled cap, all in the same sky blue colour - and under his arm was his cane!

"But the Prince..." Amanda began to stammer.

"His Highness," corrected the Princess. "His Highness planned all this - and he will be very angry if on his return he finds you still dressed as a business woman."

"Oh!" It was all so sudden. And yet so exciting, so very much what she wanted - to be the plaything of the handsome and powerful man she loved, Prince Rashid. But it was all absurd. This was London and she was a free woman again. There was no way she was going to return to the Prince's harem.

Her mind made up, she turned and ran to the door, determined never to set foot in this house again. But she had forgotten - the door was locked!

"Let me out!" she screamed. "Let me go!"

"No," smiled the Princess, gesturing to Faithful who putting down the pile of clothes came towards Amanda, his cane raised.

"Please!" Amanda begged. "Please!"

"No Sky Blue! No!" laughed the Princess. "I'm not letting you escape again! And, anyway, you know very well that you don't want to stay here in boring London. You want to come back with us, Sky Blue, don't you?"

"YES!" she shouted. "OH YES!"

Then she added, in a small voice: "Has he got a fourth wife yet?"

Extract

Here is a short extract [abridged] from BIKER'S GIRL by Lia Anderssen (who also contributed BIKER'S GIRL ON THE RUN, THE TRAINING OF SAMANTHA and THE HUNTED ARISTOCRAT to our list):-

The jailer barked an order and the guard unlocked the cuffs, allowing his hands to stray over her bare breasts and to finger her open sex as he did so, making her catch her breath.

Once she was released, the jailer ordered her to kneel, then unwrapped something he held in his hands, revealing what was a sort of vest, made of a thick stringy yarn woven very loosely, so that it was more like a net, the holes in it about the size of a penny piece. He draped it over Lia's head and pulled it down so that it just reached to below her buttocks. It had the effect of covering her nakedness without really hiding it, the firm brown nipples protruding through the holes and the dark triangle of her pubic hair showing a clear contrast with the smooth pale flesh beneath the material.

Then he stood up and shackled Lia's wrists behind her again. A leather collar was buckled round her neck, from which ran a chain like a dog's lead. Then she was ready.

Outside there must have been more than three hundred people packing the square, chattering noisily. As Lia appeared in the doorway, the noise ceased and the crowd stood silently, watching her. She held her head high and marched behind the jailer, a passage opening in the crowd to allow their progress. As she walked she glanced sideways at the faces of her audience. All were intent on her, their eyes feasting on the lithe young body that was scarcely hidden by the vest. Lia felt the hem of the garment rise up over her buttocks as she walked, but was determined not to appear uneasy. She strode on, intent only on the platform that rose up in the middle of the crowd, the place of her punishment.

As she stepped onto the platform a murmur went up from the crowd. They jostled forward for a better look, those at the front craning their necks for a view of her sex beneath the short garment.

She turned to face the crowd. She looked out at them, trying to show no fear. She was determined to give them the show they desired. All eyes were fixed upon her as she took a deep breath, grasped the hem of the garment in both hands and pulled it up over her head in a single movement. For a second she stood holding it in front of her, hiding her nakedness. Then, in a gesture of abandonment, she tossed it carelessly into the crowd below, placing her legs apart and standing, hands on hips, her magnificent breasts proud and bare, the pink slash of her open vagina thrust forward for all to admire.

A low whistle came from somewhere in the throng below, but Lia stood proudly erect. Across the centre of the dais was a bar, about four inches thick, supported by two similar bars placed upright on each side. It was there that she was now led. She stood against the bar, which was at just the height of her vagina, so that her pubis rubbed against it. The jailer took each foot in turn, stretching them out on either side and shackling them to the uprights.

Then he took Lia by the hands and pulled her forward until she was bent double over the bar, then shacked her hands to where her feet were attached. The naked girl was now completely helpless, the skin across her arse stretched taut. The crowd manoeuvred for a better look at her so delightfully splayed, her breasts hanging down invitingly.

The jailer turned and opened a long case that lay at the side of the dais. Then, for the first time, Lia saw the weapon of her punishment. It was a long cane, about the thickness of her index finger. She shuddered as she watched him take a few practice blows, the cane swishing through the air.

He positioned himself slightly behind Lia and to one side. Lia felt the gloved hand stroking the taut flesh of her backside, descending to her love hole and running along the outer lips, so that she felt the juices begin to flow within her. Then he stood back, raised his arm high and brought the cane cracking down onto Lia's raised posterior.

Thwack! The blow cut across diagonally, biting deep into the tender flesh, making the girl yelp with pain, her body convulsing with the strength of the strike. The agony of the blow was intense, surely she couldn't be expected to endure twenty?

[abridged]

Thwack! Lia was shouting out loud with the agony and the ecstasy of the beating now, her arse on fire from the hail of blows. There was almost nowhere on her posterior that hadn't been touched, so the blows were beginning to fall on areas already red and raw, redoubling the pain.

Thwack! The jailer's strength showed no sign of abating as he continued, though a small film of perspiration was forming on his forehead. He appeared to be enjoying the task, the sinews in his arms standing out as he put his full force into the punishing strokes.

Thwack! Through the mist of tears that filled her eyes, the tortured girl could still make out the sea of faces that watched fascinated as she was disciplined. She clenched her teeth, trying desperately not to let herself go completely before the crowd

Thwack! The blows kept on falling. That made eleven, Lia thought, trying desperately to keep count in an effort to retain her senses amid the cacophony of pain that racked her body.

Thwack! Her whole body was responding to the strokes now, rocking back and forth despite the firm bonds that held her down. Her feet rose completely clear of the ground in a futile effort to break the chains that held her, to allow her to escape the terrible punishment.

Thwack! Lia's naked body glistened with a sheen of sweat as the blows continued. She was emitting a long animal-like wail with every stroke now, still counting in her mind, determined to remain in control.

Thwack! Fourteen. All she could think of now was how many more to go. Six! Could she stand another six? She gazed into the face of her punisher, trying to detect a glimmer of mercy. There was none.

Thwack! Fifteen. Five more to go. The tears were streaming from her eyes, her whole body shaking as the sobs racked her.

Thwack! Sixteen. Her taut arse was burning all over, the cruel red weals criss-crossing one another in a crazy pattern, so that they merged into one another, each one agonisingly painful.

Thwack! Seventeen. Only three to go. Only! Lia felt she would have given anything in the world to avoid those last three strokes. She had had no idea that such pain could exist. The whole of her being was centred on the source of the agony.

Thwack! Eighteen. Once again the tip of the cane cracked across her open sex, making her writhe all the more at the dreadful stinging of the blow.

Thwack! Nineteen. The sweat was dripping from her onto the hard floorboards below, a fine spray arising from her with every strike. Lia craned round to look at the jailer. He was drawing back his arm, clearly determined that the final blow would strike as hard, if not harder than the first.

Thwack! The cane came down for the last time across Lia's buttocks with a terrible force, so that she screamed out loud as it bit into the punished flesh. It felt to Lia as if it was barbed wire, and not a cane that she was being lashed with.

The jailer stood back, breathing heavily with the exertion of the beating, his face now wet with perspiration. He ran his hand over the red, glowing flesh of Lia's backside, making the girl flinch as if he had struck a further blow, then bent and undid the shackles on Lia's wrists and ankles.

For a long time the sobbing girl remained where she was, heedless to the sight that her bare red arse made for the onlookers, too drained to care about anything but the pain. Gradually, however, she felt her strength begin to return and, summoning all her power, she slowly straightened up, supporting herself on the bar until at last she stood upright again.

Then, slowly, gingerly she turned and faced the crowd and, determined to show that her will had not been broken, she spread her legs, placed her hands on her hips and thrust forward her sex in the same defiant gesture she had made before the beating, throwing back her head so that the sun shone down onto her tear-stained face.

A murmur of appreciation came from the crowd...

All Silver Moon and Silver Mink titles available from shops
£4.99 or (USA $ - varies) or direct (UK) £5.60 including
postage or (USA) $6.95 + $2.95 per parcel

ISBN 1-897809-01-8 BARBARY SLAVEMASTER
ISBN 1-897809-02-6 ERICA:PROPERTY OF REX
ISBN 1-897809-99-9 BALIKPAN 1:ERICA ARRIVES*
ISBN 1-897809-03-4 BARBARY SLAVEGIRL
ISBN 1-897809-04-2 BIKER'S GIRL
ISBN 1-897809-05-0 BOUND FOR GOOD
ISBN 1-897809-07-7 THE TRAINING OF SAMANTHA
ISBN 1-897809-08-5 BARBARY PASHA
ISBN 1-897809-09-3 WHEN THE MASTER SPEAKS**
ISBN 1-897809-10-7 CIRCUS OF SLAVES
ISBN 1-897809-11-5 THE HUNTED ARISTOCRAT
ISBN 1-897809-13-1 AMELIA**
ISBN 1-897809-14-x BARBARY ENSLAVEMENT
ISBN 1-897809-15-8 THE DARKER SIDE**
ISBN 1-897809-16-6 RORIG'S DAWN
ISBN 1-897809-17-4 BIKER'S GIRL ON THE RUN
ISBN 1-897809-19-0 TRAINING OF ANNIE CORRAN**
ISBN 1-897809-20-4 CARAVAN OF SLAVES
ISBN 1-897809-21-2 SONIA**
ISBN 1-897809-22-0 THE CAPTIVE**
ISBN 1-897809-23-9 SLAVE TO THE SYSTEM
ISBN 1-897809-24-7 DEAR MASTER**
  *Direct only, £10 ($15)   **Silver Mink

Silver Moon Reader Services
PO Box CR25, Leeds LS7 3TN
or
PO Box 1614, New York NY 10156

FREE BOOKLET OF EXTRACTS ON REQUEST